David Footman was born in 1895 and
educated at Marlborough. Before going
to New College, Oxford, he fought in
World War I and was awarded a Military
Cross. He served with the Levant Consular Service in Egypt and Yugoslavia until
1929. In 1935 he joined the Foreign
Service and served with MI6 up to,
through and after World War II. He was
made a CMG in 1950 and in 1953 retired
from MI6 to become a fellow of St
Anthony's College, Oxford. He retired in
1963 and was elected an emeritus fellow
of St Anthony's. He died in 1983.

PIG AND PEPPER

A COMEDY OF YOUTH

DAVID FOOTMAN

Rc

Robin Clark
London

First published in paperback by Robin Clark in 1990
A member of the Namara Group
27/29 Goodge Street
London W1P 1FD

First published by Derek Verschoyle in 1936
© David Footman 1936

British Library Cataloguing in Publication Data
Footman, David 1895–1983
Pig and pepper: a comedy of youth.
I. Title
823′.912[F]
ISBN 0-86072-126-4

Printed and bound in Great Britain by
Cox & Wyman Ltd, Reading

'Would you tell me, please, which way I ought to go from here?'

'That depends a good deal on where you want to get to,' said the Cat.

'I don't much care where . . . ' said Alice.

'Then it doesn't matter which way you go,' said the Cat.

' . . . so long as I get somewhere,' Alice added as an explanation.

'Oh, you're sure to do that,' said the Cat, 'if only you walk long enough.'

ALICE IN WONDERLAND

CONTENTS

FOREWORD

Under some political régimes, men are liable to be denounced to the Secret Police for holding 'liberal views'. The open and tolerant mind is no longer a thing to be admired, but a social menace to be stamped out at all costs. In much the same way, it is possible nowadays to denounce a novelist to certain Gestapos of criticism by saying that his work is 'very readable'; presumably with an underlying implication that any *proper* contribution to literature can only be appreciated by sense of smell or by playing it on the glockenspiel. I do not know Mr David Footman, and can therefore denounce him without that slight qualm which even the most ardent Nazi must have felt over denouncing his mother. Mr Footman's works, I fear, resemble those of Mr Charles Dickens, Mr Defoe, Miss Austen, M de Balzac, and various other notorious deviationists, in being very readable indeed. It is possible to read him for pleasure, without sense either of duty or penance, and to feel, when one has done so, that one has been in good and stimulating company.

But the cardinal difficulty of all highly readable books, and the reason why readability is suspect, is that it is possible to read them at various levels of concentration and intellectual effort. If a poet publishes a thin volume of verses, as the fruits of twenty years' application to his art, or if a novelist chooses a theme or manner which makes heavy demands on his reader, we accept at once that he has something important to tell us, and are prepared to spend time and trouble in reading him. Like the Yorkshire farmer with the Parson, we may not know what he is saying, but we think he has something to say. But when

Mr Footman, in the person of the artless Mr Mills, takes us into a Middle European bar full of cabaret girls and members of the English colony, we are liable simply to lean against the bar with him, drinking whisky and enjoying the fatuously good natured company, without noticing what is going on around us.

Yet when a serious artist (and Mr Footman is a very serious one) undertakes the hard labour of writing a novel, it is a reasonable assumption that he is giving us more than some bright and amusing reporting; and the fact that he does not seize us by the lapel and insist on the importance of his message does not, in itself, mean that there is no message or that the message is unimportant.

I do not mean that Mr Footman's intention is heavily didactic. I doubt very much if it is. But the acuteness and subtlety of his observation, and above all the charity which is the hall mark of all good novelists, are often very cunningly concealed. There is no obligation to look for them, if we would rather go on leaning against the bar of easy reading. They are merely there if we want them. This gentlemanly refusal to push the larger emotions down the reader's throat is usually claimed, by those who have not read Stendhal, to be 'peculiarly English'. It would be more accurate to say that it is peculiarly and excellently arrogant. Anybody who reads the account of Mausi's departure to Belgrade and still feels that Mr Footman writes so amusingly, must be classed with those who think that Mr Evelyn Waugh is a scream. One can only agree, whilst reflecting that there are screams and screams, and amusement and amusement.

I do not claim that *Pig and Pepper* is a masterpiece. It was written nearly twenty years ago, and is clearly the work of a comparatively young man. But the young man has eyes and ears, and sensitive ends to his fingers. These are notable gifts, even when compared with the knack of technical dexterity and the ability to keep us amused and interested. Perhaps if the critical Gestapo were now to arrest Mr Footman and put him to the question, he might reveal under prolonged torture that his proven readability is merely a cloak to disguise the fact that he is a fine novelist. Perhaps if they were to re-read his books they would come to the same conclusion.

NIGEL BALCHIN

PART ONE

THE SENTIMENTALIST

I

GUIDE TO TSERNIGRAD

This chapter is nothing more than its name implies; so
those who want to begin the story or who object to guide-
books on principle had better go on at once to Chapter II.
Perhaps they are right, since, taken objectively, Tsernigrad
is nothing much to write home about. It is just the raw and
ramshackle capital of one of those small Balkan states who
spotted the winning side in the Great War, and consequently did well out of the Peace Treaties. It is neither
Eastern nor Western; culturally and architecturally it is
in the awkward age; and most of those who come to it
from the West are very ready to go away again as soon as
they can.

But I came to Tsernigrad from the East, after three years
of dust and boils and consular tea-parties in Aleppo. I
came, too, at the age of twenty-six, an age that I suppose is
for most of us a period of mental stock-taking. We feel
ourselves irrevocably caught up in the profession in which
we started four or five years previously, and are apt to
wonder whether we have chosen rightly. The faith of
youth that can remove mountains is beginning to wear
rather thin. No doubt in interesting and congenial sur-
roundings this depression soon passes. But how on earth
can one keep up any interest in a place like Aleppo? I
learnt Arabic and a little Turkish, and wrote the first and
only two chapters of a detective story; I made ineffective
attempts to outwit the mosquitoes, and when I could not
decently avoid it I attended the social gatherings of my
colleagues. Oh, those tea-parties! To this day I can see the

huge powdered face and strained smile of Madame Maza-
raki bearing down upon me.

'Ah, Monsieur Mills, how are you?'

'Thank you, Madame, and yourself?'

'Oh, I am always well, Monsieur.'

'You are looking extremely well, Madame.'

'Thank you, Monsieur. Your health is good?'

'Thank you very much, Madame. What news is there?'

'I have no news, Monsieur. Do you sometimes play
your gramophone?'

My consular career looked like being forty years of this
conversation with a series of Madame Mazarakis, to be
continued, after my retirement, in Tunbridge Wells or
Mentone.

I was profoundly relieved to find that my transfer, when
it did come through, was for Tsernigrad, the capital of
Vuchinia, twelve hours from Budapest and eighteen hours
from Vienna, as near to the heart of Europe as the limits
of HM Levant Consular Service will allow. I felt I was
going to live in a proper town, among Europeans, right
away from that atmosphere of sand-flies and sullen resentment and ill-used mangy dogs that I had come to associate
with the East. I set out all agog with anticipation.

Tsernigrad sprawls over three hills at the confluence of
the Danube and the Bina, with the green Vuchinian up-
lands behind, and to the north, across the rivers, the great
Danube plain stretching out towards Hungary. I first came
to it by steamer. We touched at Mohrstadt about nine
o'clock on a summer evening, and five minutes later we
rounded a bend and Tsernigrad stood up before us in
pyramids of twinkling lights above dark and hurrying
waters. The quays along the Danube and the Bina swung
out on either side in shining crescents. Here and there the
little red and blue lights of a garden restaurant glittered
like jewels. Away to the left was a great chimney-stack

standing up like a sentinel with its jet black smoke rising across the blue velvet of the sky. I am not very susceptible to landscape, but this always gave me a thrill. So did the view the other way, that is looking north from the edge of the Kezbin Park or from the balcony of Colonel Fraser's villa. The ground falls sharply; and you look down on the two great rivers with the ferry boats crawling over to Mohrstadt, a little clump of spires and trees three miles away – and around and beyond the plain, mile upon mile of growing maize reaching out to the horizon.

These two views are the show features of Tsernigrad: these, and of course the girls. Slaughter, whom you will meet later, has a curious game which consists in walking down the main street of any fresh town he visits and deciding to how many of the first hundred women he meets he would care to make improper advances. If the game were played scientifically by enough people and the results compared one ought to get an interesting table of the Coefficient of Sex Appeal in the principal towns of Europe. In Slaughter's list, I remember, Berlin and Southport come out best, with those strongholds of spiritual beauty, Oxford and Geneva, bracketed bottom. Tsernigrad comes third and I myself would be inclined to mark it even higher. I often wonder, thinking of their mothers and brothers, where it is these girls get their looks; and also, knowing how little they spend on clothes, how they manage to turn themselves out so smartly. The first problem remains insoluble; as to the second I suspect gruesome economies in underwear. Six to eight is the time for the evening *Corso*. All day long the young ladies have been sitting in their homes or their offices, filling their own or their employers' time with day-dreams of clothes, film stars, and the Eternal Male. At six o'clock they come out to be admired, and make no secret of it.

Not that there is anything lax about the moral atmo-

sphere of Tsernigrad. The Mayor and Municipal Council
have seen to that. All houses of ill fame have been banished
to Mohrstadt, twenty minutes away by the municipal ferry
service which does a roaring trade every evening in consequence. No bachelor or widower may employ a female
servant under thirty years of age; and no woman under
thirty may smoke in the public gardens. Further, when a
site had to be chosen for the War Memorial, the gigantic
statue of The Warrior, it was felt that five metres of such
magnificent virility if placed in the centre of the town
might have an unsettling effect on the young. So the statue
was set up at the extreme edge of the Kezbin Park, pointing, appropriately, to the immodest spires of Mohrstadt,
and bidding defiance to the Serbs, Austrians, Magyars,
Germans and Roumanians beyond.

Otherwise Tsernigrad has little to offer in the way of
natural beauty or historic interest; unless you admit the
claims of the forceful profile and flowing white mane of
Mr Tropoff, who can be seen any day drinking his
slivovica, the pungent local spirit distilled from plums, in
the Café Esplanade. Mr Tropoff with his own hands
strangled the last Queen of Vuchinia in the glorious revolution of 1907, and has taken his place as a national
hero ever since. Half the houses are one-storeyed Balkan
cottages (some picturesque, others merely sordid) and the
rest pretentious and jerry-built erections run up since the
war. After a storm one is always surprised that more
houses have not been blown down. The streets are crooked
and ill paved, and prolific of curious and unexpected
smells. You soon acquire the habit of polishing your fork
and your glass with your napkin in every restaurant.
Hughes-Winsor, our immaculate Second Secretary, puts
gloves on before backing his car a couple of yards into the
shade, explaining that the people from the garage brought
it round in the morning and one can't always be sure that

they wash their hands. But Hughes-Winsor is an extreme case.

I recommend you to put up at the Continental or the Bristol. In the other hotels you will probably be expected to share a room with a total stranger, who, if you demur, will think you are giving yourself unjustifiable airs because you happen to have more money than he has; or else will suppose that you have some unpleasant disease or deformity which you are anxious to hide. The Continental has a small American Bar where about eight in the evening you generally find Messrs Pemberton, Grimshaw and Slaughter with other good eggs. That, we think, is the hotel's greatest asset.

For the rest Tsernigrad has 240,000 inhabitants, three churches, a university, four secondary schools and 2,987 cafés and drink shops, a proportion which, as Mrs Brinkworth says, is all *wrong*. A ramshackle town and yet I have a feeling for it that no other place has been able to inspire. Perhaps it is because there I had my most vivid emotional experiences; perhaps I still feel the magic of that first glimpse from the river. Whatever the reason, I have a hunger for the sound of peasant carts rattling over its uneven cobbles, for the blare of gipsy music round the café doors, and for that blended smell of dust, cattle, cheap Viennese scent, petrol and *slivovica* that hangs about its streets.

2

The Vice-Consulate was in a corner of the Legation. Vice-consuls do not as a rule like this sort of arrangement, but Sir William Drexler was not one of those prowling and inquisitive ministers who make life a burden to their subordinates; he had, I think, come in once in eighteen months. Also I liked my room. It faced north, a great advantage in summer, and was clean and cool-looking. My chair was well padded, and by turning it sideways and opening the second drawer in my desk I could manage to get my legs up and read *The Times* in comfort whenever I had nothing much else to do. This happened quite often. I am not lazy but I dislike any form of unproductive effort, and in posts like Tsernigrad where there is a Legation, a Commercial Secretary and a Passport Control Officer the vice-consul's efforts are often unproductive. In any case it is pleasanter to sit with one's pipe and read *The Times*.

On this particular morning the Commercial Secretary had gone on leave and left me an elaborate questionnaire from the Department of Overseas Trade concerning possible outlets for British toothbrushes. I looked at it with pessimism. Toothbrushes are on the list of luxury articles the import of which is stopped by Vuchinian Ministers of Finance whenever they want to restore the balance of trade; and although no toothbrushes are made in the country nobody has ever objected. Vuchinians as a nation have excellent teeth and as little liking for unnecessary effort as I have. I felt the Department of Overseas Trade was wasting time.

My window looked out on a corner of the Legation garden, with an old lime-tree where jackdaws cawed with sleepy querulity. Beyond the garden wall the ground dropped, rising again half a mile away towards the Kezbin Park. On the side of the hill I could see a tumble of irregular roofs with vines clinging about the eaves. Here and there one of the big new concrete houses blazed white in the May sunshine. It was all very peaceful. I pushed away my papers, and tried to determine whether or not I was in love.

Of course in the past I had often been in love. Some sort of feminine interest is a psychological necessity for me; and

I suppose since the age of ten I had been in love on an average three times a year–except during my time at Aleppo, where, contrary to the opinion of a certain school of novelists, there is very little doing. When I came on to Tsernigrad I had a considerable store of emotion in reserve and succumbed three times in the first six weeks. There was a girl in the Tabarin, who had gone on to Bucharest at the end of the month; there was the daughter of the American Military Attaché, who gave me clearly to understand that she was out for larger game; and then there was a girl in a gramophone shop who turned out to be even more of a baggage than I had taken her for. Besides which there was the very trying incident of Olga.

Olga was the daughter of a local lawyer, and I first met her at the annual ball of the *Cercle des Avocats*. I suppose she must have been looking rather nice, or I was feeling full of beans. Anyhow I kissed her in the corner of a passage and got her to promise to come out on the river the next day. (Hughes-Winsor is always ready to lend his motor-launch on these occasions.) When the time came I found she didn't look nearly so nice in a hat as she had the night before; also it was a hot day and she ought to have worn dress-preservers. As I got the motor going and turned the boat upstream I felt I was not going to enjoy the afternoon as much as I had anticipated. Still, I was then learning Vuchinian and it would be good practice.

Olga said it was an unheard of thing for a girl of good family in Tsernigrad to go out alone with a young man, but she herself would not be bound by these absurd old prejudices.

Politely I applauded her independence.

'So that when I come out,' she said, 'I have to keep it secret from my father. He is a congenital idiot, and gets on my nerves. But then I am not happy at home. I am out of sympathy with my relations.'

'What about your friends?'

'I have no friends. I have never found anyone who could understand my character.'

I got a little anxious. I always do when a woman starts talking like this.

'I have my thoughts,' said Olga, looking at me with intense dark eyes.

'What do you think about?' I asked.

'Love. I sit and wonder when I shall find the man whom I can really love. He alone will know what real passionate love can mean. Do you think much about love?'

'I'm afraid I never think very much about anything.'

'I have always found Englishmen most interesting,' said Olga. 'I have not known many, but I have read a lot of English books. What wonderful writers you have – Oscar Wilde, E. M. Hull! How well they make one understand the passionate heart that beats beneath an Englishman's cold and distinguished surface.'

I hurriedly explained that though that might no doubt be true in some cases, yet there were many others, like myself, whose surfaces were neither very cold nor very distinguished, and who were inherently incapable of any but the most superficial emotions.

Olga's eyes grew more intense than ever.

'You like to pretend,' she said, 'but I know you better.'

Just then I began to suspect I might be the man whom Olga had been waiting all this time to love. In a panic I turned the head of the boat round, murmuring something about important official interviews. And then the damned engine coughed and died away: Hughes-Winsor's chauffeur had forgotten to fill up the oil tank.

I am a poor oarsman, and it seemed ages till we got back to the landing stage. All the way we wrangled inconclusively about my capacity to love on the grand scale. We went up into the town in a closed taxi (for fear of her father), Olga sitting very close to me so that on that summer afternoon my side was hot and moist. I dropped her two streets away from where she lived (also for fear of her father), and went back to my flat feeling like a heretic who had escaped from the Inquisition.

But that was not the end. The following day Olga rang up the Consulate twice, the day after four times. I got Mr Aquilina, the Pro-Consul, to answer the phone and say I was not there. Whereupon she took to writing me notes, dozens of them, which Mr Aquilina brought in with an air of exaggerated discretion which gradually turned to one of hardly concealed amusement, while ragged little gipsy boys who acted as messengers waited outside for an answer.

It was a dreadful time. I felt angry and resentful, the more so because my conscience pricked me – quite unreasonably: for how on earth could I have known that the girl was going to behave like this? Then one day she wrote that she had something very urgent to tell me, and that if I did not meet her in the Kezbin Park the next afternoon she would throw herself into the Danube. This made me seriously alarmed. Young Vuchinians are very unbalanced and throw themselves into the Danube on the slightest provocation; there is a crop of suicides every year when the results of the University examinations are given out. I imagined my name in large headlines in the morning papers. I wrote back at once and said I would come.

Olga turned up dressed completely in black and with her face powdered a deathly white. I asked her what she had to tell me.

'You know already,' she said, and began to sniff.

I searched desperately for some way of escape.

'My good girl,' I said, 'can't you understand that it's not really me at all that you're interested in? It's simply something that you've imagined yourself. I'm not made that way: I've no deep feelings of that sort at all. You're very young: some day no doubt you'll find what you want, but it's no good asking me for something I haven't got.'

'You're only pretending when you say that.'

At last I got her into a taxi and back to two streets away from her home. Her last words were that after she was dead I would perhaps understand.

Next day she wrote that she had not been able to say all she wanted to, and therefore I must meet her again that afternoon. I tore the letter up.

Two mornings later her father called at the Consulate. He said he had found that I was corresponding with his daughter and he wished to know my intentions.

I said I hadn't got any.

He looked very grave.

He had, he explained, called in the family doctor, who had fortunately been able to assure him that his gravest fears had not been justified. But even so it was grave enough. He realised that in London we had the so-called modern ideas. They might be all very well in London. He did not wish to express an opinion. But in Tsernigrad one still kept to the good old-fashioned ways. And then his little Olga, his timid quivering rosebud, with never a thought that she did not share with her beloved father, with never a wish outside her own dear home circle, never an inkling of this unwholesome modern talk about love – in short, what were my intentions?

I repeated firmly that I had none whatever.

In that case he must ask to see the Minister.

I rang the bell and told the porter to take him round to Sir William Drexler. Meanwhile I sat waiting, picturing myself banished in disgrace to some particularly trying post in the Red Sea.

However it turned out that Sir William (who has a re-markable talent for not receiving stray visitors) refused to see him and never learnt the object of his visit. So the indignant father retreated with the feeling that the whole British Empire was leagued against him, and took the only course left which was to pack off Olga for an indefinite stay with her aunt in Sofia. And so the whole thing fizzled out.

But this is a digression. The Olga incident was all over months before this particular morning. Now I was thinking of Jill Bingham – wondering if I was in love with her and hoping if I was that I should succeed in becoming more so. I was conscious of the need of doing something definite. My eighteen months at Tsernigrad had been pleasant, but so far singularly barren of achievement. I ought to have distinguished myself enough to get transferred to the Diplomatic Service; have written a novel; won the Irish Sweepstakes; got a job outside; somehow or other have shown myself a man of action instead of waiting as I was while the days rolled on until I should once more be swallowed up in the Levant. Failing anything else a successful marriage was something.

Jill Bingham was so suitable. Of course, Mrs Bowles, her aunt with whom she had come out to stay, regarded me as a spineless and dissipated young man; but there was no reason to suppose that Mrs Bowles could cause much trouble after her marriage. Otherwise there were no disadvantages. She had money of her own (assessed by local gossip between three and six hundred pounds a year), and expectations. Her father was on the board of the Meridian Insurance Company, and therefore in a position to find a comfortable job for a son-in-law. And then Jill herself was charming. Everybody said so. She was pretty, not quite so much as everybody made out but still definitely pretty. She wore her clothes nicely. She was intelligent. She was a thoroughly nice girl. What then was lacking? Goodness knows. Perhaps if I had to be wrecked on a desert island with either Jill or Greta Garbo as the other sole survivor I might have chosen Greta Garbo. But the practical chances of my being offered such a choice were nil. Perhaps what I have written above has been rather unfair to Jill. She really was very charming. I gazed out of the window at the lime-tree. Of course if I was seriously in love with Jill then Mausi would have to be liquidated.

Mr Aquilina brought me in a card. I looked at it with the anxiety all consuls feel when a stranger calls upon them. The caller may always want to borrow money, thus giving the consul a choice between the probable loss of anything he may be rash enough to lend and the certainty of subsequent self-reproach if he is hard-hearted. But this man seemed as if he ought to be all right. Lieut-Col C. P. Vickery, Warsaw.

'Show him in, please, Mr Aquilina.'

A tall spare man in a grey suit came in, and took a chair and a cigarette while I ostentatiously pushed away the questionnaire on toothbrushes. He seemed very young to be a colonel: but for a few grey hairs above his ears I would have taken him for under rather than over thirty-five. He was fair with very clear blue eyes and a short moustache brushed away from the mouth. His skin was tanned and gave the impression of perfect fitness, and when he spoke his voice was a pleasant one. Altogether a high-class piece of work. It ran through my mind that if he stayed any time in Tsernigrad and took any notice of Jill Bingham my own problem would be automatically solved.

'Well, Colonel?'

'Never mind about the Colonel: I only keep it up for the Poles. You must have some sort of a title in Poland.'

'What's Warsaw like?' I asked.

'Well, I dropped two thousand pounds there so I'm rather prejudiced.'

I looked sympathetic, but he did not appear to be in need of sympathy; in fact he seemed rather amused.

'It's all in the game,' he said.

'I hope nothing of the sort will happen here.'

'It won't.'

'What are you interested in?' I asked.

'What is there doing?'

'Commercially?' I assumed my best official manner. 'Well, some time or other the Government will have to build a bridge over the Danube at Mohrstadt: they've been trying to make their minds up for years. So, if you're in touch with a big engineering firm or a group that could raise a loan you might have a go at that.'

'But it mightn't come off for months?'

'Possibly years.'

'I can't wait that time. What else is there?'

'Well, really,' I said, 'I wouldn't advise anyone to put money into this country just now.'

'I haven't got any money. I had two thousand pounds but it's gone.'

I looked at him enquiringly.

'I want a job,' he said.

People who want jobs, as any consul will tell you, must be got out of the country at once, however good an impression they may make.

'I'm afraid that's hopeless,' I said. 'Especially a job that would suit a man like you.'

'Any kind of job.'

'But it's quite hopeless. There are very few British firms here and they're all reducing their staffs.'

'It needn't be a British firm.'

'But you don't know the standard of salaries here, especially with all this unemployment about. A man of relatively good education thinks himself damned lucky if he gets anything at the equivalent of ten pounds a month.

'That would do to start with.'

'But damn it all . . . '

He laughed at my earnestness.

'I've lived on less than that in my time,' he said.

'Well, I'll ring up Bowles, he's the manager of the English bank, and see what he says.'

Bowles, of course, was most emphatically of the opinion that Colonel Vickery should go back to England at once. I passed on this advice.

'I haven't got the fare back.'

That, I felt, settled it. This man must be got beyond the limits of my consular district without delay. A casual borrower is bad enough; but a British subject who stays on in the place without money and without prospects is an unlimited and indefinite liability.

'My regulations lay down,' I said with mock seriousness, 'that if after an exhaustive enquiry I am convinced that a British subject is genuinely and absolutely destitute, I may impound his passport, obtain from him a signed note undertaking to repay all sums expended on demand, and give him a third class ticket by the cheapest route to the nearest English port.'

'What should I do in England?'

'Find something to do.'

'It's just as hard there as here. Besides, as a point of pride, I don't like being under an obligation even to the Government.'

'But you couldn't live on the sort of salary they offer here, even if there was a job. This is half-way to the East. You'd be a Poor White.'

Still with the same air of amusement he took out another cigarette and lit it. In spite of myself I was finding his personality rather infectious.

'Well, look here,' I said. 'Here's an example. A creature whom I think is a scallywag came here two days ago to ask if there was an Englishman who would teach at a school of languages he wants to start. He offers nine hundred douros a month and a commission which at the outside would come to another five hundred. Ten douros go to a shilling so that the whole thing would come to seven pounds a month. You'd want more than half that to get a room which has any chance of being free from bugs.'

'Could you give me the man's address?'

'I could. But I think you'd much better go back to England.'

His eyes twinkled at me and I wrote out the address.

'Of course,' I said, 'I know nothing about the man, and I can't be sure that the job's still open.'

'We can but try. And now I want to ask you another favour.'

I knew what was coming and my heart sank.

'When I come a cropper I do it thoroughly. I arrived here this morning with two suitcases and five bob. Half of that's going on a whisky and soda. Can you lend me a pound or two to go on with? Here's my passport and this as a security.'

He put his passport and a little leather case on my desk. I looked at the passport, Lieut-Col Charles Pallant Vickery, born at Hereford in 1892. Profession commercial. Issued three years before by HM Consul General in Mukden.

'Mukden?' I asked.

'I went out East in '24. I was in the motor business for a bit, and then I fell in with General Lih Fing and ran his transport for him.'

'In the civil war?'

'Yes, I was with the old scroundrel four years. Then I'd saved a little money and wanted to get back to Europe. I always travel Trans-Siberian, and dropped off at Warsaw to see if there's a chance of making money out of road transport in Poland. There is, a damned good chance. But I missed it, and here I am.'

'Manchuria must be interesting.'

'It is, but one gets tired of it. Harbin's a good spot.'

An improbable career: but still, of course, a possible one, and here was the passport to back it up. Damn these people that want to borrow money!

'I'm afraid I've only got three hundred douros on me,' I said, 'but if that would be any good . . . '

'Ample. Keep the passport and keep that too.' He tapped the case. 'I don't know what they're worth, but they have a sentimental value. I'll be coming along to redeem them very soon. I'm awfully grateful to you.'

His eyes twinkled and he was gone. Left alone again I became vaguely anxious about my three hundred douros. I don't know that I am especially mean, but in the consular service where a man spends his life trying to keep pace more or less with people with double his income he is apt to get cautious about money matters. And although in this case I had his passport it is surprising how many people leave their passports as security for loans and then succeed in disappearing completely into the blue. I picked up the little leather case and opened it. There glittered a mass of shining metal and multicoloured ribbons.

During the war I was a small boy at school and one of the forms taken by my patriotic zeal was to amass more knowledge of the various Allied decorations than probably ninety-nine per cent of the combatants ever possessed. The sight of Vickery's collection took me back to those days. I had never before actually seen a Victoria Cross: but there was no mistaking that little bronze cross with the dark purple ribbon. Sophisticated as I thought I was it thrilled me just as it would have done in my schooldays. Apart from that there was the DSO with bar, the Military Medal (so that he must have started in the ranks) the

Mons Star, and the two ration medals; also the French Croix de Guerre, the Serbian Order of St Sava, two Italian decorations, and one which I could not place; it might have originated with General Lih Fing. Who then was this man Vickery?

Feeling unable to keep it all to myself I packed the decorations back neatly in their case and took them in to Hughes-Winsor. Hughes-Winsor received me with the slightly anxious air of an official who fears that another official is about to try and plant a dossier on him. I laid the case on the table in front of him.

'Whatever are all these?'

'Medals. That's the v c.'

Hughes-Winsor regarded the emblems of military violence with a faint disapproval.

'Where did they come from?'

'A colonel just blew into my office. They're his. He's now trying to get a job here at seven pounds a month.'

I was rather proud of my story, though, of course, I should have known that Hughes-Winsor would be the worst possible audience.

'Do you think they're genuine?' he asked.

'I hope they are. I lent him some money on the strength of them.'

'Oh dear.'

'But not very much,' I added, hoping to retain my air of worldly wisdom in Hughes-Winsor's eyes, 'I was wondering if we could find out something about him in any of your reference books.'

We hunted and discovered that Charles Pallant Vickery, then a temporary Major in the 8th Radnorshires, had been awarded the v c in the autumn of 1917.

'That's the man,' I said, 'I've seen his passport.'

'Why did he come here?'

'He had a business in Warsaw and went smash.'

'But why did he come to Tsernigrad?'

'I suppose because he had no reason for going anywhere else,' I said. 'And anyhow it's a bit thick, an ex-colonel and a vc trying to live in a place like this on thirty-five shillings a week.'

Hughes-Winsor sighed, his patient well-bred sigh at the unlovely and chaotic world which he endeavoured so persistently and so successfully to ignore. I gathered up the medals and went back to my room. What had been the particular problem before this interruption? Oh yes, was I or was I not in love with Jill? And wouldn't it perhaps be better to liquidate Mausi in any case? Not, of course, that there was really anything to liquidate. Possibly I was making my own difficulties. Very likely to anybody else it would all be simple, to a man like this fellow Vickery for instance, who drops his last two thousand pounds and thinks it is all in the game, who wins Victoria Crosses, and always travels Trans-Siberian, and organises Chinese civil wars. Whereas I . . . Abruptly I decided that I couldn't be bothered with day-dreams and turned resolutely to the task of discouraging the manufacturers of British toothbrushes from placing too great hopes in the Vuchinian market.

3

I saw Jill a few days later at the Diplomatic Tennis Club. Bowles, her uncle, is honorary Nicaraguan Consul and therefore a member. The Diplomatic Corps *de carriére* look rather askance at the invasion of the club by honorary consuls and often talk about having the rules amended. But they were all very pleased to see Jill. The club is on the side of the most north-easterly of Tsernigrad's three hills. At one corner one can look through an opening in the surrounding hedge and see the Danube rolling down towards the Iron Gates; but only in one corner, for otherwise the hedge is a thick one, with trees high enough to give ample shade to the little tables in front of the pavilion. From the river-side comes the hoot of sirens, and from the other the growl of lorries going out to the military automobile park and the slow rattle of ox-wagons along the cobbles. The disadvantage of the place is that the municipal power station with its great chimney stack is only four hundred yards away. About three times every summer when the wind is in a certain quarter the club is enveloped in nauseous-smelling black smoke, which considerably flutters the diplomatic dove-cots and causes firm representations to be sent to the Mayor. These are always courteously acknowledged but I don't think anything is ever done.

It was nearly seven in the evening when I got there and the tennis was over. There was quite a crowd at the little tables: two bridge fours and a rummy party (mostly ladies) and the heavyweights of the corps having an animated discussion at the far end. I bowed to the card players and was acknowledged. Madame Silviera of the Argentine Legation had her back towards me: a disappointment. Madame Silviera is very good-looking and always extremely smart. At one time, secretly, I had designs on her, but as I gathered she would no more think of me in that way than she would the club caretaker, I never had the courage to make advances. Then I noticed Jill. As I feared, she was surrounded by third secretaries and vice-consuls – with Pujotas, the Spanish Commercial Attaché, making the running. I do not like Pujotas. He is probably a perfectly harmless little man, but I find anglophil Spaniards very tiresome; I class them with refined barmaids, emancipated schoolmasters and actresses who talk about hunting. It is all very well for me, a minor government official, to pose as a man of the world: but other people should remain in the class to which they belong. Besides if Pujotas wants to appear like an Englishman he ought to drop that persistent and torrential verbosity that all Latins seem to think women fall for. I tried to persuade myself that Jill was looking bored. However, on principle, I never line up in a queue for a woman, so went on to the heavyweights. I was greeted elaborately in diplomatic French.

'Ah, Mr Mills!'

'How goes it?'

'What have you been doing? One never sees you!'

I sat down and listened to the conversation which was concerned with a tea-party that Madame Stepanek was giving at her Legation, and to which, apparently, Monsieur De Woutte had not been invited.

'It is strange,' said Monsieur De Woutte with suppressed feeling, 'as a rule they are very correct people, the Stepaneks. I am always on the best of terms with them. It is most strange.'

'I presume,' said Monsieur Hindström with the evident desire to smooth things over, 'it is for the youth, the extreme youth. My third secretary has been invited. Will you be going, Mr Mills?'

I said I was not, inwardly a little hurt at this implied relegation to the *extrême jeunesse*.

'It is bizarre,' said Monsieur De Woutte. 'As far as it concerns Mr Mills, who for the rest is extremely sympathetic and estimable, one might suppose that, this time, the members of the diplomatic corps are being invited, but not the members of the consular corps. But in my case . . . To-day I met Stepanek in the town, and he did not even mention the tea-party. It is most strange.'

I lost interest in the conversation, which was running

deadly true to the general form of the Diplomatic Tennis Club. I looked over towards Jill. Yes, she really was looking bored. I blessed the ebullience of Pujotas. Seized with an inspiration I went over to the group and told Jill I had a message from her aunt that they were dining out and that she must go home at once to dress.

'But people are coming to us, and anyhow dinner isn't till half-past eight.'

'Perhaps she's changed her plans.'

'Aunt Eleanor's mad.'

Jill gathered up her racquet, and Pujotas, blast him, suggested he should borrow his chief's car and run her home. I countered by saying I had a taxi waiting outside. We made our farewells with the minimum of circumstance possible in an assembly of that kind, and went. As we passed Madame Silviera I noticed her looking at Jill's feet with a slight but perceptible air of criticism. Monsieur Hindström's voice followed us down the path:

'*Mais la jeunesse,* *l'extrême jeunesse* . . . '

The gate clicked behind us.

'Where's the taxi?' asked Jill.

'There isn't one. The whole story about your aunt's a myth.'

'What on earth . . . ? '

'I wanted to show you my pet sunset, and it was the only way to get you.'

'What frightful impertinence!'

I could see she was rather pleased about it.

'This way,' I said.

We turned off the road, through somebody's back-yard (in Tsernigrad the way to almost everywhere seems to lead through somebody's back-yard), up a little path that zigzagged through allotments to a gipsy settlement: quaint little shanties hammered together with boards and flattened oil cans, and tiny gardens full of sunflowers taller than the houses themselves, and dogs and fowls and brown naked pot-bellied babies and curious smells.

'Where are we going?' she asked.

'To the top, where the President's building his villa.'

The President of Vuchinia had realised that this was one of the finest sites in Europe, and was taking advantage of his term of office to have a villa put up there at government expense.

Beyond the gipsies was a patch of waste land and the slope was steeper.

"I hope they can't see us from the Club,' said Jill.

'Would you mind if they could?'

'It would look so rude to Pujotas.'

'He's got a very thick skin.'

'Don't be rude about my young men.'

'I'm jealous.'

This was all very well; but was it going to help me to make up my mind? Perhaps if I could get the conversation going on serious or sentimental lines it would be easier. But that might take some doing. English girls are difficult, especially to one like me who had been living abroad and rather got out of touch with them. They are sentimental at bottom, but as a rule too self-conscious to allow conversation to develop to any extent on sentimental lines. Of course they are sometimes impressed with violence. The round-eyed gipsy babies would have been surprised at nothing, and there was nobody else about. But it is no good going out to do cave-man stuff in a mood of philosophic doubt. Besides the path was very steep and I was a little out of breath.

At last we reached the earth-works and heaps of stones and mortar that marked the beginnings of the presidential villa, and looked round.

'Was it worth it?' I asked.

The great plain stretched out before us green with growing maze and pricked out here and there with a spire or clump of trees that marked a village. The Danube was a band of polished steel, but the Bina, reaching up towards the west, was gold and scarlet. Down below the Diplomatic Tennis Club was a tiny orange square framed in green: beyond, the roofs of Tsernigrad in all their infinite variety caught the last glow of the sunset. On the top of the hill to our left was a little cupola, very white and dainty against the red earth.

'What's that?' Jill asked.

'That's where the Turkish cemetery was. The house just beyond is Colonel Fraser's.'

'I haven't met him yet.'

'It's a she. One of those middle-aged spinsters who go about adopting small countries. She adopted Vuchinia. She brought them into the war more than anybody else, and fought herself in their army, and rose to be colonel. After the war she refused a pension, though she's not in the least well off, so the Vuchinian Government gave her that site and she built herself a villa.'

'She must be very interesting.'

'She is. Everybody's terrified of her.'

Far below a toy train crawled along the railway bridge over the Bina.

'It's rather lovely,' said Jill, looking down at the plain.

'Do you remember the Yadil excitement?' I asked. 'They got the stuff analysed by some specialist, and he got it all divided up into perfectly ordinary components except for a curious smell at the end which he couldn't explain. That's my philosophy of life in a nut-shell: you can take all experience and analyse it down to unpleasant or ridiculous components, and then you get this view which gives you a feeling just as inexplicable as the smell in Yadil.'

'That's all rather deep for me.'

A pity. I was hoping she would play up to my opening gambit. Once you get a woman talking about Life the warm and intimate atmosphere thus engendered will generally encourage her to talk about Love. But perhaps it was my fault. Perhaps I was being too high-brow.

'Cigarette?'

'Please.'

I gave her a light, and she climbed up on one of the infant walls and sat with her legs dangling.

'How many countries can you see from here?' she asked.

'Only Roumania besides this one. The frontier's over there. It's only about twenty miles away.'

'Why, the sun's gone down.'

As we went on talking the horizon opposite turned from crimson to salmon pink, to pale gold, to a faint grey gleam. Twinkling lights shone out of Mohrstadt and crept along the river on the ferry boats. Stars came out one by one in a heavy velvet sky. From below came the deadened blare and drumming of strange music: the gipsies had a bonfire near their settlement and were gathering round to dance. Jill took another cigarette and the little flame from my lighter lit up her profile and brought out the gold in her hair. There was something very attractive about her; I was quite ready to fall if she would give me a chance.

'That story about your aunt was the best thing I ever thought of in my life,' I said.

A figure loomed out of the darkening twilight. It was the policeman on guard over the presidential bricks and mortar, come to tell us that no one was allowed here after dark. If one knows how to deal with them Vuchinian policemen are pleasant and friendly creatures. I showed this one my consular pass, explaining that we were enjoying the evening air, and slipped twenty douros into his hand. He beamed with sympathetic comprehension and left us.

'I brought you up here for a reason,' I went on. 'Not only because . . . '

Blast that policeman! Just as I was getting nicely going he reappeared, smiling and voluble.

'What ever does he want?' asked Jill, who of course did not understand Vuchinian.

'He wants to show us something.'

We followed him round some heaps of stones to a little wooden shanty. He unlocked the door and flashed his torch on an aged bedstead with a torn and tumbled blanket. He explained that it was really quite clean and handed me the key.

'Oh!' said Jill in horror.

I brusquely returned the key to the policeman (who probably to this day has doubts of my virility) and hurried back after Jill.

'It's past eight,' she said. 'I'm frightfully late already.'

I followed her down the path, inwardly cursing the policeman. She was frightened and, I think, shocked; though true enough to her generation to have died rather than admit it. She even might be supposing that the man was hand in hand with me. What an idiot the girl was! Or perhaps it was merely that she was very young. Anyhow it was a damned nuisance. One would have to start all over again.

We hurried down to the settlement at five miles an hour, past the bonfire and the gipsies (who took no notice whatever of us), through the allotments, through the back-yard and into the road again.

'I wonder where I can get a taxi.'

'Round here to the left.'

Round the corner were three taxis in a row, two very battered Citroëns and one only less battered Morris. For patriotic reasons I chose the Morris and handed Jill in.

'Don't you bother to come,' she said.

'It's on my way.'

There was much crashing of gears and the ill-used Morris started. Jill sat very much in the far corner. I suppose as a rule when a woman travels for the first time in the dark in a taxi with a man whom she knows finds her attractive her prevailing feeling is curiosity as to what he will do. In Jill's case I felt that apprehension predominated. I accordingly sat with the utmost propriety in the depth of my own corner.

'Of course our friend rather jumped to conclusions,' I said.

'I should think he did.'

The taxi took a corner much too fast and much too sharp as is the habit of taxis in Tsernigrad. Jill was thrown on to my lap. Like a perfect Galahad I helped her carefully back to her own corner.

'Of course,' I said, 'it's the practical Vuchinian mind. He couldn't see any other reason for our going up there. I hope you're going to forgive me for him.'

'It was rather amusing.' (Being half-way home she was getting reassured.) 'Of course if Aunt Eleanor heard of it she'd die.'

'I often wonder if that generation is as easily shocked as we like to think they are.'

'Aunt Eleanor is.'

'When am I going to see you again?' I asked.

'Whenever you like.'

'I want to show you the view the other way – borrow Hughes-Winsor's boat and go up the Danube.'

'Yes, let's.'

'I warn you the damned thing often goes wrong and then we just drift down to the Black Sea.'

'Well, if it does, you'll have to explain to Aunt Eleanor.'

It occurred to me that perhaps I was being too sedate.

But anyhow it was too late now. We were already in the Bowles' street, almost at the house.

'I'll ring you up,' I said.

'Yes, do. Or why not come round tomorrow? About cocktail time.'

'All right.'

The taxi stopped.

'And then we'll make plans. It's no good asking you in now. The American Minister's coming to dinner, and Aunt Eleanor's sure to be hot and flustered.'

'I'll draw up a programme,' I said. 'You're staying here three months and I'm not going to give any of it away.'

The taxi-man looked round at us enquiringly.

'Well,' said Jill, 'I suppose I'd better get out.'

'What about a little drive along the quay and round by the Wilsonovi?' (I was now convinced I had been too sedate.)

'I can't possibly; I'm late as it is.'

We got out.

'Well, so long.'

She squeezed my hand – definitely squeezed it – was up the steps and through the door, waving to me as she disappeared.

'Well,' I said to myself, 'I'm damned.'

At that moment I decided I was in love with Jill.

I climbed back into the taxi. Of course it might be the reaction once she had realised she had been rather silly to get scared about the policeman. Perhaps she had the instincts of a baggage. Not that I cared in the least. My mind was made up.

The taxi-man made interrogative noises.

'What does it matter where?' I asked him. 'You are a chauffeur. Just drive!'

His back bristled in repudiation of an implied insult. The gears groaned and rattled. In two minutes we were doing forty, roaring along the ill-paved street scattering hens, dogs, children and citizens, leaving a trail of imprecations behind us.

I was in love with Jill.

On we went, switchbacking up and down hills, bumping into gutters, fouling kerbs as we rounded corners, past quays and customs yards and lighted cafés and wide deserted market-places. I put my hand on the corner where she had been sitting; it was still warm. How intimate! It was the best of possible worlds, and everything was just beginning. The air was full of a spring or Kruschen feeling. I myself felt like Mickey Mouse in one of his more idyllic conceptions. I pictured Jill hunting for stockings; wishing the Bowles' had lights in more sensible places; dabbing at the back of her neck with her powder-puff; regretting that it was the American Minister who was coming to dinner and not me. Or at any rate I hoped so. Never mind; I was on my way. To travel hopefully is better than to arrive.

My ecstasy must have lasted about twenty minutes and then I noticed that I was hungry and that the meter was showing eighty-five douros. I told the chauffeur to go to the Continental.

4

The American Bar at the Continental Hotel is on the first floor, in what used to be one of the smaller and cheaper bedrooms. On one side of it is the barber's shop and on the other a little den used by the first floor staff. It is not easy to find and not very impressive when one gets there. Much of the furniture had originally been in the cheap bedroom. The corridor has a close and stuffy smell and the single window looks on a courtyard that also contains the laundry and is heavy with the aura of other people's dirty washing. At one end of the room is the bar, gaudy with bottles of Balkan liqueurs, and Mr Weiss, the barman, poring over the football news in the evening paper. At the other end are nearly always half a dozen members of the English colony.

I don't know why it is we are so faithful. The place often lacks the fount and origin of bars, that is, gin; for the Continental at this time was in financial straits, and Mr Weiss quite often had to go down and borrow one hundred douros off the porter and send round to the dealer's before we could get our dry Martinis. Perhaps we went because Englishmen are clubbable souls and there was no other club in Tsernigrad. For the bar of the Continental is a club. Strangers may come in and are always politely received, more or less, by the regulars. But either they are accepted and themselves become members, or else for some reason they never come again.

There were five there when I arrived this evening: Bowles, Pemberton, Grimshaw, Slaughter and Glover, playing poker dice.

'Hullo, you look very pleased with yourself. Where's that damned fellow Weiss? Here, bring this gentleman a drink!'

Why have bars never inspired great poetry? Perhaps because they only came in after poetry had ceased to be the food of a nation to become a hobby for the cultured; or perhaps because if poets frequent them they get affected with the jealousies and intrigues of literary society and lose their essential spirit. A pity: for there could be no more splendid subject for an ode, nothing so gloriously and immortally mellow as Pemberton over his fourth gin and French. Pemberton was in Machinery and Heavy Metals. He originally came from Islington, where there still lived a vague and shadowy Mrs Pemberton who occasionally wrote to say she was coming out to Tsernigrad. Where-

upon Pemberton would be rather grave and thoughtful
for the next few days. But she never came. Next to him was
Slaughter (Insurance), with a small dark moustache and
horn-rimmed glasses: the wag of the party, especially full
of jokes against himself – a lovable creature. Beyond was
Grimshaw, lean and ginger-headed, who dealt in Tea,
Whisky and Provisions; then Clive Glover, Pemberton's
second in command and husband of Beryl Glover who is
one of the nicest women I have ever met. To complete the
circle was Bowles, tall and growing slightly bald, with that
precise and rather harassed air that is natural to a bank
manager who has married a woman of spirit.

'How's business?' I asked.

'Waiting for this damned government crisis to finish.'

'I hear the Nationalists are coming in.'

'Don't you believe it.'

'That's what they're saying in Parliament.'

Pemberton smiled omnisciently at me and shook his
head. He had that quality of self-sufficing omniscience,
possessed by many successful business men, which I have
so often envied. Even if convicted to his face of gross in-
accuracy he could carry on with equal assurance and without any loss of dignity. But I wasn't in the least interested
either in the state of business or the government crisis. I
wanted to talk about Jill.

'I met your niece this afternoon,' I said to Bowles.

But mention of his family reminded Bowles that he had
a dinner-party on at home and would probably be late, so
that he reached for his hat and took a hurried leave of us.

'He'll catch it!' said Pemberton as he disappeared.

We all smiled. There had never been the best of feeling
between Pemberton and Mrs Bowles. He regarded her as
the ruin of what might otherwise have developed into a
good egg. She thought he was vulgar and immoral. There
is still a legend of the evening of some dinner or other,

after which Bowles had been taken down to the Tabarin by Pemberton and Grimshaw and had returned to an indignant wife at 4.45 a.m. 'Mr Pemberton,' Mrs Bowles is reported to have said the next time they met, ' I cannot understand what satisfaction you can derive from inducing my husband to sit up all night drinking with a set of prostitutes.' 'Well, hang it all, Mrs Bowles, they weren't prostitutes; and as a matter of fact your husband only talked to one of them.' 'Mr Pemberton, I will try to forget, but I can never forgive.' Neither, apparently, could Pemberton.

Ten minutes later Glover went, after an ineffective attempt to pay for a round of drinks: Pemberton who knew he could ill afford it hardly ever allowed him to pay. When the four of us were left the atmosphere got more mellow, or perhaps it was that the gin was beginning to work. Slaughter was full of the story of how the Rector of the University had been held up by brigands about twenty miles out of town. They had taken away his car and everything else, so that he and the chauffeur walked back with one pair of inadequate pants between them. Pemberton had just returned from a business trip to the wild and woolly frontier districts beyond Vladikop, and in the train coming back had found seven live geese in the lavatory: 'Seven of them, damn it, and the bloody things hissed at me!' Grimshaw, whose thoughts were apt to run on basic pleasures, was admiring the ingenuity of a young American in one of the Oil Companies, who had commissioned a taxi-driver to bring a fresh woman every Monday, Thursday, and Saturday: and was wondering how soon it would end in disaster.

The poker dice went round again. At 10.15 Mr Weiss was sent down to the kitchen to see if there was any dinner left. We started our meal just after eleven. About midnight we went down and watched the programme in the

Tabarin, Pemberton for the eighth, Slaughter and Grimshaw for the sixth, and myself for the third time. Nine girls, more or less undressed, waved their arms and legs about to the strains of the band. The audience, nearly all German or Czech or Jewish commercial travellers, watched with impassive boredom or lechery according to their mood. The last turn consisted of the well-known acrobats Carlo and Bogey, who always moved Pemberton to great enthusiasm. But even acrobats come to an end. The band and audience packed up and moved across to the dancing floor next door. I imagined that Jill would now be going to bed; walking round her room with a Flit machine and inspecting the various corners for mosquitoes; wondering perhaps if I was thinking of her. Well, I was. I became rather disgusted with the Tabarin.

'This is very dull,' I said.

'I suppose you want to go along to the Apollo and see Mausi.'

'It's better than staying here.'

'Come along then.'

As a matter of fact I did want to see Mausi. As things were now I supposed she ought to be liquidated; not, as I kept on saying to myself, that there was really anything to liquidate. And anyhow Mausi was a very good sort and I was anxious not to hurt her feelings.

We got our hats and went out into the night. It was pleasantly fresh after the stale atmosphere of the Tabarin. Tsernigrad seemed deserted. Half-way down the Wilsonovi was a café still open, with lights shining through the door and the rancid smell of *slivovica* and the whine of a gipsy band. Now and then in the distance a dog barked. Otherwise it might have been a city of the dead. Close to the entrance to the Apollo a tall lean figure met us.

'Hullo.'

It was Vickery.

'Going to bed?' he asked.

'Very soon, I expect,' I answered.

I wanted to ask him to join us. I liked the man and would have been proud to show him off: my own generation which just missed the war has a slight inferiority complex about it, so that to be able to produce a real VC is doubly gratifying. But I was held back by an unworthy fear that if he came I would have to pay for his drinks.

'Are you going down here?' he asked, indicating the Apollo.

'Yes,' I answered, and then after a pause, 'why don't you come down and have a night-cap?'

'Won't I be butting in?'

'Not at all.'

I introduced him to the others and the five of us went down. It occurred to me suddenly that Mausi might fall in love with him so that the problem would be solved; but then I realised if she did I might have to support both of them.

Salaries are paid in Tsernigrad on the first of every month, and to-day being the 26th business was slack in the Apollo. The waiters rushed to collect our hats, and Zacharias himself, who was really the proprietor but who found it paid to carry on as head waiter as well, came up rubbing his hands and enquiring after our healths. And well he might, since Pemberton and his friends had probably spent over two thousand pounds here in the last four years. Some of the girls were sitting at the bar, but Zacharias shooed them away to make room for us. We climbed up on the high stools and I looked round for Mausi. She was in one of the pew-like boxes and I brought her along; it was one of her good points that she never came up unless invited. I introduced her to Vickery and watched for the reaction. There was none, though some of her colleagues were obviously interested. We ordered drinks, five

47

whiskies and sodas and for Mausi a *feingespritz*, that in-
nocuous mixture of white wine and soda water that en-
ables cabaret girls to carry on till four a.m. When she
drank she held her hand under her glass to prevent drops
falling on her dress. The dress to-night was a new one, a
blue that set off her childish fairness. I wondered if I
mightn't just as well say nothing about anything, and wait
for the end of the month when she would be going in any
case.

The band started playing again at our arrival. Two of
the girls got up and danced. I felt comfortable and at
home. Vickery to my satisfaction seemed to be getting on
very well with the others. Mausi suddenly touched my
elbow.

'*Du, ich bin prolongiert!*'

She had managed to get her contract renewed for
another month. What on earth was to be done now?

'Aren't you pleased?' she asked.

'Of course I'm pleased,' I said, thinking desperately.
'The trouble is I may be away next month.'

'Where are you going?'

'To Sofia.'

It all sounded very feeble and improbable.

'How long for?'

'I don't know; I expect most of the month.'

I don't know whether she believed me. Luckily at that
moment I was temporarily rescued by guffaws from behind
and thumps on the back.

'Here, old man, listen to this one.'

It was the one about the cinema and the finger-bowls
which Vickery had brought with him and which was new
to all of us. I began to translate it for Mausi; it was rather
difficult, as I didn't know the German for finger-bowls and
Mausi had never moved in circles that use them. Suddenly
she interrupted me.

'Do you like that girl?'

'Which girl?'

'That one you keep staring at.'

I did not know I had been staring at anybody, but now she drew my attention I noticed there was a tall good-looking dark girl in a box opposite.

'If you want her,' said Mausi, 'send the waiter for her; I don't want to be in the way.'

'Mausi, don't be an idiot.'

'Well, don't keep looking at her.'

The trouble of course was that Mausi was still hurt at my reception of the news of her stay. I called in Slaughter to help.

'Slaughter, do you see that black-haired trollop over there?'

'Ilonka?'

'I don't know what her name is. Go and dance with her.'

'But I can't dance.'

'Of course you can. Besides it'll help me out. Mausi's being rather trying.'

'Is she? Naughty girl!'

'Go on, man.'

'I'm sure she doesn't want to dance with me.'

I pushed the bashful but not unwilling Slaughter off his stool.

'That girl's a Hungarian,' said Mausi in a voice of scorn. She herself was an Austrian, and Austrian cabaret artistes have a contempt for their Hungarian colleagues equal only to that felt by the Hungarians for the Czechs.

We watched the two dance. Slaughter's style of dancing is peculiar. Even the waiters smile discreetly when he takes the floor, and his partner is apt to look ridiculous. Mausi's spirits improved, only to freeze into dignity when Ilonka broke off after a couple of rounds and came back with

49

Slaughter to the bar. Ilonka was in high fettle and her voice dominated the conversation.

'The Vuchinians,' she said, 'are a lot of savages. A man came up to me in a café this afternoon and offered me a hundred douros!'

Grimshaw said she was damned lucky to have found a Vuchinian with a hundred douros to offer.

'Men of any breeding or education behave quite differently,' Ilonka went on. 'If they like a girl they arrange to meet her in town the next day, and take her to dinner or out in a car somewhere. Of course quite platonic. This sort of thing goes on for at least three or four days. Then, when they have got to know each other and he has had an opportunity to give her to understand what material assistance he is in a position to offer, then of course he can ask her if she thinks they are sufficiently mutually congenial for their relations to become more intimate.'

Ilonka looked towards Vickery, but he was engrossed in a conversation with Pemberton; her eyes passed over Slaughter, who was scraping out his pipe, and met mine. Yes, my dear, I thought, we quite understand each other and one might do a lot worse; but I've got too much on my hands. Nothing doing.

Ilonka took hold of Vickery's arms and made him dance with her. Afterwards, encouraged by a couple of brandies, she danced again with Slaughter. Mausi became reassured and cheered up. The night wore on. Snowball, the black jazz drummer, looking rather foolish and self-conscious, did his special turn which was to sing *The Song is Ended* in Hungarian. We are rather proud of this in the Apollo, as we feel there are very few niggers in the world who can sing this sort of song in Hungarian. I myself became cheerful. After all, a happily married man, son-in-law of a director of the Meridian Insurance Company, would not have many chances of a night out. One must make hay while the sun shines. The only cloud on my horizon was that Vickery seemed to be drinking a great many whiskies and sodas and I was anxious about the bill. At four o'clock, official closing time, my fears became vocal.

'Let's pay and go,' I said.

Mausi whispered to me to wait for her and slipped out to change. Zacharias produced a pencil and calculated. Twenty-six whiskies and sodas at twenty douros, four brandies at twenty douros, three *feingespritz* at fifteen douros . . .

To my astonishment Vickery pulled out a note-case full of hundred-douro notes.

'This is on me,' he said.

'No, everyone pays his own whack down here.'

'Anyhow, I owe the Consul three hundred.'

As he pushed the notes across he must have noticed the surprise on my face, for he explained that he had been down to the races that afternoon and got a winner at thirty to one. I reflected that if I had been in low water and gone to the races I would certainly have lost. But I was glad to have my three hundred douros back.

'Come on, you fellows. Slaughter, are you coming with us or going home with your girl friend?'

'Good Lord, no.'

They went off on foot and Mausi and I got into a taxi.

'We're both rather sleepy to-night, aren't we?' I said.

'Yes.'

The taxi stopped in front of the hotel where she was staying, a tall grimy building in a side-street behind the Continental.

'You're not angry?' she asked suddenly.

'Why should I be?'

'About my making a fuss this evening.'

'You were rather upset.'

51

'Yes, I was jealous. I can't help it. Are you angry?'
'Of course not.'
'Tell me, are you glad I'm staying on?'
'Yes.'
'Say, "I'm glad you're staying on." '
'I'm very glad you're staying on.'
'*Du* . . .'

I felt her arms tightly round my neck. Then she jumped out of the cab and disappeared in the big doorway. I stared at the back of the chauffeur's head. There was something vaguely familiar about it, and I recognised him as the man who had driven Jill and myself eight hours before. Probably he was thinking I was a bit of a lad. I gave him my address. On the way home I decided that if I ever had a son I would advise him to have to do only with women of such unpleasant and repulsive characters that he would be able to throw them off at once and without the slightest compunction whenever he wanted to.

5

I may have given the impression that in each of the last three chapters I claim to have made a fresh conquest, and it may be asked what on earth they could all have seen in me. I hasten to reassure the reader that I have little success with women. A self-appointed lady killer is an unpopular character. Also I am not one. Of the three girls mentioned Olga was a fool, Jill's encouragement had been very non-commital, and Mausi is a type who will get fond of anybody who is reasonably kind to them.

When we divide the world into rich and poor we all of us like to class ourselves among the poor; though when the dividing line is between those of good family and others we like to think of our own family as good. However, I have to admit that all my life I have done less work and for a higher salary than ninety-five per cent of my fellow beings; and also that my family is entirely undistinguished. My father is a solicitor with a not very affluent practice in Leicester. I have one brother who is married and has gone into partnership with my father, and one sister who lives at home, but hopes in time to have a chicken farm in Wales.

I am very fond of my family, but have grown away from them. When I go back there to stay I seem very soon to have said all that I have to say. Perhaps I have more in common with my sister-in-law than with the others. I was rather frightened of her at first; she is one of these very capable and managing young women. But she always treats me with great deference. I imagine the reason is that she has that curious geographical inferiority complex which people who live in places like Leicester often feel when they meet people who live in places like Aleppo. They are afraid of appearing provincial and stuffy. Goodness knows why; a fortnight in Aleppo would certainly cure them.

In appearance I like to think I resemble a photograph of Aldous Huxley which I once saw in the *Sphere*. But no one else could see the likeness. When in funds I am rather dressy, but haven't the knack of looking after my clothes, so that they soon wear out. I am not shy and am quite a useful guest at parties. When I was at Oxford I read a great deal and was always in the van of literary fashion, but nowadays read very little beyond newspapers. I am a great movie fan and have a weakness for slender blondes. I have a fair head for spirits, but too much wine affects my stomach. The only thing I have ever really been ashamed of is poverty. Such is myself.

*   *   *

As I lay in bed with my cup of early tea on the morning after that night at the Apollo I decided that things were not really as difficult as I had imagined. I was, of course, in love with Jill, but not as yet by any means definitely committed: until I was, there was no need to do anything drastic about Mausi. As I have said I hated the idea of hurting Mausi's feelings, and after all girls nowadays rather like a man to have an eventful past. I pictured Jill telling the story to a bosom friend: 'And then there was an Austrian dancer who was desperately in love with him. My dear, I thought every moment I should have a knife in my back!' And the bosom friend being properly impressed. Really there was no need for me to worry myself. For the present I would just wait until something definite happened.

But nothing did. A cabinet was formed (including the Nationalists, so that Pemberton was wrong after all), but my private affairs showed no progress whatever. When I went round to the Bowles' at cocktail time that evening the house was full of third secretaries and resounding with the voice of Pujotas. I went again two days later and found the same thing. I felt slightly peevish. Then Hughes-Winsor's motor launch went wrong so that the Danube scheme was definitely off. Meanwhile Vickery never turned up at the Consulate to reclaim his medals, and I heard nothing of him until one day I ran into Beryl Glover in the Wilsonovi, who demanded to be taken and given a beer.

'I'm so thrilled,' she said. 'I was terrified I wouldn't find anybody to talk about it to.'

'You've got Clive at your mercy all the evening.'

'Oh, he doesn't count.'

'Surely women marry just to have a listener on tap.'

'Why do men marry then?'

'Goodness knows; perhaps to have someone to attract the mosquitoes.'

'Oh, you're awful!'

One of the many reasons I am fond of Beryl is that even when I am at my most inane she gives me the impression I am being rather bright. I steered her to an unoccupied table on the pavement of the Café Esplanade.

'Well?' I said.

'I suppose I really oughtn't to have beer. Do you know I've put on five pounds since Easter?'

'It doesn't matter. You aren't really fat. Just voluptuous.'

'How horrible! But I will have beer after all. I like beer.'

'Well, here I am waiting to be talked to.'

'My dear, I'm thrilled, absolutely thrilled. And really I was thinking I should never be thrilled again. But I've just met a man ... '

'Lieut-Col C. P. Vickery, VC, DSO.'

'It was!'

'Where did you meet him?'

'At Miss Fraser's.'

'Miss Fraser's?'

'I went up to call, and he was there. The very last place you'd expect to find a man like that!'

Beryl takes her calling very seriously. She is anxious to maintain in Tsernigrad the high standard of social observance which prevailed in the northern suburb where she used to live before Pemberton offered her husband his present job. She has an enormous number of cards printed and regularly goes round leaving them even on such unlikely recipients as Miss Fraser.

'What did you do to him?' I asked.

'Don't be silly. I asked him to dinner. Tuesday week. He's interested in some scheme and I expect Clive could help him. Will you come?'

'I'd love to.'

55

'I'll get Miss Bingham for you. I suppose she can come without her uncle and aunt. And I'll have to find another woman for Clive.'

'What about Miss Fraser?'

'Oh, she's dreadful!'

'But you haven't told me what Vickery was doing up there.'

'Oh, they were talking about some transport scheme.'

'But he was teaching at a language school.'

'This motor business is a side show at present. He's still at the language school. It's awful to think that all these ridiculous Vuchinian girls can go and talk to him for fifteen douros an hour. I want to go and have lessons myself.'

'So you've really fallen.'

'Utterly, my dear.'

'It's rather sad for your old admirers like me.'

'You! As if you ever took any interest.'

Poor Beryl. Her tragedy, unknown to herself, was that nobody (except perhaps the mild and faithful Clive) ever did take any interest, that is, in the way she meant. Everybody liked her; everybody was ready to squeeze her hand in a taxi or even, if there was enough whisky about, tickle her in the course of a game of sardines. But that was all. Quite apart from considerations of time and place and possible complications, which after all are the best safeguards of marital fidelity, no one was ever prepared to go any further. Many women like to believe in their heart of hearts that if they had not been kept in the path of rectitude by force of circumstance or by their own iron wills they would have made a tremendous success of the profession of courtesan. I am sure Beryl thought so; and I would never forgive anyone ill-mannered enough to disillusion her.

I gave Beryl another beer and saw her into her tram.

When I got back to my own flat, Agnes, my cook-house-keeper, told me rather tartly that '*das Fräulein*' was in the sitting-room. Agnes and Mausi did not get on. Agnes disapproved of cabaret girls, and Mausi considered that Agnes did not look after me properly; and made no secret of it. I found her curled up like a kitten in my largest arm-chair with a pile of my socks.

'Doesn't that woman ever darn your socks?' she asked indignantly.

'Nobody ever does. I wear them till the holes start showing above my shoes and then throw them away.'

'But that's very extravagant.'

'Not very. I only buy cheap socks.'

'Well, they're all done now except the brown ones. That woman says she hasn't got any brown wool.'

'Perhaps she hasn't.'

'Anyhow I'll get some in the town to-morrow.'

Mausi was looking rather nice curled up in the chair: an ornament to any gentleman's sitting-room.

'*Du*,' she said suddenly, '*ich werd' dir was sagen*.'

'Well?'

'That Hungarian girl is very common.'

'Who, Ilonka?'

'*Sie hat den Kellner geküsst*.'

Kissing a waiter is regarded as the depth of social and moral degradation.

'Which one?' I asked.

'Zacharias.'

'You shouldn't call him a waiter. He's the proprietor.'

'*Der Stritzi!*'

She gave further details of this horrid affair, which had taken place at Mirko's, a dirty little café-restaurant half-way down the hill towards the Danube. Thither the artists and staff of the two cabarets, the Tabarin and the Apollo, would often resort in the early morning after closing time in order to drink soup, play cards, quarrel and generally work off the slight muzziness resulting from consuming inferior alcohol from 9.30 p.m. to 4.30 a.m. But it made me rather suspicious to hear that Mausi had been there again; for Mirko has a sideline that is more profitable than the sale of coffee or gulyas soup.

'Have you been buying cocaine?' I asked sternly.

She got very red.

'Yes.'

'You promised me you'd never get any more.'

'I know.'

'And I told you if I found you getting it I'd have nothing more to do with you. You're too young to let yourself go to pieces.'

'I'm not young any more.' (Mausi was just twenty-two.)

'If ever I find you again ... '

'I didn't mean to get any more. You know I haven't for a fortnight. Only I was worried. I thought you were getting tired of me. I haven't taken any of it, really I haven't.'

'Where is it?'

'Here in my bag.'

She gave me the little fold of paper. I took it to the window and the evening breeze scattered the white powder over the roofs of Tsernigrad.

'How much did you pay for it?'

'Forty douros.'

I counted the notes out on the table.

'No,' she said.

'Don't be an idiot.'

'No, I won't take money from you.'

Very well then, I would respect her pride. I put the money back in my pocket, worried not so much because my conscience would not let me rest until I had got her a bottle of scent or chocolates that would cost at least sixty douros (I am not quite as mean as all that), as because I vaguely felt she was laying me under a moral obligation. The emotional atmosphere in the room was becoming more charged.

'Let's make some tea,' I said.

'Yes, let's.'

Making tea with Mausi on the little electric heater was always rather fun. I used to maintain, quite rightly, that she knew nothing about making tea. She, like all her kind, regarded the beverage as dangerous, and thought that tea as I insisted on having it was rank poison. She classed it with other curious and dangerous habits of mine such as sleeping with the window open. When our usual wrangle began the emotional tension relaxed. I rather enjoyed her fussing over me; and wondered if I would enjoy Jill fussing. Regretfully I decided that probably I would not. I am an undomesticated animal. I enjoy, at intervals, what I might describe as amateur domesticity – the domesticity of a cabaret girl in her spare time. But the whole-time professional domesticity of a respectable married woman (which doesn't come to an end at the end of the month) might become tiresome.

After tea we turned on the radio, and later, when the ether seemed to hold nothing but Bach, we did a crossword puzzle out of a Viennese weekly. After a time I began to wonder about dinner. I hadn't ordered any; and if I did now Agnes in her present mood might make a fuss, and it was too hot for a fuss. On the other hand now that I was, so to speak, in the running for Jill, it would be rude to Jill if I was seen dining a dancer in the town. I hoped there were some eggs in the house so that we could send Agnes out for the night and let Mausi do her worst with a frying-pan.

Mausi noticed I was not being very helpful with the crossword puzzle.

'What's the matter?'

'I was wondering if there was any food in the kitchen.'

'I must go back. I've got a rehearsal.'

This last was said with some pride. I remembered that the fact of her staying on another month meant that there were four new dances to be rehearsed. Mausi had no more talent than ninety-five per cent of her colleagues, whose gyrations are merely to allow the Czech and German commercial travellers to get a better view of their legs. But like all the others she regarded herself as an artist, and took the rehearsals (which were merely to get the band synchronised) very seriously indeed. I went down with her to the door.

'Are you coming to the bar this evening?'

'No, not to-night.'

'Just for a few minutes; it's dull when you don't come.'

'Not to-night. I'm rather tired and very hard up.'

'Don't go down to the Tabarin!'

'They're all far too ugly.'

'I'll bring some brown to-morrow.'

'What?'

'Brown wool; for your socks.'

I watched her slim figure disappear round the corner and then went back upstairs. She really was a dear, was Mausi. But it was rather a relief when she had gone. I have never been able to understand the tendency to regard philanderers as idlers. The miner, at the end of his shift, hands over his pick and shovel to his relief, and the harassed accountant can lock up an unfinished balance sheet in a drawer till Monday morning. But a woman can neither be locked up in a drawer, nor, as a general rule, handed over to a substitute. Although the mental, physical and nervous output is often far greater than in coal-mining or accountancy, respite is uncertain and fortuitous.

I felt it nice to sit in a large chair in an empty room and read *The Times*.

6

I would have liked that night to have gone to the Continental Bar, but an evening that starts there generally costs from two to three hundred douros, and my funds were rather low. So I went and had a lonely dinner at the Bristol. The restaurant was full of hard-faced well-nourished men sitting in twos and threes, glowering at each other, and becoming restive when a member of any of the rival groups went out to the telephone. They were all so exactly like the villains of American film dramas that one got the impression that twenty minutes before they had been clutching Jean Harlow or Tallulah Bankhead or some such other intensely beautiful and virtuous young lady in an unwelcome embrace. Unconsciously one scanned their faces for traces of the avenging fist of a Gary Cooper or Clark Gable. I wondered at first who they were; and then remembered that whenever a chauvinist government comes into power in a Balkan country there is a possibility of contracts for war material, and representatives of all the armament firms swoop down like vultures.

The present government was distinctly chauvinist. Three weeks before there had been a coalition composed of the Liberals (who correspond to our Conservatives), the Progressives (who correspond to our Liberals), and the Jewish Party (who always vote with the group in power). Then had come one of those squabbles which occur every six weeks or so in Vuchinian cabinets, and after a good deal of lobbying and intrigue a fresh coalition had been formed consisting of the Liberals, the Nationalists (who correspond to the Hitlerites), the Independent Anti-Semites (who correspond to nothing whatever), and the Jewish Party. It may seem odd that the last two should become political allies; but then there is much in Vuchinian politics that is very odd indeed.

The only difference this reshuffle made to me personally was that the new government decided to make a big show of the Annual Congress of the FIV. The FIV (*Fédération Interalliée des Vainqueurs de la Guerre Mondiale*) is the noisiest of the various ex-servicemen's organisations. Every year it holds a congress in one of the ex-allied capitals, when there is always a good deal of speech-making, flag-waving, and general stirring-up of the bellicose spirit. The decision to hold it this year in Tsernigrad was the only occasion I have ever known to make Sir William Drexler really angry.

Sir William was close on retiring age, and, one felt, almost reconciled to the fact that his career had not been much of a success. He had been Counsellor for so long that at one time it seemed unlikely that he would ever get an independent post; indeed it is quite probable that he was given Tsernigrad not so much because it was thought he would make a success of it as because the Foreign Office had charitable wishes for his pension. Not that Sir William was stupid. He simply had no interest in anything except Oriental carpets, of which he had a magnificent collection, and on which, as soon as he retired, he was going to write a book. At Tsernigrad we had a very able and energetic First Secretary who did all the work. When he was on leave (as he was at the time of which I am writing), and there was only Hughes-Winsor left, a calm settled over the Legation, only to be disturbed by interruptions such as the FIV Congress.

Sir William was obviously in a bad temper when he sent for me.

'The Government are going to give a dinner to the FIV,' he said.

'Will I have to go?'

'Of course you will.' When Sir William suffers he likes his staff to suffer too. 'Now, about this Congress. Do you know the French are sending two sections of Senegalese machine-gunners?'

'No, I didn't.'

'Well, they are. So of course the Italians have got to send a company of Bersaglieri. The French want to go one better and they're sending a blinded air officer as well. And now I hear that the Italians have found up a sergeant-major who lost both arms and legs and has to be carted about in a wheel-barrow and fed with a spoon. They bring these wretched creatures here and lead them about in a show just to stir up international bad feeling.'

'What are our people sending?'

Sir William pushed a letter towards me. I picked it up and read that while it was hoped that Colonel Goodman would be able to attend if his business engagements permitted, the British Delegation would consist of Dame Helen Whittington, Mrs Prout, Miss Baldock and the Hon Mrs Travers-Bones.

'Do you know who they are?' I asked.

'Goodman I believe has something to do with Moor-sides. I know nothing about the others. I suppose some of these pestilential women who have nothing to do but found leagues and sit on committees.' Sir William in his heat got up and walked up and down the room. 'I disapprove, mind you, of our taking any part in these things at all. But if we do we ought to do it properly. The people will simply laugh. Here are the French and Italians and I suppose everybody else turning out with half a regiment of soldiers, and I have to walk with four middle-aged women.'

'You might get Miss Fraser,' I suggested.

'Then there would be five of them.'

'Well, the people here have some respect for her.'

'Very well, you can ask her if you like.'

'And then we've got a v c in the colony.'

'Who?'

'A man called Vickery. A colonel, or was. He's just come.'

'Is he a gentleman?'

'I think so.'

'Very well, you can ask him too.'

'Though I'd sooner back Miss Fraser if you want someone to cope with Mrs Travers-Bones.'

Sir William grunted. He was himself a little frightened of Miss Fraser, and in any case was not fond of jokes. He once made one himself. It was when an English football team came to Tsernigrad, and the night after the match at 12.30 a.m. they had stopped in front of the British Legation on their way from the Apollo to the Tabarin and sung *God Save the King*. At 3.20 a.m. (on their way from the Tabarin back to the Apollo) they did it again; and Sir William remarked next morning that he had caught cold through springing out of bed so many times during the night and standing to attention. But that is the only joke of his recorded.

7

I liked Miss Fraser, and though she regarded me as very young and foolish she was, I think, in her way fond of me. She had hardly any friends, except perhaps Mrs Brinkworth who ran the Girls' Friendly Society. Not that Miss Fraser had any sympathy with the g f s: she disapproved of all forms of religion, being of the type that rejects the testimony of the Scriptures, the Fathers and the Churches, while retaining implicit faith in the integrity of Balkan politicians. But she had stepped in soon after Mrs Brinkworth's arrival (when the local authorities were suspecting the GFS to be an instrument of international intrigue and making trouble) and had more or less adopted her as a protégée. Probably it would be right to say that Miss Fraser had no friends at all, and divided the world into protégées, enemies and neutrals.

I suspect that things were not altogether too easy for Miss Fraser. The war had been over a long time and the British public had lost what interest it had ever had in gallant little Vuchinia. Although Miss Fraser was a recognised expert I imagine she was now finding it difficult to get her articles accepted. Her last book I know was published at her own expense, and I doubt if it sold more than four hundred copies. Even the Vuchinians were beginning to find that her name carried less weight than it used to and were rather neglecting her. Only when money was required for some charitable purpose and they couldn't get anyone more important they came to her to issue an appeal; and she always did.

She was unfortunate too in that her case was wearing rather thin. The Vuchinians are a sturdy and likeable people, but there are many skeletons in the cupboard of their public life. They have broken almost as many treaties as they have made, and political murders have been common. In face of the flood of post-war disclosures it was becoming more and more difficult to maintain that the inner history of Vuchinian governments from 1912 to 1918 had been either glorious or creditable; and of course rival apologists, pro-Serb, pro-Hungarian, pro-Bulgar, or pro-Greek, snatched at the many opportunities to lay the blame for those years at the door of Vuchinia. Still, Miss Fraser never faltered. For her, ever since she first came to

the country in 1895, Vuchinian Infallibility was both a
Creed and a Call, just as for Mrs Brinkworth was the in-
culcation of strict Anglican principles upon Vuchinian
girlhood. Sometimes I used to think that both of them
were to be envied. It is better, perhaps, to have a vocation,
even a ridiculous and improbable one, than to drift
through life aimlessly as I was doing.

No one but Miss Fraser could have built a villa up
there; for no one else would have had the relentless driving
force to urge a lazy local contractor with the materials up
that slope. There was no road, merely a mud track, which
after rain turned into a morass where one lurched and
slithered and sank knee-deep. I had once taken an hour to
climb it when I had gone up there one winter, and only
succeeded by floundering from gravestone to gravestone
up the side of the old Turkish cemetery. Now of course the
ground was baked hard and red, with great cracks in it
where lizards lurked. All the same it was a stiff climb.
Miss Fraser had used her military instincts when estab-
lishing her stronghold upon that site. The enemy arrived
exhausted and completely at her mercy.

I found her sitting outside on the vine-covered verandah, hammering away at her typewriter. She looked up
and noticed me.

'Do you want anything?' she asked.

'I've come to see you.'

'Then come in and sit down.'

I joined her on the little verandah.

'About this FIV business,' I began. 'The Minister wants
to know if you would care to walk with the British delegation.'

'Does the Minister happen to know that I served with
the Vuchinian and not with the British army?'

'Of course he does.'

'Then why does he ask unnecessary questions?'

66

'He wants to make his own little party rather more impressive. But I'll tell him there's nothing doing.'

'Who are the British delegation?'

'Apparently four ladies.'

Miss Fraser got extremely angry.

'What absolute rubbish!' she said. 'Women have no business to take any part in things of that sort. They ought to stay at home.'

This I felt, coming from Miss Fraser, was a bit thick, even though many of the Vuchinians had, and still have, grave doubts as to her sex.

'I'm not being inconsistent,' she went on, interrupting my thoughts. 'Anything I may have done myself I simply did because there was not a man there to do it. As soon as there was an officer available to take on my battalion I handed over to him.'

'I see.'

'There are hundreds of ex-officers in England who would have been only too glad to come. And if the Minister wants anybody, why doesn't he get this man Vickery?'

'I'm going to ask him.'

Miss Fraser clapped her hands and a big long-boned peasant girl brought us out half a litre of the sour and heady red wine grown in Miss Fraser's own vineyard.

'I hear you know Vickery,' I said.

'How did you hear that?'

'Mrs Glover told me.'

'A common little creature. Goodness knows why she keeps coming up here to leave her ridiculous cards.'

'I'm very fond of her.'

'I dare say.'

I began to wish, as I always did, that Miss Fraser's chairs were not quite so hard and uncomfortable.

'How did you meet Vickery?' I asked.

'He came up here. He had read two of my books before

67

he came to this country at all, and wanted to talk to me about them.'

'It's real fame people in Mukden and Harbin reading your books on Vuchinia.'

'Why shouldn't they read them?'

I realised I had said the wrong thing, and became rather confused.

'Perhaps he read them in Warsaw,' I suggested, and at once felt the suggestion was an idiotic one.

'I really have no idea where he read them.'

'Is he still at that language school?'

'He won't be there much longer,' said Miss Fraser shortly.

'He's a pretty live wire, I imagine.'

'He's the only man I have met since the war with enough brains to see the possibilities of this country and enough character to make use of them!'

I looked at Miss Fraser. This was not her usual tone. It was the voice of a prophet, such as she must have used on that legendary occasion when she burst in upon the assembled Vuchinian cabinet in the spring of 1915 and told them that Austria-Hungary must be destroyed; the voice that did not perhaps launch a thousand ships (Vuchinia has no navy) but which sent three hundred thousand peasants to their deaths between Lake Ohrid and the swamps of the Dobrudja. I felt a little embarrassed.

'He's lucky,' I said.

'Why?'

'To see something he can go all out for.'

'Indeed,' said Miss Fraser.

There is something about Miss Fraser that makes me always want to discuss with her the ever fascinating problem of the relation of my own personality to the universe. But I never seem able to get very far.

'Take my own case,' I said. 'I'd be only too willing to

go all out for something. But so far I haven't got what the Victorians used to call a Cause.'

'The best thing for you would be to marry some sensible young woman with a little money of her own.'

Could she be referring to Jill? I became most interested.

'Do you really think so?' I asked.

'I do. And now I must turn you out because I have to get my letters finished in time for the post.'

Somewhat disappointed I got up to go.

'I'll come up again before long if I may,' I said. 'I know you think I'm very young and rather a half-wit, but I can't help that.'

'At least you have one good quality.'

I pricked up my ears.

'You have a certain recognition of your own short-comings.'

With that I had to be contented.

As I went two goats came down from the little cupola that marked the last resting-place of Ali Moustafa, one time Vali of Tsernigrad, and eyed me superciliously. I pondered over my conversation with Miss Fraser. 'A sensible young woman with a little money of her own.' If that was a fair description of Jill how very uninteresting it made it all seem. I felt vaguely disappointed. I looked at my watch. Not quite six. A silly time: too late to find anyone to give one tea, and too early to find anybody to give one a cocktail. I wondered if there was any chance of catching Vickery at his school of languages.

8

The school of languages was at the corner of the Kolod-vorskaya, in a big new building that in itself seemed to contain the whole of Tsernigrad's Edgware Road. The

street frontage was taken up with shops for cheap haber-
dashery, bicycle lamps, umbrellas, wireless sets and other
articles that when retailed always seem so particularly
untidy. In the centre a long and dark arcade ran in for
about seventy yards, its sides lined with barbers' shops,
rubber goods, more radios, and mildly pornographic
literature. The place seemed to be entirely populated with
perspiring and rather unshaven young Jews. At three
points along the arcade were stairs leading to the floors
above, which were mostly occupied by small and strug-
gling offices, pensions and furnished lodgings. These last
were of the type known in Central Europe as *sturmfrei*,
that is to say there were no questions asked and tenants
were free from prudish interference. There were no lifts
and the stairs were at an awkward and tiring angle.

The school of languages was on the second floor according to Vuchinian ideas, but as they have a *hochparterre* and
a *mezzanin* we should call it the fourth. At any rate there
were more than eighty steps, and before I was half-way
up I was wondering how the denizens of the *sturmfrei*
lodgings ever got sufficiently rested to have any zest for
their revels. When I arrived I knocked and rang for some
time without getting any answer. At last a very old man
came out of one of the other doors on the corridor, bringing
with him a strong smell of garlic, and asked me what
I wanted. I said the language school and he told me to
go in.

I found the door was unlocked and went into the first
room I came to. It was bare and small, with an uneven
boarded floor, two rickety chairs, a wooden bench, and a
table stained with ink and scarred where lighted cigarettes
had been left along the edges. The walls were discoloured
and pocked with little holes. The only ornament was a
gaudy calendar with a coloured portrait of the Vuchinian
President. It seemed a most unlikely room to house a man

like Vickery. But there were no signs of anybody. I looked out of the window; it opened on a shaft-like courtyard and gave a commanding view of all the wc windows of the flats opposite. There was a step outside and in came a bullet-headed young Vuchinian with a dirty collar. He looked at me angrily.

'I came half an hour ago and you were not here,' he said. 'You will have to give me an extra half-hour without paying.'

'That has nothing to do with me.'

'You are the new English teacher.'

'No, I am not.'

'Then you are his assistant.'

' I have nothing to do with the school.'

'Who are you then?'

'I am the British Consul.'

He didn't believe me, but wasn't sure enough of himself to contradict. We sat for a couple of minutes in hostile silence. Then there was another step outside and Vickery came in.

'Hullo!'

'I came to look you up,' I said.

'That's awfully nice of you.'

'I have been kept waiting more than half an hour,' said the young man. 'I shall complain to the director.'

I said I thought I was rather in the way, but Vickery told me to stay.

'You will now have to give me a two-hour lesson, or I must have all my money back.'

'Well,' Vickery said to him, 'to-day you aren't going to have any lesson at all.'

'But I have paid my money.'

'You can talk to the director about your bloody money. There's nothing doing now.'

'But I have paid for six lessons!'

'Get out!'

'This is a swindle. You are all here common thieves . . . '

Vickery took him by the scruff of his neck, dragged him through the door and threw him out into the corridor.

'Damned little swine,' he said as he came back.

'He's rather worried about his money.'

'He'll be lucky if he gets it. You were quite right when you said that the man who runs this place is a crook. I've finished with it. I've only come back to get my things.'

He opened the drawer in the table and took out some letters. As he did so he told me he was now in charge of a garage, and he was just going to try out a new car. Would I care to come along? The idea appealed to me. We went out of the squalid little office, past the smell of garlic in the corridor, and down the endless spiral of the stairs. At the mouth of the arcade the young Vuchinian was talking excitedly to a friend. He shouted at us as soon as we appeared. Vickery hailed a passing policeman and gave him in charge. The young man of course objected noisily and a crowd began to collect. I became anxious lest my vice-consular name and dignity should be mixed up in a row. However the young man lost his temper with the policeman (who was paying more attention to Vickery than to him) and tried to push him into the gutter. That of course was the end. He was arrested and marched off to the police station, and Vickery and I slipped away unnoticed.

'I'm really rather sorry for that young man,' I said. 'He misses his lesson, he'll probably lose his money, he's thrown out of your office, and now he's locked up for the night.'

'Serve the little swine right.'

As he went along Vickery told me his news. One of his pupils had been the daughter of a garage-owner. She had told him that her father had just had to sack his manager for incompetence and dishonesty and was rather short-handed. Vickery had gone along as a volunteer. For the last ten days he had gone every morning to the garage at a quarter to six so as to be on duty when the night taxi chauffeurs came in to hand over their cars to the day men. From eight till half-past twelve he was teaching at the language school. At half-past twelve he came back to check over any repair jobs that had come in during the morning, and to demonstrate a car to possible customers. From three to seven he was in the language school again. Then he came back to superintend the shift over from the day men to the night men. After that he helped old Sonnenschein with his correspondence and went through the books.

'When do you get away?' I asked.

'Oh, those accounts are in a frightful mess. I'm generally there till about midnight. Then I go down to the Tabarin or the Apollo and have a whisky and soda.'

'Do you ever eat or sleep?'

'I get three hours, from two to five. I never want much sleep. And when I'm hungry I send out for a sandwich.'

'Well, I'm damned.'

'As a matter of fact it is a bit too much. Anyhow I'm dropping the school now.'

I felt that if ever there was a man who deserved to win through here was one.

We turned under an old Turkish archway and arrived at the yard which formed the garage. It was littered with the rusting entrails of forgotten cars. Along two sides were temporary buildings run up out of unpainted boards and flattened petrol tins. Two nondescript youths were changing the wheel of an ancient Ford. Old Sonnenschein waddled out of his office to greet us. Under the bonhomie natural to his race I thought I noticed a certain nervous-

73

ness towards his new manager. There was none, however, about Mlle Sonnenschein, a very dressy and perfumed person, who came out almost immediately to join us. I think she expected Vickery to ask her to come with us. But he didn't. We got into the new car, a Mervyn Dominion, and drove off.

'Where are we going?'

'The Danube road's the best.'

I like the Danube road. It runs due east from the town, towards the Bulgarian frontier. For the first two miles, until one gets clear of the sprawling suburbs with their brick-yards and tram-lines, the going is atrocious, but after that the road is as good as most that can be found in the Balkans. For over fifteen miles it runs along the line of a crest, with the great river down at the bottom to the left: flashing reaches of muddy silver, willowed banks and green islands, and beyond marsh land and the endless plain with its little dotted villages and the growing maize. To the right lies an undulating country of orchards and meadows and copses that might almost be Somerset. It was all very pleasant and I lay back luxuriously. We met no one. Except on market-days one can travel for miles in Vuchinia without seeing a soul. Mervyn springs are good and the thick carpet of dust smoothed out the little irregularities in the road. I watched the speedometer crawl round from fifty to sixty, to seventy, to seventy-five.

'You can always have a car for an afternoon if you want one,' said Vickery.

'Thanks very much.'

It was a pleasant prospect, but for the moment I was quite satisfied as I was. I am a poor and diffident chauffeur full of visions of sheep or school children round the next corner. I seldom venture on more than twenty-five miles an hour with any internal comfort. To be driven like this, freed from all responsibility, was perfect enjoyment.

And then, very suddenly, there occurred the incident of the Danube road.

As we rounded a turn I saw that a tree trunk blocked the way in front of us. Behind it was a big peasant with a rifle. I heard Vickery curse under his breath as he jammed on the brakes and the car skidded in the dust. Someone shouted and Vickery whipped out an automatic pistol and fired. At that moment the following wind enveloped us in the cloud of dust. There was a rifle shot and a bullet crashed through the windshield.

'We can't turn round,' said Vickery. 'Make for the ditch.'

In my bewilderment I had realised that this was a hold-up by local bandits who are nasty customers if resisted. I was thoroughly frightened, jumped out; tripped against the footboard; and fell on the road with an intense pain in my ankle. Vickery caught my shoulder and dragged me to the side; a figure loomed out of the clearing dust; Vickery fired again. As we dropped into the ditch came three shots close at hand and the bullets pinged over our heads.

'Are you hit?' he asked.

'I don't know. I think I've sprained my ankle.'

I suppose I should have been impressed by his gallant rescue of me. As a matter of fact I was conscious only of fear, of the pain in my foot, and of a furious resentment against Vickery for having opened fire and thus causing us to be in our present predicament instead of by now walking safely if ingloriously back towards Tsernigrad in our pants.

The dust had nearly all cleared away. Vickery peered over the top, fired quickly and ducked.

'Is it very painful, old man?'

'Rather. Do you think they're going to rush us?'

'They'll be damned fools if they try.'

He pulled out a cigarette for each of us. I in my turn

peered cautiously through the weeds. Our enemies were about eighty yards away. There were four of them. They seemed to have been rather surprised by our resistance and uncertain what to do. Every now and then they fired some shots in our direction, but if they came nearer Vickery fired back and they hesitated. I remembered an idiotic exercise called 'advancing by sectional rushes' I had so often had to perform in the OTC at school. If anything of the sort occurred to the brigands we were done for. I wondered if it would be any use holding up a handkerchief as a flag of truce; and at once decided it would be merely futile. After about ten minutes I heard the hum of a motor-car in the distance and felt a thrill of hope. But the hum stopped; then started again and died away in the distance.

'How many rounds have you got left?' I asked.

'About twenty. I always carry spare fills.'

That was all very well, but it was not going to keep them off indefinitely. Besides which it would soon be getting dark, and goodness knew what would happen then. The bottom of the ditch was dank and moist; I suspected the presence of noisome crawling things. The pain in my ankle grew worse.

'They're off,' said Vickery suddenly.

I looked myself and saw that it was true. All four of them were making their way up a little hollow to the left. One, who apparently had been hit, was being helped along by the others. At the top of the hollow they stopped and fired a couple of shots back in our direction. Then they disappeared into a wood. We were safe!

A bullet had gone through one of our tyres, and before Vickery had changed the wheel a car came up with a party of gendarmes and a police dog. Apparently the occupants of the car which we had heard had guessed what was happening from the sound of the shooting, and had gone back to the first telephone and called up for help. We pointed out the spot where the brigands had disappeared and the patrol went off after them. Forty minutes later, just as it was getting dark, we were back again in Tsernigrad.

*   *   *

Such was the incident of the Danube road. I have tried to describe it and the part that I personally played as honestly as I could, because the subsequent fuss has made me rather sceptical of published accounts of acts of heroism. Of course my official position made it all a splendid story for the Tsernigrad Press. The morning papers next day came out with a glowing account of the murderous attack upon the British Consul. The evening papers went one better and explained that I had been on a diplomatic mission, carrying secret despatches to Bucharest; and the hold-up had been instigated by the unspeakable Bulgars (the opposition papers said the unspeakable Serbs), who wished to obtain the documents and precipitate another world war. The story got through to Vienna, and the various correspondents there – whose highly coloured versions of Balkan happenings so often cause such intense annoyance in the Balkans – fairly let themselves go. Most of the papers at home gave it half a column; and the most enterprising of the London dailies had a leading article in which the cowardice and inertia of Downing Street was contrasted with the dash and initiative of the British Vice-Consul at Tsernigrad. As a result of course I had several anxious wires from my family; and my Aunt Esther, who is ninety-one and lives in Wiltshire, wrote me a very angry letter to say my behaviour had been extremely foolish and I must insist at once on a transfer to a safer post.

What made me feel so foolish about it all was that no mention was made of Vickery. I told him so when he came up to see me.

'Oh hell,' he said, 'I don't want my name in the papers.'

'But it's damned uncomfortable for me.'

'Why? After all you people can't advertise, and it might do you some good. Whereas if I set up in business here it might do me harm; firms at home would think I'm a sort of buccaneer.'

'Yes, but look here, all I did was to trip over and sprain my ankle. You kept the lot of them off single-handed.'

'Yes, old man, but that was simply because I happened to have the pistol. If you'd had it it would have been the other way round.'

The only thing I could think of doing was to ask Watterson, who was correspondent of a big news agency, to write in and explain what really had happened. He did so, but meanwhile there had been an international crisis and a distinguished actress had slapped the face of another distinguished actress in the grill-room of the Savoy Hotel; so that the matter was no longer of interest.

I was laid up for a week with my ankle. The Continental Bar contingent rolled up in force on two occasions, each time bringing with them a bottle of gin which they proceeded to consume. Pemberton told me that the contract hunters had this time gone away empty; for the moment there was nothing doing except a contract for wire for the Telegraphs Administration, which he, Pemberton, was going to get. Things were all much the same at the Apollo and the Tabarin. Slaughter was steadily falling for Ilonka (which Slaughter himself stoutly but unconvincingly denied). Mausi had got flue and had been away for the last two nights. I was sorry to hear that Mausi was ill, but a little relieved that she could not come round and look after me. I might have felt I was having almost too much of her.

Any looking after that I wanted I had from Beryl, who

is always wonderful in any emergency. She came up every day, coped with my bandages, and brought me all the gossip of the town. Jill came up with her once, and then again later with her aunt, each time looking so nice and obviously so full of interest that I remembered very definitely that I was in love with her. Miss Fraser came up once with Mrs Brinkworth, and Sir William and Lady Drexler called and left a *Blackwood's* and four back numbers of the *Sphere*. Altogether I rather enjoyed my convalescence. I noticed that while the men all took the line that it had been a very uncomfortable experience, the women were so convinced that I was a hero and that my disclaimers were to be put down to a manly modesty that in the end I almost began to believe it myself. Of course there were exceptions. Miss Fraser, I am sure, realised exactly what had happened. And then Mrs Bowles said that when her brother was attacked by seven bandits in Burma he shot three of them and brought the other four back to justice single-handed. But of course Mrs Bowles has always regarded me as a spineless and dissipated young man.

Meanwhile the gendarmes succeeded in catching the wounded brigand though the other three got clean away. It was found that he was already wanted on other scores, and in due course according to Vuchinian legal practice he was sentenced to death and to four hundred and eighty-two years' penal servitude. When I heard the news I remembered the hard wolfish looks on the face of the sergeant of gendarmes as they set out in pursuit; and I had an irrational and uncomfortable feeling that somehow the man's blood was upon my hands.

9

The first time I left my flat was to go to Beryl's dinner. I like dining with the Glovers. There is something very delightful about the serious way in which Beryl takes her parties. Everything has to be very up-to-date and correct. The table of course is polished and clothless, with little mats; the napkins are folded in gothic shapes, each containing a card to ensure that we sit in our right order. Generally to begin with there is a certain nervousness. Beryl is preoccupied with the possibility of calamities in the kitchen, and Clive is busy uncorking the bottle of sherry, the bottle of white wine, and the bottle of port which he is later to hand round in their proper order. But soon the sherry begins to tell – in justice to Clive I ought to say that it is nearly always good sherry – and the tension relaxes. The white wine carries on the good work; and by the time the port is reached there is an atmosphere of cheerful ribaldry, which is probably much more in keeping with smart society than the rather mannered opening. For me Beryl's parties have another charm; I always seem to shine at them.

It was therefore in a cheerful mood that I hunted for my stud. I wondered who the other woman was going to be, and hoped it would be Mrs McLean. She was the young widow of an Air Force officer and had just come out as Secretary to Torrens, the new Passport Control Officer. I had been introduced to her, and found her not unattractive. I think I have said already that I have a weakness for slender blondes. Of course I was really going to meet Jill, with whom I was in love; but all the same it would be nice to get to know Mrs McLean. Thinking of Jill reminded me that it might be a good plan to ring her up and see if I could take her. I did so. Mrs

Bowles came to the phone and told me that though it was nice of me to have rung up it had been arranged that Jill should go to the Glovers with Miss Phipps.

Miss Phipps? Oh yes, of course she had come out in some vague connection with the Anglo-Vuchinian War Orphanage, now being wound up. So she was going to be the sixth. I was disappointed. Then I tore two of my collars and arrived late and rather hot.

The beginning was unpromising. As I feared I was next to Miss Phipps: Beryl had previously ascertained from me that vice-consuls rank with but after majors, and therefore Vickery sat on her right, while at the other end Miss Phipps, being the elder, sat on Clive's right. To begin with Beryl and Clive were taken up with the mechanics of the dinner; and Vickery, who seemed to be one of those men who do not talk much until they know the company, was merely replying to Jill's rather conventional gambits. With grim determination I turned to Miss Phipps and asked her how she liked Vuchinia.

Miss Phipps said she loved it all, especially the people. They were so Arcadian, she thought, so like the ancient Greeks; they had such respect for women.

I felt there were possibilities in Miss Phipps after all, and tried to lead her on to tell me more about the ancient Greeks. But she eluded me and we had to come back to Vuchinia. Tsernigrad itself she had found rather disappointing; one had hoped for something historic and romantic instead of just rather ugly modern buildings and trams. And then these taxi drivers here were so dangerous! One was almost afraid to cross a street.

'Almost as bad as Paris,' said Jill.

'Oh, those taxi drivers in Paris,' said Beryl, who could now devote herself more to the conversation. 'Whenever I have to cross over to the Gare de Lyon I'm terrified out of my life!'

'But of course they drive wonderfully well in Paris.'

'Yes, they certainly do drive well.'

I suppose there are few people living who have not heard a conversation to this effect in almost the same words at least ten times. I myself must have heard it thirty times. And there is really no reason why anyone should object. We none of us have anything original to say except perhaps twice in a lifetime; and it is all to the good that there should be a stock of these hardy conversational evergreens to facilitate social intercourse. But at that moment I was out of tune with the universe and it annoyed me. However a whole crop of them was to follow. Miss Phipps thought that some of the Vuchinian girls – like other foreign girls – were pretty when they were quite young, but lost their looks very quickly: they got so dreadfully fat. Clive remarked that it was strange that foreigners seemed to take so little exercise, though of course some of the younger ones were beginning to take up games. Miss Phipps thought it was a good thing that people were travelling more nowadays – it tended to broaden the mind. Beryl, starting off on a new line said how trying people were who were bright and talkative in the early morning. Miss Phipps suggested that no doubt they meant well.

'I always think,' said Jill, 'that one can't say anything worse about anybody than say they mean well!'

I looked at her in real alarm. In my inner circle of friends are at least five people who on an average of once a month announce that one can't say anything worse about anybody than say they mean well, and always bring it out with the same bright air of originality. And of course, as I have said, there is no real reason why they shouldn't. But then I hadn't got to live with any of the five. One must remember that Jill was very young, and presumably capable of learning. But even so . . . It was not until the second round of the wine that I began to cheer up again.

At Beryl's of course the men are left behind to finish their port. Clive brought his glass down to our end of the table and sat between us. He began to talk to Vickery about the motor business, and I remembered that one of the objects of the dinner was that he should offer his help. Vickery listened politely, but I got the impression that he already knew a great deal more about the motor business in Tsernigrad than Clive did. Clive's advice was extremely cautious. One had to be very careful about one's local staff, he said, and very careful about the authorities, who would make trouble wherever they could; and as to credit, never give a Vuchinian credit except against a bank guarantee, and there weren't many banks in the country whose guarantee he'd care to accept. In fact Vuchinia was rather a country to keep out of.

'The other day,' I said to Vickery, 'I heard you described as the one man since the war with enough brains to see the possibilities of Vuchinia.'

He laughed.

'Was that old Miss Fraser?'

'Yes.'

'We're great allies. I cracked up her books to the skies and now she's returning the compliment.'

'Do you really think there are possibilities here?' I asked.

'I do.'

'In spite of its being a poor country with a bad financial reputation, a rotten government, corrupt officials, on the worst possible terms with all its neighbours, and nobody having any idea what may happen in five years' time?'

'Well, if you want safety you buy Consols and get four per cent on your money.'

Clive looked very earnest and shook his head.

'I don't know,' he said. 'In times like these I should prefer a nice safe job with a firm with a big reserve fund and a pension scheme.'

'It's more fun to make a hundred thousand quickly and be your own master.'

Vickery's eye caught mine as he said it, and I felt he was talking to me rather than to Clive.

'Are you going to do it?' I asked.

'Very probably.'

I began to think. Of course such things had been done. I had heard of a young American who had arrived in Belgrade just after the war with five dollars in his pocket and had done it. And it sounded so infinitely more interesting than to marry a sensible young woman with a little money of her own and eventually retire into decent mediocrity at Mentone or Tunbridge Wells.

'Will you have some more port?'

'No thanks.'

'Then shall we join the ladies?'

We went into the next room where Vickery was immediately claimed by Beryl. Jill beckoned to me, and I went over and joined her. Her invitation rather flattered me. With Vickery in the room it was pleasant to be singled out.

'Let's go out on the balcony,' I suggested.

'Yes, all right.'

We went out. The others didn't follow us which was lucky, as there were only two deck chairs. The night was balmy and there was a fat lazy moon. The Glovers live in one of a row of small houses each with a little garden in front, some way from the centre of the town. From far away came the hum of traffic on the main road.

'You were an awful time in there,' she said. 'Whatever were you talking about?'

'Business mostly.'

'How dull.'

'It's sometimes rather romantic; fishing in troubled waters I mean, and making a lot of money quickly.'

'When it comes off.'

'Well, it's romantic just because the chances are a hundred to one that it won't come off.'

'That's not romantic, that's simply a gamble.'

It would be a mistake, I realised, to sit in judgment upon Jill simply because she had on one occasion used a much repeated phrase at a dinner-table. Also it was very pleasant to be sitting by her in the soft night air, watching the glow of her cigarette and listening to the croak of the frogs in the ornamental basin the next garden but one. I told her so.

'Why?' she asked. 'Because it's dark?'

'Partly.'

'Thanks very much.'

'It's not an insult. I find it pleasant because I can sit here knowing that you're rather lovely. And whenever I begin to doubt it your cigarette burns up again, and I can see the tip of your nose and am reassured.'

'When are you going to take me on the river?'

'As soon as Hughes-Winsor's damned boat gets going again. It ought to be soon. Do you think you could come one evening after dinner?'

'I doubt it, unless we have Aunt Eleanor.'

'I'm very fond of her, but I'd rather she stayed at home. And I want you to see the town at night, when it's all lit up. We'll have to go out in the afternoon and arrange for a breakdown.

'All right.'

Suddenly a way of solving my problem dawned on me. Though married life might be tedious if I had to spend all my time running after Jill, yet, if she was desperately in love with me – stranger things had happened than that – and carried, so to speak, most of the emotional weight, it might be quite pleasant. After all apart from being so suitable she was very charming in herself. The chances were that I should be happier married to her than otherwise. Of course if the impossible happened and I ever made a hundred thousand pounds and became my own master I might be unfaithful now and then – that was only to be expected – but I should remain very fond of her. It only remained to be discovered if she was desperately in love with me. Perhaps I could kiss her on the way home in a taxi and see how she reacted.

'Here you two,' Beryl called from within, 'are you going to sit out there all night or are you coming in to play rummy?'

Beryl knew that nobody in England played rummy any more, but one had to do something after dinner and she hadn't got a roulette board. Usually I play that sort of game with great seriousness; I find it hard to hide my discomfort when I am losing more than a shilling. But to-night I was light-hearted; it was a weight off my mind to have shifted the responsibility of a decision on to Jill.

After about an hour (when I had lost twenty douros) Beryl suggested vingt-et-un as being more exciting. So we played vingt-et-un.

Of course, I reflected, there was the difficulty of how to get rid of Miss Phipps on the way back. She might conceivably imagine it was her duty personally to see Jill into her aunt's door. But I doubted it. After all in this age of progress and enlightenment, when girls go wrong through fear of appearing cold-blooded, when husbands are expected to go astray every three months or so to keep themselves fresh, when virtuous women apologise for resisting improper advances, surely a travelled and broad-minded lady like Miss Phipps could not run the risk of being thought old-fashioned.

I played so dashingly that I lost a hundred and eighty-seven douros, and Miss Phipps said archly that I must be lucky in love.

When the time came to go, I had no trouble whatever. Vickery, who had probably noticed how the land lay, pointed out that Jill and I lived in one direction and he and Miss Phipps in the other, and it was all settled before she had any time to discuss it.

So Jill and I started off side by side in a taxi. I determined that the climax should occur just as we got into the road where the Bowles' house was – not before, because if she didn't like it and made a fuss the rest of the journey should be as short as possible to avoid embarrassment. On the other hand if she liked it and responded enough one could always tell the driver to go on, and we could go for a long ride in the light of the moon locked in each other's arms, and become officially betrothed, and the next day I would finally liquidate poor Mausi, and eventually be as good a husband to Jill as circumstances might permit.

We talked on indifferent subjects.

'Did you fall for Vickery like everybody else?' I asked.

'He's very good-looking.'

She had nothing more to say about him, and we discussed our host and hostess. She loved Beryl, and thought Clive rather a dear, but dull.

We crossed the Wilsonovi. Two minutes more, I thought.

I asked her if she played bridge.

She did a little, but disliked playing with her aunt, who took it so impossibly seriously. There was a grim bridge-party on at home to-morrow afternoon, and she was going to the Tennis Club to escape it.

The corner of the road was in sight.

Jill wondered why I never came to the Tennis Club nowadays. I said I would probably go to-morrow.

Now for it.

I seized Jill firmly in my arms and kissed her.

Eagerly I looked for the reaction. There was no reaction whatever.

Now what the dickens did one do? In the usual run of novels one tells the girl that one loves her. But one has to say it with some conviction, and in my present mood of baffled curiosity I felt it wouldn't sound right.

The taxi stopped in front of the house. There was a light in one of the upper windows.

'Aunt Eleanor's waiting up,' said Jill.

What, if anything, was one to deduce from that? Jill's voice was somewhat strainedly normal. I opened the door and handed her out. We said good night as if nothing particular had happened. Jill's latchkey clicked in the lock and she disappeared. I got back into the taxi and went home.

I lay still dressed on my bed and tried to tidy up my thoughts. My scheme had been a fiasco. Jill hadn't actively objected, but nothing was established beyond the fact that she quite liked me, which I knew already. That was hardly enough. Matrimony is a serious matter. I remembered how Grimshaw had once got very confidential at about three o'clock in the morning and told me how depressing was the prospect of returning to England and having always to go to bed with the same woman. And of course that isn't the only snag. One can never tell in advance what will be the loss of personal liberty in other ways. I took out a coin: heads, all out for Jill, tails, tactfully fade away. It came down heads. Very well; perhaps something would turn up. I felt extremely sleepy and went to bed.

IO

I had never been inside the Hotel London until the next day when I went round to see Mausi who was still laid up. I wished she had been staying somewhere else. Although the London is fairly new it is already squalid and depressing, and I reproached myself for not having insisted more effectively that Mausi should move into better quarters. Like all Balkan hotels of its class the porter's lair is up two flights of stairs, a curious arrangement which Slaughter explains as being due to the fact that if the porters lived on the ground floor their repellent aspect could be seen from the street, and intending guests would be frightened away. There would certainly have been this danger with the porter of the London. I asked him the number of Fräulein Radenk's room and he looked at me with suspicion.

'Are you the gentleman who owes me forty douros?'

'No, I am not,' I said.

'Because there is a gentleman about your build who owes me forty douros.'

'Then it must be somebody else.'

He looked at me wistfully as if hoping that on second thoughts I might confess.

'It is very unfortunate,' he went on. 'Of course I always like to do what I can to help, but it is very disagreeable to get mixed up in trouble with the police. And in this case I not only didn't get a tip, but I lost forty douros of my own.'

'All that has nothing to do with me.'

'The day before yesterday,' said the porter, 'a gentleman came back here at five o'clock in the morning with one of the artists.'

'Well, I'm sure it wasn't Fräulein Radenk.'

'No, it was one of the others. He wanted to go up to her room with her. Well, you know as I do that that sort of thing is not allowed. But I always like to do what I can to help; and besides I didn't know where else the girl was going to get the money from to pay her next week's rent. So I told the gentleman that if he liked he could take the next room on the same floor which would cost forty douros and he was very pleased and promised me another twenty for myself. I thought nothing more about it but half an hour later the Morality Police came and made a raid. Well, of course, you know what the Morality Police are, a lot of blackmailers and swindlers. But one can't keep the police out and they went up to the girl's room. Well, it happened the gentleman wasn't there at that minute. He'd gone down the passage to the lavatory. But there were his braces lying on the floor. Of course the police asked the girl whose the braces were, and she got frightened and said they belonged to the proprietor of the hotel. The fool of a girl thought that if it was the proprietor the police wouldn't mind. So the police went up to the proprietor. Meanwhile the gentleman came back and when the girl told him what had happened he got so scared he ran straight out of the hotel, just as he was, without stopping to put his braces on, just holding his hands in his pockets to keeps his trousers up. I was sitting here and saw him. I shouted at him as he went past, but he took no notice and I couldn't catch him.'

'This is all very regrettable,' I said.

'While all this was going on,' said the porter, 'the Morality Police went up to the proprietor's bedroom and woke him up and asked him what about his braces in the girl's room. Then the proprietor's wife woke up and began to scream and shout about her husband going with girls, though as a matter of fact he's too old for that sort of thing. And then they all went down to the girl's room again and the proprietor's wife went for her and the fool of a girl got more frightened and began to cry so that they couldn't get any sense out of her at all. Then they sent for me and shouted and said it was all my fault, which was not fair or just because I only wanted to help.'

'What happened in the end?'

'Oh, the girl gave the police six hundred douros, which was all she'd got, and they let her go. But as she hadn't got any more money of course we had to turn her out of the hotel. I haven't seen the gentleman again. I don't mind so much about the tip but I think he ought to come back and give me the forty douros for the room, because I'm responsible for money for the rooms and had to pay it out of my own pocket. The gentleman was rather your build and I thought at first it might have been you.'

'Well,' I said, 'it wasn't.'

'No,' said the porter. 'I can see it wasn't now. The gentleman was rather stouter than you. Fräulein Radenk's room is No 28.'

It was a long climb up to No 28. In hotels like this of course the top floors are the cheapest, and Mausi was too independent in regard to money matters not to have to economise. The room was a small one, uncarpeted, with dingy distempered walls. Like so many rooms in Tsernigrad it looked out on a pit-like yard that smelt of drains and cooking. There was a small iron bedstead, one wooden chair, a chipped enamel wash-stand, and that invariable adjunct of Balkan hotel bedrooms, an unlidded and unemptied slop-pail. Mausi was lying in the bed looking very unkempt and unwell. When she saw me her eyes became radiant.

'You've come!' she said.

'Of course. How are you now?'

'Much better. But how about your foot? I heard all about that.'

'That's nothing. But are you really better yourself?'

'Much better. I shall be up again to-morrow. Do you know the colleagues told me you wouldn't come?'

'Why?' I asked. 'Have they been up to see you?'

It surprised me because as a rule continental cabaret artists, unlike English chorus girls, leave their sick colleagues to fend for themselves.

'Yes,' said Mausi. 'Lya came. You know, that Czech girl with the fat legs. She wanted to borrow my new dress.'

'Did you lend it to her?'

'Of course I didn't. The impertinence of it! She simply wanted to pretend to the others that it was hers and that she had lent it to me. If I hadn't been in bed I'd have smacked her face.'

Mausi was certainly getting better.

'And then,' she went on, 'she said no man was fool enough to waste his time and money on a woman who was ill and couldn't be any use to him, and that you certainly wouldn't come round and see me. But I thought you would and now you've come!'

Suddenly I noticed a small photograph of myself in a cheap frame by her bedside.

'Where did you get that?' I asked.

She hid her face in the pillow.

'But tell me.'

'It was in a drawer with all your socks. Are you angry?'

I remembered I had had half a dozen taken for passport purposes and left them lying about somewhere.

'Of course I'm not angry,' I said, 'but why didn't you tell me?'

'I wanted one so I took it.'

As a matter of fact it did worry me. It was another sign of a devotion for which I could offer her nothing in return. It made me feel mean.

'Have you decided where you're going next month?' I asked.

'I've got an offer from Belgrade. Shall I take it?'

'The Palace?'

Conversations with Mausi and her like during the last two years had given me a good second-hand knowledge of all the cabarets from Vienna eastwards.

'Yes,' said Mausi, 'the Palace.'

'Then you should take it unless you get anything better.'

'Zacharias won't prolong me again. He says he never keeps a girl more than two months. And I went to the Tabarin and asked, but they'll only take me on as an *Animierfrau*.'

An *Animierfrau* is a girl who attends every evening at a purely nominal salary, does no turn, and subsists on what she can get out of the clients whom it is her duty to animate into drinking. She is regarded with a certain contempt by the artists who do turns.

'What are they offering you at Belgrade?' I asked.

'Four thousand dinars. They'd have offered me five thousand if I'd gone last month. They were short of girls.'

'Why didn't you go?'

'I wanted to stay here.'

There was a pause, and then she said suddenly:

'I'd much better go to Belgrade. I know quite well you'd rather I went away at the end of the month.'

'Don't be silly.'

'Yes, I know it. It's only natural. I know quite well you'll never care for me in the way I care for you. You didn't really want to come and see me to-day. You only did it out of pity.'

'Don't be ridiculous.'

'I know.'

There were tears in her eyes. I took her hand and felt her

hot answering squeeze. I felt extremely guilty and embarrassed.

'Will you promise me one thing?' she asked.

'What?'

'Will you promise me?'

'All right.'

'That for the rest of this month, until I've gone, you'll never go down to the Tabarin.'

'You know I practically never go there.'

'And will you promise you'll have nothing whatever to do with any other woman at all, even a *Privatfrau*?'

A *Privatfrau* is a woman in any of the private walks of life, as opposed to actresses, dancers and *Animierfrauen*. Jill of course would be one. Still, it was unlikely that I would want to do anything decisive in that direction for the next few days.

'I promise,' I said.

'*Du süsser!*'

There was a short pause.

'It's only to the end of the month,' she added, as if to relieve the prospect of my monogamy of some of its terrors.

'And now,' I said, 'you must promise me something.'

'Of course.'

'That whenever I come to see you like this you must powder your nose.'

Mausi, a little disappointed that I had not extracted a vow of life-long fidelity, reached out for her bag. She had no proper looking-glass and the result was not very successful. I was finding the interview depressing and hoping I would soon be able decently to go away.

'What's the news from the Apollo?' I asked.

'Nothing. Ilonka, that Hungarian girl you liked, had a row with Lya. They began to fight in the dressing room.'

'What about?'

'That friend of yours.'

94

'What, Slaughter?'

'No, the one with the moustache.'

'But surely Slaughter was after her.'

It was an unwritten law among those of the English colony who visited the Apollo and the Tabarin that one would no more think of approaching a girl on whom a friend had staked out a claim than of snatching the food off his plate at dinner. There was none of this rubbish about expecting the girls themselves to have any say in the matter. It was impossible that Vickery could be guilty of such a breach of manners.

'Oh! that was all before,' said Mausi. 'Of course Ilonka is Zacharias's friend as well. And Lya says Vickery is going with a girl in the Tabarin.'

I felt it was all too complicated for further discussion. I tried to cheer up Mausi by painting her prospects at Belgrade in a very rosy light. But it was very hard work. I became more and more depressed and at last got up to go.

'You mustn't take me too seriously,' I said.

'Is that what you think?'

'I'm no good to you. You missed the big salary in Belgrade and now you've been ill. I've only brought you bad luck.'

'You have only brought me good luck.'

On my way down I gave the porter twenty douros and told him that he must arrange for the slop-pail in No 28 to be emptied immediately. Then, to ease my conscience further, I went into the town and ordered five shillings' worth of flowers, half a kilogram of peaches and a German translation of *The Constant Nymph* to be sent up to Mausi's room.

II

Modern science must at least be given the credit of having taken the wind out of the sails of those lugubrious philosophers who maintain that happiness is an illusion. Knowing as we do now that we ourselves, physically and mentally, are reducible into conglomerations of states of becoming with no basis of being, we are no longer disheartened to hear that happiness is a changing and ever receding carrot held before us on the end of an invisible stick. We ourselves are changing and ever proceeding donkeys, attached by the stick to the carrot: if these only seem near enough and succulent enough we are happy. But of course we have to imagine that the semblance of a carrot is there and that it is appetizing.

The philosophical reflections were induced by the contemplation of my official mail and misgivings as to whether I should ever be able to raise any zest for my work. That particular morning I had a query from the Finance Officer of the Foreign Office about an alleged discrepancy of fourpence in my accounts for the quarter before last. The Chief Clerk reminded me that my annual Return of Government Typewriters was now overdue, and the Chief Passport Officer sent elaborate instructions as to how to deal with applications from natives of Nigeria who had become converts to the Jewish Faith and wished to proceed to Palestine for permanent settlement. An obscure Russian refugee wrote that he had an invention, the nature of which was too confidential to be disclosed, but which he was willing to hand over to the British Government for ten thousand pounds. There was an acrimonious letter from a Miss Jones in the interior, in answer to one of mine complaining that she had altered the date of her birth on her passport. Then there was another letter from Mr Dutt. Mr Narwanjhee

Dutt was a British Indian subject, who originally set out to ride round the world on a bicycle. Three months ago he had got as far as Salonika, had run out of funds, and had left his bicycle with the Treasurer of the British Benevolent Society there as security for a loan of five pounds. Later he had sent back the five pounds, and asked for the machine to be forwarded on to Tsernigrad; but before it arrived Mr Dutt himself had already left. I had now become a target for heated letters from (a) Mr Dutt, now in Barcelona, who refused to pay any more than the five pounds he had refunded and demanded that the bicycle should be sent after him, (b) the Treasurer of the British Benevolent Society at Salonika, who was trying to recover the cost of carriage to Tsernigrad, (c) the forwarding agent at Tsernigrad who pointed out that the bicycle was certainly not worth more than thirty shillings and wanted to know who was going to refund him for the Customs duty into Vuchinia and for the storage charges which were steadily mounting, and (d) various consuls along the route from Salonika to Spain who had somehow or other become involved.

I felt it was too hot to cope with the problem of Mr Dutt's bicycle, which as far as I could see was in any case insoluble. I had no private letters, and as it was a Thursday and the post takes four days from London there was no *Times*. I was bored. I was glad when Mr Aquilina announced that Mrs Brinkworth wanted to see me.

Mrs Brinkworth, after her fluttering introductions, produced a case that was almost as baffling as that of Mr Dutt. An English girl had married a Vuchinian in Bolivia. It wasn't a proper wedding, Mrs Brinkworth explained, only a civil ceremony, but the girl had done what she could and got married again next year in the American Methodist Church at La Paz. There was now a little boy and they had come back to live at Tsernigrad. But the husband had turned out to be a bad lot. He had told the girl he did not regard her as his legal wife, and had even (Mrs Brinkworth became very red and hot) got another woman in the house. The girl wanted to go back to England, but the husband had made trouble and the Vuchinians wouldn't give her a passport. She was even afraid they would take the child away. What could I do?

I looked very wise, and said that as the British law recognised a Bolvian civil marriage as valid the girl had lost her British nationality and I could not issue her a passport. On the other hand Vuchinian law lays down that a Vuchinian subject must be married in a Vuchinian Orthodox Church; consequently under Vuchinian law the marriage was not valid, the girl had not acquired Vuchinian nationality, and the local authorities were quite right in not giving her a passport. Similarly with the child; under British law he was Vuchinian, under Vuchinian law he was either Bolivian or British, in either case illegitimate; and not eligible either for a British or for a Vuchinian passport. I would, however, write to the Foreign Office and ask for permission to issue an emergency *laissez-passer* to enable mother and child to go back home.

Mrs Brinkworth beamed at me with gratitude. She was sure I could arrange it: I was always so kind and so clever. I began to think that perhaps I was and got into a very good temper. I enquired solicitously after the G F s. The news was not very good; the authorities were making trouble again, one of Mrs Brinkworth's favourite girls had turned out to be not at all nice, and then there was that growing indifference to good works on the part of the general public that seemed to be getting more marked every year.

'Of course the Minister is very kind,' said Mrs Brinkworth, 'but it always seems so difficult to find a time when he is free if one wants anything done. If only there was an

Englishman here who would not only come to committee meetings but also be willing really to put in some work on it as well . . . '

'If only I wasn't so busy . . . ' I began in self-defence.

'Of course I know what a terrible lot you have to do,' said Mrs Brinkworth. 'You do such a lot already and we're so grateful. No, I was thinking of Colonel Vickery. I was telling him all about our work the other afternoon at Miss Fraser's, and he seemed so interested and willing to help.'

Very soon after she had gone Vickery himself came in. I rallied him about Mrs Brinkworth, and we agreed that she was rather an old dear. But he had some real news to tell me: he had got rid of Sonnenschein.

'Got rid of him?' I asked.

'Yes.'

He explained that while going through Sonnenschein's books he had found, as he expected, a great deal that was very fishy indeed. The Vuchinian taxation authorities had been swindled right and left, and there had been grave irregularities about the remission to the Mervyn Company of instalments for cars sold on hire purchase. Vickery had made enquiries until he was quite sure of his ground, and then he had gone to Sonnenschein with an ultimatum: either the business with the premises and the stock were to be handed over at once at a price and on conditions named by Vickery or else criminal proceedings would be started.

'In other words, blackmail,' I said. He laughed.

'You can call it what you like, but you've got to be pretty sharp with an old scoundrel like Sonnenschein.'

'How are you going to pay him?'

He told me he had raised a loan from one of the local banks by mortgaging the garage, so that some of the purchase money was already paid over. The balance was payable in six months' time. There had been a real fight, he said. Sonnenschein knew that the price was dirt cheap, and had argued and wriggled for all he was worth. At their last interview they had sat up all night before the old man had given way: but he was frightened of the police and couldn't help himself. Now it was an accomplished fact.

'That's pretty quick work,' I said. 'You arrived here just over three weeks ago with five bob in your pocket, and now you've got a business of your own.'

'It's a beginning.'

When he left me I felt quite exhilarated. It is stimulating to meet men who do things even if one does nothing oneself.

* * *

Two days later I had a visit from Mr Sonnenschein himself. He had come he told me, to appeal to the warm heart and keen sense of justice of the British Consul. There had been a young Englishman starving in Tsernigrad. Normally in such cases one refers these young men to their consuls; but Mr Sonnenschein had realised that the time of the British Consul in Tsernigrad was taken up with high affairs of state and should not be encroached upon by these minor worries. Also his daughter, who was always full of pity for the unfortunate, had interceded. In short Mr Sonnenschein had offered him a job. Now this same young Englishman was turning him out into the street. Was that fair? Was it just? Was it humane?

I told him that as far as I could make out all that had happened was that he had sold his business, and in any case it was not a matter in which I could interfere. Besides all which I had been given to understand that he had not been conducting his business to the best advantage of the British firm of Mervyn.

Mr Sonnenschein raised his hands and appealed to Heaven to witness that throughout his life he had been actuated by an admiration of British ideals in general and by a devotion to the interests of the Mervyn shareholders in particular. The efforts he had made to increase the sale of Mervyn cars in Vuchinia had caused him to lose many more profitable opportunities in other directions. They had even permanently impaired his health. There might have been one or two minor errors in book-keeping, but how could a poor weak ignorant old man be expected to look after everything at once? All could be put right at once. And was that the reason why his greying hairs should be brought down to the gutter? Must he see his beloved wife and daughter starve before his very eyes? His voice grew tremulous; finally he removed his spectacles, produced a large bandana handkerchief and burst into tears. I was thoroughly embarrassed and could think of nothing to say. Probably my silence in turn embarrassed Mr Sonnenschein; for he wiped his eyes, replaced his glasses, besought me once more to consider the justice of his cause and went away.

Vickery was highly amused when I gave him an account of this interview. The next time he came to see me was to get a certificate to the effect that he was registered at the Vice-Consulate, and that we had no record that he had ever been convicted of a criminal offence. He had to show this certificate to the police before he could get a permit to carry on a business. He also brought along the account books and asked me to look through them and see if I agreed with a report on the position which he was sending to the Mervyn people.

'But I'm not an accountant,' I said.

'Neither am I. Of course these books are in such a mess that it would take years to clear them up properly. But I want to give the Mervyn people an idea of how it all stands and anyhow your opinion will be very useful to me as a check.'

'I see.'

He laid some very dirty and almost illegible ledgers on

my table, brought out his own report and plunged into explanations. I felt it was up to me to try not to appear a complete fool in his eyes. I assumed as best I could the bearing of an alert man of business, and hoped he would not realise that I knew nothing whatever about the difference between returns outwards and returns inwards, and between net profit and trading profit.

'Do you agree with me?' he asked when we had finished.

'Yes,' I said boldly, 'I do.'

'Could you drop the Mervyn a line and tell them so?'

This of course would be committing myself officially, and I got nervous.

'I don't know that my opinion would be worth much.'

He looked rather disappointed.

'Of course,' I said, 'I might write through the Department of Overseas Trade, and say you'd shown me the books and that while of course I am not an accountant and not qualified to give an expert opinion, yet I have no reason to suppose that the position as given in your report is not substantially correct.'

'That would do perfectly. It would show the Mervyn people that I'm trying to go straight with them.'

'How's business?' I asked.

'I sold a car this morning. It's rather fun.'

'It must be.'

'Have you ever thought of going into business?'

'Yes but not very seriously.'

'The Consular Service may be all very well, but a man like you should be making two thousand a year.'

After he had gone I wondered what he had meant by his last remark; he had looked at me rather curiously. Of course I entirely agreed with the sentiment. For some time I had secretly been thinking the same myself.

I started drafting the letter about Sonnenschein's accounts.

12

The moment that Lady Drexler rang me up on the house telephone and asked me to stay on to lunch to meet Colonel Goodman I felt it improbable that I would like him. Whenever the Drexlers had somebody really nice they invited nobody else. They called on Hughes-Winsor to help them out with well-connected bores, and when they roped me in it was nearly always something particularly tough.

I felt it was a pity about Colonel Goodman, as up till then I had regarded him with sympathy. I had not yet seen him, but at least he had had the grace to be prevented by his business engagements from arriving with the other British delegates to the FIV Congress at the grisly hour of seven-thirty in the morning. He had not been there to add to my difficulties as I piloted Dame Helen Whittington through the Customs. He had booked his own room at the Continental, and had not blamed me, like Mrs Prout, because it had no view over the Danube, or, like Miss Baldock, because the charges for baths were unreasonable. He had not been there to back up the Hon Mrs Travers-Bones when she told me that for the four days of the Congress I ought to wear a miniature Union Jack in my button hole. In fact he had given no trouble whatever.

I had also a secret reason for wanting to like Colonel Goodman. The influence of Vickery and perhaps other things had made me restless. Just before I left Aleppo the Vice-Consul who had been for eight years at Bitlis was transferred to some post in Italian North Africa. and I put him up for a couple of days on his way through. He was a moist-skinned little man in a crumpled cotton suit, with rather dirty finger-nails. He shouted at my servants, drank all my whisky and kept me up most of the night, his eyes getting wilder and wilder, explaining that but for malice and nepotism at the Foreign Office, he ought by now to be a consul-general. Ever since I had been haunted by the nightmare that I myself might be transferred to some loathsome little village at the back of beyond and left to rot in the same way. Now Moorside, Kempton and Goodenough Ltd, the firm with which Goodman was connected, may not have been particularly prosperous: no dividend had been declared on the ordinary shares since 1921, and the last working year (after allowing for Debenture interest and depreciation) had resulted in a loss of nearly £150,000. Nevertheless, they were a great firm and a household word in British industry. And I pictured Colonel Goodman saying to me: 'Young man, we have been looking for you for years. Stay here at Tsernigrad and work for us on a salary of two thousand pounds a year and appropriate allowances!' Of course it was grotesquely improbable; but seen from the angle of an outsider there was so much in the business world that was grotesquely improbable. I remembered the odd numbers of various trade journals that lay about in our waiting-room and which I had occasionally looked at in moments of boredom. They were all full of photographs of fat-faced hawk-eyed young men with rimless pince-nez and remarkable names: 'Mr Vernon Snell, who stands behind the publicity of the Cheeseby Throttle' or 'Mr Roy Bustard who built up the distribution of Lavender's Dress Preservers.' Mr Snell and Mr Bustard must have begun somehow. But the first thing for me was to get on with Colonel Goodman.

I went along to the private part of the Legation wishing I was not quite so hungry. The Drexlers give one an excellent lunch but there is so little of it that one has to hurry home and get some bread and cheese. All down the passage I heard the indistinct boom of Colonel Goodman's voice. As I opened the drawing room door it became articulate.

' . . . with a lot of preposterous ideas in their heads already and not the slightest desire to trouble to find out what the country really wants!'

'This is Mr Mills, our Vice-Consul.'

'Oh yes.'

I was offered an uninterested hand and received the impression that Colonel Goodman was used to having rather more important people invited to meet him.

'Look at the mess they made of things in two years. If they were to come in again, which Heaven forbid, there'll be nothing left for us but to sell out our holdings and go and live abroad.'

I understood now. Of course he was talking about the Labour Government. But the audience was a poor one. Both Sir William and his lady disapproved of socialism as much as anybody else, but Sir William had passed beyond the state of imagining that any good would come of any alternative, and Lady Drexler would be quite unmoved at the prospect of Colonel Goodman having to sell out his holdings and go and live abroad.

'Have you been doing any more cross-word puzzles, Mr Mills?' she asked.

'No, not lately.'

I think I have said I have a certain facility for languages and a few months ago I had distinguished myself by winning a prize in a competition in a Vuchinian paper. The chief result had been that ever since Lady Drexler had asked me the same question every time I went to lunch there. We were fond of each other, Lady Drexler and I, but seemed to have nothing in common to talk about. I liked her partly because I was sorry for her; her whole life since her marriage nearly forty years ago had so obviously been built round the hope that one day Sir William would become an ambassador. Now there was no possible chance of that

and she had not even a passion for oriental carpets to fall
back upon. Why she liked me, goodness only knew. Or
perhaps she didn't like me after all (one is so prone to flat-
ter oneself), and merely found it convenient to have me to
ask about cross-word puzzles when people whom she
had to ask to lunch began to get boring. But in this case
it was unsuccessful; Colonel Goodman continued to hold
forth.

'Of course if you have a Government in power which
prides itself on putting a premium on idleness . . . '

The butler came and announced lunch.

'One of the most depressing signs of the times,' said
Colonel Goodman between mouthfuls of soup, 'is that the
so-called labour leaders attach so little importance to the
views of the only men who know anything about labour.'

'A barber once told me . . . ' I began.

'What?'

'Oh, nothing.'

I have an unfortunate habit of thinking irrelevantly and
aloud. It had come into my mind that when I was last at
home my barber had told me what a depressing sign of the
times it was that young men seemed to attach so little
importance to their hair. Of course I had no business to
think of things like that. Colonel Goodman looked at me
as if I was an idiot and continued. No one, he said, realised
more than he did the importance of treating work people
decently. Only last year when his Progress Department had
evolved a new process which had enabled him to dismiss
nine hundred workmen, he had arranged with the local
branch of the FIV that those of them who were ex-servicemen should have two months of their subscription excused.
In addition he had given each of these same ex-servicemen
his photograph. One really didn't see what more he could
have done. But to think that the British workman of to-day
had so little self-respect that he was ready to sit about in

idleness and live on charity when there was so much empty space in Canada. . . .

I left off listening, and concentrated on trying to catch the butler's eye to get him to bring me some more bread. The only time when I paid any attention to the conversation was when Sir William happened to mention that we had a vc in the colony. Colonel Goodman did not know Vickery personally, but at the beginning of the war he had spent two months at the depot of the Radnorshire Territorials before going on to more important work at the Ministry of Munitions; he had ever afterwards regarded the Radnorshires as his own and had heard of Vickery's various achievements. The fact that I knew him better than anyone else in Tsernigrad made Colonel Goodman almost regard me as within the pale for two or three minutes. But he soon got back again to the Labour Party, and stayed there till Sir William took him off to look at his carpets. I then left, and called in at the first café on my way home and ordered some scrambled eggs. As I ate them I pondered over Colonel Goodman, and wondered, in spite of Arnold Bennett and H. G. Wells, whether all big business men are quite the supermen it is the fashion nowadays to make them out to be. But what he had said about Vickery had pleased me, I liked what I had seen of Vickery immensely; but in some ways he had seemed almost too sensational to be genuine. Perhaps I was still affected by the doubt Hughes-Winsor had cast on his medals the day he arrived. Anyhow I was glad to be reassured by meeting someone who knew all about him.

13

Big dinners are always a mistake. The average human mind is incapable of taking in more than a certain number

of people all at once. Four is the ideal number for a dinner.
When there are six one can still manage to appreciate the
other five personalities. With eight the outlines begin to
become blurred, and anything more than twelve is a mob.
At the dinner given by the Vuchinian Government to the
FIV Congress there were a hundred and ten.

For me it began very badly. I was feeling rather worn
and harassed after the speeches and processions of the last
three days, and felt I needed a tonic of a couple of gins and
a few minutes of the atmosphere of the Continental Bar.
But half-way up the stairs I walked into Colonel Goodman.

'Oh, yes,' he said, 'you've come to show me the way.'

I had not got the moral courage to tell him that I hadn't.

All the way there Colonel Goodman complained of the
very meagre help offered to British business by His Majesty's representatives abroad. He got a little of his own back,
however, by leaving me to pay for the taxi.

As the Hotel de Ville was being used for the ball that
was being held afterwards the dinner took place in the hall
of the Postal Employees' Co-operative Society. It was a
large barn-like room and extremely stuffy; Vuchinians
never open windows, logically desiring to keep out the cold
air in winter and the hot air in summer. There was some
muddle as to how we were all to sit. The dinner had been
planned on the assumption that all the guests would be
male. When it was realised at the last minute that four-
fifths of the British Delegation were ladies, a few wives
of generals and Ministers had to be invited to keep them
in countenance. This meant a reshuffling of the whole
table, and for nearly forty minutes the guests stood about
like a flock of hungry and rather disorganised sheep while
a very hot and wrathful Minister of War and two very
frightened secretaries went up and down rearranging the
cards.

'Now,' said Colonel Goodman, endeavouring to extricate himself from the wheels of the legless Italian's trolley, 'I want to be introduced to the leading Vuchinians.'

I saw a leonine head towering above the crowd.

'That's Mr Tropoff,' I said.

'Who's he?'

'He was one of the big men in the revolution.'

'Has he any business interests?'

Colonel Goodman, I felt, was very disappointing. As a rule I had a good deal of success with the story of how Mr Tropoff strangled the queen. I enjoyed telling it. Luckily I saw Vickery and introduced him. They seemed to get on very well together, but I couldn't listen to the conversation for long as I was buttonholed by Monsieur De Woutte. Monsieur De Woutte was very upset because two days before some minor official of the Vuchinian Ministry of Foreign Affairs had called to see him, and finding him out had left his card. But the card had been turned down in the top left-hand corner. Of course cards should be turned down when left in person, but as Monsieur De Woutte explained everyone should know that the manner in which it is folded gives an indication of the relative social position of the two parties concerned. If the whole of the left edge is folded over then they are equals. The bottom left-hand corner is to be turned down when one calls on a superior, the top left-hand corner when one calls on an inferior. In this particular case the implication was that Monsieur De Woutte ranked lower in the social scale than *un petit fonctionnaire de bureau.*

'Perhaps he did not know,' I suggested.

'But yes, he knew very well, and even if he did not know he ought to learn.'

Poor Monsieur De Woutte got hotter and hotter in his indignation. I looked round eagerly for someone who would take him off my hands, but all his friends (who had doubtless heard the story many times already) seemed to be keeping out of the way. There was nothing for it but to await the beginning of dinner.

We sat down at last, faint with weariness. I had had a presentiment that my immediate neighbours would be duds from the point of view of company, and duds they were. On my left was an unshaven Vuchinian patriot from the backwoods, who looked at me once with disgust and afterwards confined his remarks to a second unshaven patriot who was on his left. Opposite was a lean and scraggy member of the French Delegation whom I took to be a schoolmaster, sitting between two obsequiously francophil young Vuchinians. The only bright spot was Mr Yoshogi, the Japanese Consul, who was on my right. But even Mr Yoshogi is not very exhilarating company; he hides himself behind a rampart of very gold teeth and very thick glasses and inexhaustible courtesy, and one never seems able to get to grips with the man himself. Besides he spoke all European languages with such difficulty that I could never be sure he understood anything I said to him.

We sat down at eight-fifty, and by five minutes past nine the very inadequate staff of waiters had handed round the soup. I said the weather was very hot, and Mr Yoshogi after thinking it over very carefully told me my remark was profoundly true. One of the obsequious young francophils hoped the Professor was liking his soup; though of course it could not pretend to compare with the soup one got in France.

'*Ah! La cuisine française!*'

The Professor gave us a short lecture on French cooking, so appetizing, so wholesome, so conducive to physical strength and mental brilliance. But, he added politely, there was no need to despair of Vuchinian cooking; with the spread of French influence no doubt Vuchinian cooking might in time become quite passable. His two young friends wriggled with delight at the compliment.

At 9.20 the waiters took away our soup-plates and handed round large dishes of cheese, salami and sardines. One of the young francophils asked the Professor if he did not find the Vuchinian language very difficult. The Professor answered that while he was interested in foreign languages he had no need to learn them because he spoke his own beautiful French: the liberality of the French in the matter of language was most marked, they were only too willing that foreigners should have the privilege of learning French; this was one of the many benefits that the friendship of France would confer upon Vuchinia. Mr Yoshogi, who was finding this almost too much for him, asked me what was the annual value of the exports of British Honduras, and I completely at random told him about nineteen million pounds.

At nine thirty-eight the waiter came back and offered us a second helping of cheese, salami and sardines, and Mr Yoshogi who had been converting sterling into yen looked extremely puzzled and said he had no idea that British Honduras had so large an export trade.

At 9.57 my plate was changed and I was given a large portion of cold suckling-pig. The Professor opposite was expatiating on the sacrifices made by France for the cause of Disarmament, and I began to wonder how many years I should survive of consular life exposed to functions like this.

At 10.15 came limbs of turkey. Mr Yoshogi looked sternly up the table towards Mrs Travers-Bones and said that in Japan ladies did not attend public banquets. One young francophil asked the Professor if he intended to dance at the ball which was to follow. The Professor said he did not dance, but some of his fellow delegates did, and he could well understand how thrilled the ladies of Tsernigrad must be at the prospect of dancing with a Frenchman. I enquired if the Senegalese were going to the ball, which seemed to displease the Professor, who turned to his two satellites and explained that the signal success of the French colonial system was due to the fact that the French, unlike certain other nations, offered true liberty and brotherhood to the coloured races.

At 10.55 the turkey came round again, and Mr Yoshogi asked me whether General Booth or Mr Asquith had been regarded as the greater public speaker and for what reason. I said General Booth, because his speeches had been on spiritual matters whereas Mr Asquith had been merely worldly.

At 11.10 we were given a very sticky pudding, and Mr Yoshogi told me that the reason I had given had been an extremely good one.

At 11.33 we had dessert. One of the francophils told the Professor that it was hoped to open the first Vuchinian air route next year. The Professor pointed out that while the great benefits to mankind, such as steam engines, aeroplanes, motor-cars, antiseptics, radio, X-rays and anaesthetics had all been invented by Frenchmen, it had been left to Americans and others (looking sternly at me) to make money out of them. That, however, was merely another proof of the unswerving generosity of France.

At 11.51 coffee was served, and a tin mug was passed down with the message that it was for tips for the waiters. The Professor looked very surprised and uncomfortable and said he had understood he was the guest of the Vuchinian Government. His two satellites tried to apologise for the primitive habits of their countrymen, insisted that of course the Professor was not to contribute, and passed the mug on to Mr Yoshogi who (not having understood a word of the discussion) put in fifty douros and gravely handed it back to the Professor. At which, of course it all began all over again. Finally the Professor produced a handful of coins and after long enquiries as to the exact value of Vuchinian currency in French francs put in the equivalent of a halfpenny. For the rest of the evening he sat glaring daggers at Mr Yoshogi.

At twelve midnight the speeches began. They all sounded like articles from the popular Press of the countries concerned during the war; except of course the British Minister's speech, which was completely inaudible.

At 12.45, during a lull, Mr Yoshogi told me that owing to the war there were now many more women in England than men. Accordingly when I next went home on leave I should look out for a wife, as I now had the opportunity of getting a better one than would otherwise be possible.

At 1.30 it was all over and the whole company went on to the ball.

Official balls are less trying than official dinners, if only because after showing oneself one can always collect a congenial party and go on elsewhere. But while they last they are pretty trying. The room where this particular ball was held was almost as barn-like as the one where we had had dinner. It was very big and decorated with the allied flags. Around the walls were alcoves, reserved for the serving of supper to FIV delegates, diplomats and other big game. At one end was a platform on which were perched the bandsmen of the Republican Guard, probably of all musicians in Europe the most unfitted to play modern dance music. Not that there was really any room to dance in, for the social cream of Tsernigrad (dressed, as prescribed on the invitation cards in *uniforme, frack, redingote, smoking, ou habit de gala*) with their wives, daughters, mothers and aunts covered the floor in a dense and perspiring mass.

After a long search I caught sight of Jill who was dancing with Pujotas. She waved her hand to me and then disappeared again in the crowd. I could see no signs of Beryl, and of course Pemberton, Slaughter and Grimshaw refused on principle to attend this sort of function. So there was nothing for it but to go round and do the polite to my colleagues' wives. They all enquired after my ankle, which served me of course as a heaven-sent excuse for not dancing with them. I bowed to Madame Silviera and rather hoped that she would enquire after my ankle. But she didn't. Then I was caught again by Monsieur De Woutte who had noticed that the alcove reserved for the FIV delegates contained twenty-one cushioned chairs and fifteen hard chairs whereas the alcove for the diplomatic corps had seventeen hard chairs and only nine soft ones. Monsieur De Woutte was properly indignant at this lack of consideration shown to diplomatic backsides, and wanted to know if there was any chance of Sir William, as doyen, taking the matter up officially. I was at last rescued by Jill.

'I thought you were never coming,' she said.

'The dinner lasted for ages.'

'Where's Beryl?'

'I haven't seen her. Is your aunt here?'

'She got tired and went an hour ago. I wish I could find Beryl.'

'Why, do you want her very specially?'

'Yes.'

'Perhaps she's in the wc.'

'No, she is not!' said Jill, getting rather pink.

'Why, have you looked?'

'There's the band there.'

'What?'

'Fifteen of them, my dear, all standing round and drinking beer!'

I remembered how badly the hall was provided with vestibules where honest bandsmen could retire and drink their beer during intervals. It was only natural they would jump at the opportunity provided by the ladies' lavatory.

It suddenly occurred to me why Jill was in such urgent need of Beryl's advice.

'We'll go along to the Continental,' I said.

'The interval will soon be over.'

'It may last an hour.'

'How awful!'

'Come on. It's only two minutes in a taxi.'

'If anyone at the Continental sees us my name's mud!'

Two minutes later we were on our way. Jill was radiant with the consciousness of daring and adventure; so much so that I almost might have been tempted to forget my promise to Mausi. On the way back, of course. I asked her if she had any small change.

'Yes, plenty, and anyhow it's costing you enough as it is!'

Jill was enjoying herself right enough.

Once inside the Continental she slipped into the lift and I went on into the lounge. There to my surprise I found Vickery and Goodman sitting in armchairs with whiskies and sodas and looking as if they had been there for some time.

'Here's the man,' said Vickery when he saw me.

Colonel Goodman, too, gave me more of a welcome than I would have expected from him and told me to sit down and order a drink. I said I couldn't.

'Surely your lady friends can wait half an hour. I want to talk to you.'

'Really I can't wait,' I said.

'He's a bad lad,' said Vickery.

'I could come back in ten minutes' time.'

'All right. If you're sure it won't be more than ten minutes.'

I went back to the entrance to the lift. All the time I waited there and all the way back in the taxi the vision of two thousand a year and appropriate allowances danced before my eyes. There was nothing else that Colonel Goodman could want to talk to me about. No more official banquets, no more official balls, no more nightmare of that loathsome little village in the wilds of Persia! Jill must have found me rather preoccupied. When we reached the hall I told the taxi to wait.

'Aren't you ever going to ask me to dance?' she said.

'Well, there's my ankle.'

'You poor hero, I keep forgetting. Well, talk to me.'

Just then Pujotas appeared all ready to bear her off.

"No, I don't think I can,' Jill began.

'Don't you bother about me,' I said. 'You go and dance.'

I left Pujotas triumphant and went back to the taxi.

When I was in the Continental once more Colonel Goodman put me through a long cross-examination about government contracts in Vuchinia. He wanted to know which came under the Ministry of Public Works, which under the Ministry of Communications and which under the Ministry of War; what Ministers or officials were the decisive factors, and how far any of them were open to bribes; how public utility works were financed; what credits were generally given; what contracts were likely to be placed in the near future; who had been getting the business in the last few years; what special pull the French or Italians had; and so on. I answered to the best of my ability, partly from personal knowledge, partly from what I remembered of the Commercial Secretary's reports, partly from gossip picked up in the American Bar of the Continental. When I did not know I guessed unblushingly, having the feeling that this would be more likely to impress Colonel Goodman than a confession of ignorance. On the whole I thought I went through the ordeal extremely well. I was just going to enquire where I personally came in when Colonel Goodman abruptly said good-night and went upstairs to bed.

'What's all this about?' I asked Vickery.

He called to the waiter for two more drinks and told the man to leave us the bottle. Then he explained. He had succeeded in getting Goodman thoroughly interested in Vuchinia: from now on he could feel that he had the great organisation of Moorside, Kempton & Goodenough Ltd behind him. (My two thousand a year and appropriate allowances faded away to join all those other forgotten daydreams; of course Goodman had no use for me whatever. I was a fool ever to have thought of it. I took another pull at my whisky and soda. Well, it would be rather fun to watch Vickery's progress.) Vickery went on to say that now he would have a go at any big engineering or constructional contract that came along. There was no reason why he shouldn't get the Mohrstadt bridge. Then Tsernigrad would soon want a fleet of modern motor-buses; Vladikop wanted a new electric power station; the army wanted tanks; the railways wanted all sorts of things. Meanwhile there was the wire for the Telegraphs Administration.

'But tenders had to be in two days ago,' I objected.

'That doesn't matter in a country like this.'

'Pemberton thinks he's going to get it.'

'Pemberton's representing some Belgian people, and it's about time an English firm got something for a change. Which ministry looks after the wire, Communications or Public Works?'

'Communications. Old Marinsky's the Minister. He was sitting next to Sir William at the dinner to-night.'

'Will you come along with me and see him to-morrow?'

'All right.'

He went on to tell me more about his plans. The total cost of the Mohrstadt bridge would be nearly a million pounds: the rake-off ought to be very comfortable. What with all these figures and the whisky I got rather dizzy. It was half-past three before we had finished the bottle and went back to the ball.

But we found that the ball had ended rather abruptly half an hour before. Large gatherings of vanquishers are inflammable material, and as far as I could gather an Italian colonel had imagined he overheard a Serb major in the buffet making derogatory references to spaghetti, and accordingly spat in his coffee. Whereupon the major spat in the colonel's face. Tempers rose, and the major knocked the colonel down. (It may have been the other way round, but I think it was as I have described.) Partisans rushed up on either side, and the situation was beginning to look very ugly when the bandmaster with great presence of mind played the Vuchinian national anthem so that everybody had to stand to attention for three minutes and then go home.

'I don't want to go home yet,' I said to Vickery.

'Lord, no. What the hell's the use of going to bed?'

What indeed was the hell the use of doing anything? Life is only to be lived once. Nearly a million pounds! We went down to the Apollo, where Mausi who had quite given up hope of my coming down that night was overjoyed to see me. Her pleasure was increased by the fact that Vickery did not invite any of the other girls, not even Ilonka who sat pouting and trying to catch his eye in the box opposite. We were along the bar on the high stools. I sat patting Mausi's knee and listening to Vickery's various schemes. Suddenly he stopped and looked at me.

'Look here,' he said, 'if I get this show really going, would you care to chuck the Service and come in with me?'

I can see him now as he said it: his lean sunburned face with the thick close-cut hair and the eyes very clear and very blue, and his lazy voice, and his hand perfectly steady after a dozen whiskies and sodas; the man who had come with five shillings in his pocket and who was now going to pull off a million-pound contract. It did not matter what his past might have been. It did not matter if I should be doomed to play second fiddle for the rest of my life. Here, I knew, was my great opportunity.

'Of course I would,' I said.

Then I made a suggestion that had been in my mind for the last few days.

'Until you get a place of your own why don't you came along and share my flat?'

'I'd love to.' He reached for his glass and raised it. 'Here's to our partnership,' he said.

14

Next morning I rang up the Ministry of Communications and made an appointment with Mr Marinsky for eleven o'clock. Vickery and I duly went round, and after a lot of walking about in passages – nobody in a Vuchinian government department can ever tell a caller where anybody else is to be found – we were shown into a waiting-room and waited. Twenty minutes later we were shown into another room and an elderly gentleman with a white beard asked us what we wanted.

'But this isn't Marinsky,' said Vickery to me.

'No, he's next door. This is the Chef du Cabinet.'

'That's no bloody good.'

I told the old gentleman we wanted to see Mr Marinsky, with whom we had an appointment.

Most unfortunately, it appeared, Mr Marinsky was not available. Yes, he was in the building, but he had a series of very important conferences. He had really no time. Further he was far from well, and his doctor had forbidden him to receive any visitors whatsoever. . . .

'Oh hell,' said Vickery.

He pushed a thousand-douro note into the astonished Chef du Cabinet's hand and marched through the connecting door, myself after him. We found Mr Marinsky, who looked like a rather old and mangy wolf, staring out of the window and picking his teeth. He was very surprised to see us and asked who we were. I reminded him that I was the British Consul. He then shook hands and explained that though he was extremely busy he would be pleased to give us a few minutes. We sat down.

'We want to speak to you . . . ' I began.

Mr Marinsky interposed that he was quite sure that he knew the object of our visit. Through the ages, he said, in the very darkest hours of her history, Vuchinia in lonely vigil had held aloft in the Balkans the torch of civilisation and progress. Material motives had never swayed her, she had striven ever for the highest ideals of humanity. At the outbreak of the great war, realising that the noisome canker of Austrian Imperialism was threatening all that life holds holy, Vuchinia had fearlessly exposed her breast to the bayonets of barbarity in arms. Now that the war was over, unbowed though bleeding from a thousand glorious wounds (Mr Marinsky paused to open the bottom drawer of his desk and spit into a cuspidor neatly concealed there), though surrounded on every side by brutal Serbs, rapacious Greeks, treacherous Rumanians and malignant Bulgars, Vuchinia still stood conscious of her destiny.

'We just wanted,' I said, 'to speak to you about . . . '

'In vain,' interrupted Mr Marinsky, 'have we looked for a gleam of encouragement or help from the Greater Powers. The megalomania of Fascist Italy, the self-interest of France, and, I regret to add, the indifference and commercialism of Great Britain have so far turned a deaf ear to the groans of our martyred nation. Nevertheless with unfaltering step and unclouded brow, beneath the eye of Heaven and upon the soil reeking with the blood of her slaughtered sons, Vuchinia presses ever forward towards those flaming goals of Progress, Civilisation and Humanity, which are her Proud Duty and her Sacred Mission.'

'Yes,' said Vickery, but what about this wire contract?'

Mr Marinsky was taken out of his stride and blinked at him.

'The tenders were all in three days ago. We can't discuss that.'

'Oh yes we can.'

Mr Marinsky thought rapidly.

'Be at the Café Esplanade at six o'clock this afternoon. My brother-in-law, Mr Gorkin, will be there. You can talk it over with him.'

'Good.'

We got up and left.

'I shall get that contract,' said Vickery as we went down the passage.

*　　　*　　　*

Vickery moved in to my flat on the 29th of June, and two days later we gave a house-warming. On the same day, July 1st, Mausi left. She should by rights have gone off at 6.15 in the morning after a night's work in the Apollo, so as to arrive at Belgrade fifteen hours later and be just in time to start the night's work at the Palace. Such is the life of a cabaret girl: she works seven nights a week and has two holidays a year, on Christmas Eve and Good Friday. But at 6.15 Mausi and her colleagues were still busy trying to get the balance of their salaries out of Zacharias, always rather a lengthy process. So she stayed on to have a few hours' sleep and go off by the evening train.

She came to tea of course, and as I was frightened of the possibility of emotional scenes I prevailed on Vickery to stay in too. It was rather mean of me as Vickery was very busy and a few tears would probably have done Mausi a lot of good. As it was I could see she keenly resented his presence although he had got her a bag as a parting present. We sat and made conversation; wondered how many of the British colony at Belgrade she was likely to meet, pretended that before long she would be coming back to Tsernigrad, and made plans for then. Every ten minutes Agnes would come in and make some enquiry about our party that evening, or the bell would ring and a gipsy porter would stagger through with a case of whisky or a load of ice; and I wished that Mausi might have been spared these signs of coming revelry.

But she behaved wonderfully well, and showed no signs of faltering even after Vickery had to go on to the garage. She went round to say good-bye to every piece of furniture, played her favourite record on the gramophone, and had a final and most meticulous review of my socks.

'When I come back again I will bring proper wool with me from Vienna.'

I promised her I would carefully save up all my damaged socks until that should come to pass.

Her train left at five minutes past seven. At half-past six we took a taxi and went to the Hotel London to collect her poor little luggage. As the porter brought it out he looked at me suspiciously, and I imagined he had not yet succeeded in recovering his forty douros. The taxi set off down towards the station. It would soon be over. Mausi kept opening and shutting her new bag.

'It's a very nice one,' she said.

Then suddenly she turned and hid her face in my shoulder and began to sob.

'*Du*, I am just as uneducated as Tessa, but I can love as much as she could!'

Tessa? Oh yes, *The Constant Nymph*. But it was a long time since I had read the book and my recollections of it were dim. What was it all about?

'Don't cry,' I told her, 'you'll be back here again before long. And anyhow I'm not worth worrying about. You don't know me really: the person you want is simply something you've imagined yourself.'

(My words sounded strangely familiar. Had there been some such speech in *The Constant Nymph*?)

She still kept her head against my shoulder, but the sobbing stopped. When the taxi turned the corner into the station boulevard she sat up straight again and took out her powder-puff.

'I must behave myself,' she said.

And she did, marvellously. She might almost have been a girl whom a brother was seeing off for the week-end. She was very sharp with the porter who took over her cheap little hat-box and basket trunk, and was very particular in choosing her compartment. I had not been able to get her a sleeper as they were all booked by the time I had heard she was taking the evening train. She eventually got in with two very stout ladies from Constantinople. It was rather smelly inside so I got out and bought her a box of chocolates, and told her not to eat them all at once as I didn't like fat women. Then I stood by her window and waited for the train to start, wondering what to say. I was just by the indication plate: (*Ankara*) – *Istanbul* – *Sofia* – *Tsernigrad* – *Beograd* – *Budapest* (*keleti*) – *Wien* (*Ost*) – *Wien* (*West*) – *Passau* – *Frankfort a/M* – *Köln* – *Bruxelles* – *Ostende* – (*Londres*). I remembered how during one of my long vacation trips I had seen this train in Brussels station and how I had felt a romantic thrill as I read the route.

'Look there,' said Mausi.

I looked in the direction she was pointing, and sure enough about thirty yards down the train was Zacharias at another window saying good-bye to Ilonka.

The whistle blew.

'Good luck,' I said, 'and *au revoir!*'

123

I took her hand and kissed it, and as I did so the train gave a jerk and pulled her away from me. It glided out of the station, and Mausi's face as she waved back to me seemed very small and very pale.

Zacharias caught sight of me as we went towards the exit and he took his hat off.

'Good evening, *Herr Konsul*.'

'Good evening, Zacharias.'

He made a deprecating gesture towards the vanishing train with its cargo of frailty.

'It costs a great deal of money, *Herr Konsul*.'

'Sometimes, Zacharias.'

I did not want to lower my consular dignity by driving up to the town again with Zacharias, nor did I wish to hurt his feelings by refusing to do so. Accordingly I turned into the station café to have a cup of Turkish coffee and a cigarette.

I knew quite well that probably no woman would ever care for me quite in the same way that Mausi did; that now that I had let her go away she would certainly take to cocaine again and go to the devil; that my feelings for Jill were superficial and not entirely disinterested; and that although the world at large (and certainly Mausi herself) would consider I had behaved very decently towards her, this was not enough to still my conscience. All the same, my predominating feeling at her departure was one of profound relief.

15

Parties in Tsernigrad are generally more amusing than parties at home, chiefly, I think, because there is more drink about. Very likely there are parties in Mayfair or Chelsea or Bloomsbury where the high level of social and intellectual sophistication brings about a constant state of drunkenness. But I cannot speak of these, never having attended one. I can only speak of parties among the brighter set in Leicester. When my sister-in-law has friends in for the evening the general average age is lower (if that is an advantage). The guests are better-looking, the women better-dressed and the men less inclined to be pot-bellied. They dance infinitely better. They have more interest in art and literature and the drama. They are most conscientiously broad-minded, sometimes even conscientiously daring. And yet parties seem to go better in Tsernigrad. As I say, I put it down to drink; or perhaps in Leicester we are afraid of waking up the servants.

There were twenty-four of us altogether at our party, and we had laid in twelve bottles of whisky and twelve bottles of champagne. This was not really as extravagant as it sounds, for my consular position enabled me to get it free of customs duty and they both worked out at about seven shillings a bottle. All the British colony came, all that counts, that is, except Sir William and Lady Drexler who never go to that sort of party, and Mrs Bowles who had a headache. The Legation was represented by Hughes-Winsor, and Jill came with her uncle. The Glovers were there of course, and Pemberton, Grimshaw and Slaughter. Slaughter brought with him a large Junoesque female with very intense dark eyes who held one's hand very tightly when she was introduced; she was stopping the night on her way out to Egypt by the overland route and Slaughter had been enjoined by some relations of his at home to look after her. Then there was Torrens, the Passport Control Officer, and Mrs Torrens, and his new Secretary Mrs McLean who looked distinctly attractive in evening dress. We had two men from the Danube Commission, and Cookson, a chartered accountant who often came to Tsernigrad, and a Mr Hooper who travelled in nutmeg, whom Cookson had picked up somewhere. Then there was Miss Phipps, and Watterson the pressman who brought some Vuchinian girl with him. We weren't particularly pleased at this, as we had wanted the party to be purely Anglo-Saxon, but the girl wasn't bad looking and we were short of women so we let it pass. Then there was a young American from one of the oil companies who arrived so drunk that the only thing we could do with him was to put him in a little lobby we used as a cloak-room, where he slept soundly till the party was over. But the great triumph and surprise was when the company found we had secured Miss Fraser and Mrs Brinkworth.

'Gaw!' said Pemberton when he saw them and his face dropped with alarm. But the cause was not Miss Fraser as might have been expected, but Mrs Brinkworth. It was the genuine alarm felt by red-faced worldly-minded men like Pemberton when confronted by clergymen, mission-helpers, Sunday school teachers or others whose lives are devoted to good works. They are fearful of a professional attack on alcohol and the other good things of life which they feel they have not the resources to defend. However a generous whisky and soda convinced Pemberton that this at any rate was not a teetotal party, and it all started in good order.

I wound up the gramophone, and, having no colleagues' wives to bother about, began to dance with Jill. She was looking quite nice – well, very nice. Only I couldn't help thinking that later on in the evening when things were warmed up a bit I should thoroughly enjoy dancing with Mrs McLean.

'What have you been doing these last few days?' I asked Jill, 'I've seen nothing of you.'

'You haven't tried very hard.'

I remembered I hadn't. I hadn't even bothered to ring her up. Perhaps my remark had been rather tactless.

'Well,' I said, 'I've been frightfully busy in the office the last few days, and there was an awful lot to do getting this place ready for Vickery to move in.'

'I dare say there was. That gramophone wants winding.'

'Mr Hooper's going to do it. He seems to like making himself useful.'

'I expect you like people like that.'

Her tone was sarcastic, and I felt she was displeased at my failure to follow up the encouragement she had given me on the night of the ball. Well, if she wanted to be independent and stand-offish she could be. I wasn't going to follow her about like a dog. I felt she was being extremely foolish to endanger her chances of securing a partner in a firm that pulled off million-pound contracts; quite apart from my uniquely interesting personality. Time would show her. I was not in the least disappointed when one of the Danube Commission men claimed her for the next dance.

I looked round the room, conscious of my responsibilities as host. Things seemed to be going quite well. They were all dancing except a little knot of heavyweights round the drinks. Miss Fraser was on the sofa talking to Vickery. Only Mrs Brinkworth seemed a little out of it and I went over to her.

'What about a cigarette, Mrs Brinkworth?'

'Oh, I never smoke. I'm not modern, you see.'

'A drink then?'

'Oh, I hardly think I . . . '

'Pemberton!' I shouted across, 'bring the lady a glass of wine.'

Pemberton was very surprised when he saw who the lady was, but he brought it over. After one sip Mrs Brinkworth nearly choked and said it was very strong. However we encouraged her and she eventually finished it. This impressed Pemberton so much that he asked her to dance, and after a little jibbing she agreed. By that time Vickery had got up and I moved along next to Miss Fraser.

'Well, young man?' she said.

I pointed to Mrs Brinkworth and Pemberton.

'That's rather a triumph.'

'What is?' asked Miss Fraser.

'Getting those two to dance together.'

'Why is it a triumph?'

I realised this was another unfortunate opening gambit on my part. In my heart of hearts I had meant Miss Fraser to think how kind and clever I had been to find Mrs Brinkworth a partner. But if one will butt in and start protecting other people's protégées, one should never boast about it: the other people don't like it.

'Well, I don't know,' I said lamely. 'They're such very different types.'

Miss Fraser was graciously pleased to leave it at that.

'When are you going to marry that Bingham girl?' she asked abruptly. I wished that Miss Fraser's voice was not so loud. Fortunately there was a very noisy record on and nobody seemed to have heard.

'Probably she wouldn't have me,' I said.

'I don't see why she shouldn't. She has nothing else to do except get married.'

'The Foreign Office may send me off East again.'

'She could go with you. There's no difficulty whatever in travelling nowadays. Thirty years ago when I wanted to go from Elbasan to Nevrokop I had to walk, but now you simply send for a motor car.'

'Miss Fraser,' I asked, 'why are you so anxious for me to get married?'

'I'm not anxious in the least.'

'But you keep suggesting it.'

'Twice, I believe.'

'Well, twice. It sounds as if you think I ought to be put down in a suburb with some capable young woman to look after me and see I get my breakfast every morning in time to catch the 8.15 to town.'

'Well?'

'Do you think it's a good enough reason to get married simply because you've got nothing better to do?'

'For some people it's an excellent reason.'

'Yes, for some people.'

I felt Miss Fraser was laughing at me.

'I may come to that in the end,' I said. 'One never knows – I might even get to like it. Quite a lot of people seem to. But I should like to have a shot at doing something else first.'

'Well,' said Miss Fraser, 'you can fetch me my cigarettes.'

She left very soon afterwards taking Mrs Brinkworth with her. Pemberton by this time had conceived such a friendship for Mrs Brinkworth that he interrupted his fifth whisky and soda in order to be the first to fetch her coat.

'She's a damned good sort,' he explained later. 'We were dancing and I bumped into your bloody door, and forgetting who she was I said "hell." And believe me she didn't mind a bit!'

This particular 'hell' was the foundation of a lasting and mutual regard. I believe even that Pemberton subscribed to the GFS.

However, it must be confessed that things livened up when Miss Fraser and Mrs Brinkworth had gone. My recollections are vivid but somewhat disjointed. Jill seemed always in the middle distance; my instincts told me that she was waiting for me to return and give satisfaction and eventually be taken back into favour. But I couldn't be bothered. I danced with Beryl and with Mrs Torrens and then with the female Slaughter had brought, who clutched me so tightly that I heartily wished she was fifteen years younger, or at any rate not quite so Junoesque. When at last I broke loose it took some time to recover my breath. I was always catching Mrs McLean's eye and never seeming to have the chance of getting her to myself. I remember Hughes-Winsor standing in a corner and talking very loudly and volubly to Beryl about expressionist French poetry, and Beryl gallantly trying to play up to it; and Mr Hooper tirelessly winding up the gramophone; and Grimshaw and Cookson playing that ridiculous game of sitting in a chair and trying to take a pin out of the back with your teeth; and Clive and Watterson's girl-friend sitting on the sofa and holding the following dialogue:

Girl-friend: 'Do you love me?'

Clive: 'Look here, steady on, I've got the wife here.'

Girl-friend (whose English was rather sketchy): 'Please?'

Clive: 'I mean it's a bit public.'

Girl-friend: 'I like it public. Do you love me?'

At midnight the champagne was all finished but the whisky was still going strong. We turned out the lights and played sardines. Mrs McLean, egged on by Beryl and Slaughter, hid in my bed, which collapsed under the weight of the eighteen people who found her there before the lights went up again. So we left Mr Hooper to repair the bed and I went back and danced with Mrs McLean and then took her out on the balcony. Ten minutes later Pat (for that was her name) told me I ought to behave myself or people would see us.

'Would you mind if they did?' I asked.

'Not in the least.'

However, all things have their limits and after another quarter of an hour we went back to the others. We arrived at the tail end of a curious little scene: Pemberton, rather red, and Vickery eyeing each other, and Beryl with one of her shoulder straps torn, and Clive watching them from a corner. But Slaughter took off Pemberton to have another drink, and his Junoesque female snatched at Vickery.

'What's it all about?' I asked Beryl.

'Oh, nothing.'

'It must have been something.'

'My dress got torn and Vickery thought Pemberton should have done more than just say "Sorry," but I'm sure he didn't mean to be rude. Let's go and dance.'

Beryl was sensible enough not to like rows, though perhaps human enough to be flattered that they should be about her if they took place at all. But I never found out what had happened.

Anyhow the little incident soon blew over. By this time there weren't any more clean glasses, and nobody minded in the least, though Mr Hooper wanted to go into the kitchen and wash them. My recollections of this part of the evening are still vivid but even more disjointed. I remember Jill becoming more and more taken up with the men from the Danube Commission and being rather haughty whenever I spoke to her; and my not caring in the least. And the Vuchinian girl asking Hughes-Winsor if he loved her, and Hughes-Winsor's horror. And the soda-water giving out. And my dancing a great deal with Pat McLean, and her exquisite cattiness about all the other women in the room; Addison may have damned with faint praise, but Pat's fulsome panegyrics were far more deadly. And Slaughter's female telling Bowles that everything in life was mean and commercial except Love. And Pemberton declaring that Hughes-Winsor had given him the glad eye and he didn't feel safe. And Mrs Torrens, a little bewildered but determined to be bright and talkative, telling me how difficult it was to get a scullery tap repaired in Tsernigrad: so different from Cologne where they had last been stationed.

At a quarter-past two the whisky gave out and Vickery

produced another three bottles from a secret store in his bedroom. To celebrate this Torrens, who had been a year in Durazzo, offered to do an Albanian dance if he could find approximately the right costume. So, to the evident misgivings of his wife, he was taken off to my bedroom to forage; and came back and did his dance. During which Miss Phipps went and hid his trousers, enjoining me not to whisper a word to anyone because Mr Hughes-Winsor would be so shocked. By three o'clock there was only half a bottle of whisky left and the tempo had become perceptibly slower. People were sitting and standing about in little groups and every now and then came a guffaw of laughter. I remember Grimshaw explaining to Watterson that if you put a coin under a table-cloth and apply the end of a lighted cigarette the cloth won't burn, and my slight annoyance when the cloth did burn owing to his having forgotten to put the coin there. And then people began to go, and fumbled for their hats and coats over the body of the sleeping American. And then it turned out that Torrens' trousers had really and completely disappeared, to the extreme discomfort of Miss Phipps, so that I had to lend him an old pair of plus-fours to go home in. The mystery of those trousers was never cleared up though next morning a pair of cami-knickers, which nobody would own to, was found attached to the back of Bowles' car. And Cookson came to me with tears of sentiment in his eyes to thank me for a marvellous evening, but especially for my having been so particularly kind to dear old Tommy Hooper. And Slaughter set out to escort his female back to the Continental, and we all shuddered to think what might happen to him in the taxi on the way. So that eventually only Vickery and I, and Pemberton, Grimshaw and Watterson were left, who said it was bloody rubbish to think about going to bed, and we must go round to the Apollo for a night-cap.

We went out into the cool night air. Vickery and Pemberton seemed to have forgotten their little incident. As we walked along I thought of Mausi, now trying to get to sleep amid the odours of the stout ladies from Constantinople, with Serbian ticket collectors coming in and growling at her every half-hour. And then I wondered whether I would have got on as well as I did with Pat McLean if she had been six years younger than I was instead of six years older.

Going down the steps of the Apollo I caught sight of myself in a glass and noticed that it was nineteen hours since I had last shaved and that I had a large smudge on my shirt-front. Downstairs the atmosphere was very stale and sweaty, rather like that of an unventilated Turkish bath with the addition of tobacco smoke. The place was full; salaries are paid on the first of the month in Tsernigrad and people wanted to see what the new lot of girls were like.

Pemberton suggested a spot of brandy now, but I was cautious and stuck to whisky.

'Christmas, look at that!' said Watterson suddenly.

'Some bit!'

I looked round and followed the glance. It was a girl sitting in one of the boxes with a fat little Jew with whom she was obviously rather bored. She was wearing a black dress with long sleeves, very simple and extremely well made, fitting close and cut very low at the back. A mass of heavy dull red hair hung to the nape of her neck; a rather long face, very pale against the crimson of the full mouth. At that distance I could not see the colour of her eyes: green most probably. I became extremely interested.

'I like that,' I said. 'Greta Garbo out of Nineveh.'

'Damned good!' said Grimshaw. 'Did you hear that?' And he repeated my *mot* to the others. But as it was very late and Grimshaw at the best of times was rather shaky on Bible history his version of it was 'by Great Garbo out of Nebuchadnezza', which was not what I meant besides sounding vaguely derogatory to Miss Garbo.

Pemberton said he didn't like red-haired women as they all smell foxy.

'Who is she?' I asked Zacharias, who was fussing round us.

'A Russian from Berlin.'

Zacharias continued that the gentleman she was with was probably going away very soon, and if I would only wait till then he would send her over. Pemberton said he didn't know about that; anyhow, apart from her, perhaps, and that little dark girl who was dancing they were a bloody poor lot and what did Zacharias mean by it? Zacharias was very apologetic and explained how difficult it was to get suitable artists at this time of year. However, there were two extremely beautiful Hungarian grls now in a private room; the gentlemen they were with would probably be going very soon, and if Pemberton would only wait till then . . .

I sat watching the couple in the box. The girl looked over in our direction; her glance rested for a moment on Vickery, passed on, went back to the cigarette in her hand. The little Jew called for the waiter; I thought he might be going. But no, he was ordering another bottle of wine. The girl yawned.

My nerves were all jigging, but my brain became as clear as crystal. I realised suddenly what a frightul mess up it would have been if I had in any way got myself committed to Jill. I had been on the wrong tack; I had been taking my desires and my emotions at second hand. That must all stop. From now on I would be a hard-boiled realist: know what I wanted and go for it; be my own master; make a hundred thousand pounds. Meanwhile if I couldn't get the red-headed Russian girl from Berlin to myself I wasn't going to stay on here looking at her.

'Let's go somewhere else,' I said.

Pemberton wanted to stay and dance with the little dark girl, so Vickery came with me, leaving the others in the Apollo. Outside once more a grey dawn was breaking over the cool and deserted Wilsonovi. In the distance a peasant cart rumbled over cobbles. But within me all was a jangle of excitement; a new era was beginning and I wanted some experience with more punch in it than any I had ever had. An occasional orgy is a physical and psychological necessity; it was so for me then. The trouble is that except in very sophisticated places like Berlin or Paris orgies cannot be ordered at short notice. However we did the best we could at the Tabarin, and apparently also afterwards in the flat. I only remember that in the morning Agnes, with a tact and a tolerance unheard of in the days before Vickery moved in, brought two cups of early tea into my room, and I looked round with some bewilderment at a mop of brown curls on the pillow beside me.

It showed no signs of animation, so I drank both cups of tea. Perhaps it was ungallant of me; but never in my life had I needed tea so much.

PART TWO

THE REALIST

16

Vickery held that if you did a thing at all you should do it
properly. In consequence he took a suite of offices bang in
the middle of the Wilsonovi and engaged a staff. All this
expense rather took my breath away, but he pointed out
that if one wanted to do business with government departments in the Balkans one had to impress the officials,
and that anyhow one good contract would wipe out over-
heads for a couple of years. He was very optimistic. Mr
Gorkin had turned out to be not only Marinsky's brother-
in-law, but also a second cousin of the Mayor and a friend
and relation of someone of importance in nearly every
Ministry. He was further a live wire and ready do to a
lot for a five per cent commission.

The staff consisted of three. There was a young Czech
from Mährisch-Ostrau, who, if he should prove himself
capable, was destined to take complete charge of the
routine side of the office. He was a fat young man with a
shaven head and a round childlike face, with enormous
visiting-cards printed Jaroslav Krompek, *Diplomierter
Kaufmann*. I never found out exactly what the diploma was
or where he had got it. Mr Krompek took life very
seriously and went about in tremendous awe of Vickery,
whom he always referred to as *Herr Generaldirektor*; thereby
raising the prestige of the firm and making it possible for
himself, Krompek, to be addressed as *Herr Direktor* by Mr
Boranovitch the junior clerk. After about a week these
two were joined by no less a person than Miss Tsernigrad.

Like all their neighbours the Vuchinians make a tremendous business of Beauty Competitions. Every town and

village elects its queen, and nearly every woman and girl competes except those whose reputation for beauty is so established that they would lose caste if the fickle jury were to choose somebody else. Then there is a national rally of all the local queens in order to elect a Miss Vuchinia; who goes to Paris to compete against Miss Jugoslavia, Miss Portugal and so on for the title of Miss Europe, and if successful eventually goes on to the States in the hope of becoming Miss Universe. This year the national rally was held in Vladikop, the second largest town in the country and Tsernigrad's bitter rival. Miss Tsernigrad (who worked in a flower shop in the Wilsonovi) was escorted to the station by the municipal band and an army of cheering supporters. When next day the news came through that the prize had been awarded to Miss Vladikop the anger and disappointment was intense. On Miss Tsernigrad's return a crowd collected outside the flower shop, booed and jeered and threw over-ripe tomatoes. Miss Tsernigrad burst into tears and the propeietor of the shop had a summons from the police for causing an obstruction to the traffic. The only thing he could think of doing was to sack the cause of all the trouble, whereupon Vickery engaged her. Mrs Brinkworth quoted this as just another instance of Vickery's chivalry. I was now beginning to know Vickery well enough hardly to agree, that is not in Mrs Brinkworth's sense of the word chivalry. But in any case next time I went to the office I found a handsome and sulky brunette sitting behind a typewriter. Miss Tsernigrad was not an efficient typist and nearly drove poor Mr Krompek to despair. But Vickery thought it wasn't a bad thing to have a girl like that in the office; she might be useful with a certain type of business visitor.

In due course I got the Mervyn Company's answer to my esteemed favour of the nineteenth. They deeply appreciated my kind attention to their interests and were writing by the same post to Colonel Vickery to insist upon the immediate remittance of all outstandings. Their Mr Scarfe was shortly proceeding to Tsernigrad and they hoped he might count on my good offices. Meanwhile they would be grateful if I would kindly forward all information as to Colonel Vickery's status and what credit he was good for. Assuring me of their best services at all times, etc, etc. They added in a postscript that they were enclosing their latest lists which they would thank me for bringing to the notice of my business and social connections.

I took this letter round to show Vickery. In the outer office Mr Krompek was holding forth with great weight and dignity to a rather hot and sheepish Mr Boranovitch.

'This will never do, Mr Boranovitch,' he was saying. 'You must try and acquire the proper commercial spirit. You must think, Mr Boranovitch, you must show initiative. It is no use merely to write to the clients and tell them we can offer accessories of good quality at a competitive price. The clients will not respond. No, Mr Boranovitch. You must put yourself in the position of the client. You must understand his psychology, Mr Boranovitch. Finish your letter with the words "we now await your esteemed order", and the client will remember and will sit down and write out his order. You must show originality, Mr Boranovitch.'

Mr Krompek, suddenly seeing me, dismissed Mr Boranovitch and came up with many apologies for having kept me waiting and enquiries after my health. I asked how business was. He said he was not unhopeful, but it was very difficult having to rely on an employee like Mr Boranovitch who had no grasp of the true commercial spirit.

'When you write that you are awaiting their esteemed orders,' I asked, 'do the clients always sit down and send you one?'

Mr Krompek sighed.

'We must do what we can, *Herr Konsul*.'

As I went on to Vickery's room I had a horrid suspicion that the world of business might after all be just as idiotic as any other one.

I showed Vickery the Mervyn people's letter and he was rather amused.

'What am I to write back?' I asked. 'I can't tell them you've got any capital.'

'Why not refer them to Goodman? He knows me.'

'Yes, I will.'

'And now I've got some news for you. We've got the wire contract.'

'Good work!' I said. 'What's it going to be worth?'

'We shan't clear more than two hundred and fifty pounds after Marinsky and Gorkin have had their whack. Still, it's a beginning for us.'

'I like the way you say "we" and "us".'

'Damn it, old man, you did the most important bit by introducing me to Marinsky.'

I wanted to go out and have a cocktail to celebrate the event, but apparently Vickery had to hurry off to lunch at the Argentine Legation.

'Why,' I asked, 'do you know Madame Silviera?'

'Yes. She's rather a pet.'

I was afraid I might look as envious as I felt, and to try and cover it up I remarked that there were too many women about and it was all getting very complicated. But Vickery said it was always perfectly easy to get rid of them if one was drastic enough.

17

Next day Vickery came round to the Consulate with an official from the Ministry of Communications, and I had to attest his signature on various documents to do with the wire contract. Soon after they had gone Pat McLean rang me up and said she wanted to see me about something.

'Well,' I asked, 'what about a cocktail at the Continental this evening?'

'Too public.'

'Up at our flat then.'

'Still too public.'

'Good heavens!'

'Can you call for me about seven and we'll go to a café or somewhere. I can't possibly tell you over the telephone.'

For the rest of the day I felt very curious.

I took Pat to Uncle Bozha, who is my wine merchant. His place is in one of those narrow side streets that zigzag steeply down from the centre of the town towards the quays along the Danube. You go through an old Turkish archway, down two steps, and find yourself in a little courtyard surrounded by high blank walls and paved with flagstones. There are two acacias there and a vine untidily trailing over a kind of pergola. In one of the walls is a cavernous opening that exudes a curiously cool smell of *slivovica* and much-breathed air. Down at the bottom when your eyes get used to the darkness you may see Uncle Bozha himself, in shirtsleeves and with a three days' beard, poring over his books. In the courtyard near the mouth of the cellar was the charcoal stove of Kosta, the *chevapchiya*. (A *chevapchiya* is a purveyor of *chevapchichi* which are rather like small sausages about the size of the top of a man's little finger.) Flies cluster in swarms over Kosta's stock in trade of raw meat and entrails, and also over Kosta's face as he slept beside them. Every now and then he would wake up and drive them away or else repulse the three cats of the establishment. It was a very peaceful place. Under the pergola were arranged three little tables with cloths almost as dirty as Kosta's hands, but hardly any one ever came there. Now and then there were two or three peasants from up country, drinking *slivovica* and eating Kosta's *razhnici* or *chevapchichi*. They would talk in low tones, being rather overawed with the town of Tsernigrad. At night the three cats defended the walls against invading cats or carried on strident love affairs. Nobody but myself ever seemed to buy any wine. I used to come every now and then when I was too hard up to afford rounds of gin at the Continental. It was also a good place to bring visitors to, as they were always delighted and used to declare that this was the real East at last. They would even order *chevapchichi*, though they seldom ate them if they had noticed Kosta's methods.

Pat and I sat down at one of the little tables, and as she is the sort of girl who can drink anything, I ordered two double *slivovicas*, and asked her what it was all about. She found it rather difficult to begin.

'It's about Vickery,' she said.

'What about him?'

'Well, we seem to know so little.'

'We know he was in the army and then he was out East, and then he was in Warsaw for a bit and now he's here.'

'That's not very much.'

'We know he turned up here with nothing at all and made a position for himself in under a month And I know I was with him in a very tight corner on the Danube road and he was perfectly magnificent. I don't know what you're getting at.'

Pat looked at her glass. The three cats came out from the cellar and advanced towards us in extended order, their long thin tails erect. They took up a position about four feet from our table and watched us hopefully.

'Well,' said Pat, 'some of your friends are getting rather anxious.'

'That's very good of them. Why?'

'You've done such a lot for him and taken him in to share your flat and everything, it would be awfully disappointing for you if he didn't turn out quite first-rate.'

'Well, really these friends of mine can mind their own bloody business. Who are they, by the way?'

'Oh, a lot of people.'

'Pemberton, I suppose.'

'Yes he was one of them.'

'Pemberton's used to being more or less cock of the walk here, and I suppose he's jealous now somebody's come along who's likely to make more of a splash than he can. Though honestly I can't understand his starting stories like that. I suppose he's rather sore about losing the wire contract.'

'Of course you helped Vickery with that.'

'It was my job. It was English wire against Belgian wire.'

'But you must admit Vickery didn't behave very well.'

'How?'

'Well, waiting till the tenders were all in and bribing the officials to tell him the lowest offer so that he could cable home and get a better price.'

'My good girl, if you want to get business in the Balkans you've got to remember you're in the Balkans.'

'I don't think you'd have done a thing like that yourself, not if another Englishman had practically got the contract.'

'It's all in the game.'

'Well, I don't know. Can't we give these cats anything to eat?'

I shouted to Kosta to bring us ten *chevapchichi*. As soon as they arrived the cats, as is the wont of Balkan cats, ceased to be dignified friends and danced round us screeching with the threatening and importunate whine of the oriental beggar. Pat held out a *chevapchich* gingerly on the end of a toothpick and was attacked *en masse*. She swore and held her finger.

'Don't give any more to that big one, damn him. He bites.'

But this is an unjust world and in spite of our attempts at discrimination the big cat got more than his share.

'So you wanted to see me,' I said, 'to pass on this solemn warning about Vickery?'

'Well, to wish we knew something more about him. Partly, of course for Beryl's sake.'

'Why for Beryl's sake?'

'Well, she is seeing a great deal of him, asking him to the house and going out in cars and having him in for drinks.'

'She sees no more of him than she does of me.'

'Yes, but you're different aren't you?'

'Why, am I perfectly harmless?'

'One knows you'll play straight.'

I was not completely mollified by this tribute.

'Damn it all,' I said, 'Beryl's old enough to look after herself. Besides she's not the type to do anything silly. Underneath all this brightness of hers she's really very domesticated.'

'I thought you were going to say suburban.'

'Well, suburban in a nice sense.'

'Of course in a very nice sense.'

'And then,' I went on, 'she's really extremely fond of Clive. Of course you'll say Clive's dull. He is dull. But if she's fond of him that's enough.'

'It isn't. She wants romance.'

'Still?'

'Good Lord yes. All women want romance and go on wanting it till they're ninety.'

And so probably do all men, I thought to myself; but they haven't got the moral courage to admit it or they're too muddle-headed to know where to look. However, I wasn't going to give my sex away to Pat.

'Perhaps she finds romance in Clive.'

'She may be trying to think she does, like millions of women all over the world. Lord, don't I know it; trying to make the best of things, trying to imagine he isn't just a commonplace second-rate little man, trying to persuade herself he's really devoted when as a matter of fact he's merely used to her and naturally polite. She'll go on trying, I suppose. But she can't really deceive herself. In her heart of hearts like everybody else she knows it's all damned eyewash.'

'Are you a philosopher,' I asked, 'or a woman with a very lurid past?'

'My dear, I'm rather drunk. Let's have some more.'

So we ordered some more, thereby causing a flurry among the cats who thought that more *chevapchichi* were coming.

'Anyhow,' I said, 'you're quite wrong to let yourself get worried about Beryl. I'm certain Vickery doesn't think of her in that way at all. He's out for bigger game.'

'That won't prevent her burning her fingers. He is extraordinarily attractive to some women; personally I don't care for these frightfully good-looking fair men, but I can quite see what it is. And then, I know he's a friend of yours but I can't help saying it, he gives me the impression of being quite unscrupulous.'

'My dear, you simply don't know the man. I grant you he's got no respect for conventional rules, but you can't expect that any more than you could expect a tiger to behave like a poodle. He makes his own rules. Big business isn't a Sunday school, at any rate not in the Balkans, and he's not going to give any quarter or ask for any. It's the same with women. If he wants to go to bed with one he does. I know of four already here in Tsernigrad, and I'm quite sure there'll be others.'

'I have heard something about that,' said Pat. 'Didn't he play rather a dirty trick on Slaughter?'

'If you mean Ilonka, I'm quite sure he didn't know Slaughter had any interest. In any case, Ilonka was Zacharias's bit as well.'

'I should hate to sleep with Zacharias!'

'I hope you never will. But to come back to Vickery, he'll stand by his friends, not because he thinks he ought to or because it's the thing to do or because he'll get anything out of them, but simply because he chooses to. Look at the way he behaves to Miss Fraser, or even more, to Mrs Brinkworth. Only two days ago he was on his way to a very important business appointment and he saw Mrs Brinkworth in the distance trying to stop a lot of nasty little boys from throwing stones at a dying cat. He went up and caught and spanked the small boys and got a car and took Mrs Brinkworth and the cat right to the other end of the town to a chemist's, and got some strychnine and put the cat to sleep. In the end he missed his appointment and just laughed. Mrs Brinkworth told me all this, of course he didn't mention it. Now Mrs Brinkworth couldn't possibly be the slightest use to him in any way. It's just the same with Beryl. He likes her, just as we all do, and he knows they're damned hard up and it pleases him to take her out and give her a good time. And if ever she was in a really tight corner and wanted someone to see her through he'd be more use to her than all the rest of her so-called friends put together.'

'Well,' said Pat, 'I only wish we knew more about him.'

'Damn it all, I know him well enough to ask him to come in and share my flat.'

'As if you cared tuppence who or what anybody was!'

That was better: that was a tribute to the careless and dashing personality I so desired other people to take me for. We each had another *slivovica* and then Pat said she supposed it was time for her to get along home to her sardines. She would obviously have liked me to ask her out to dinner somewhere, but I didn't take the hint. I liked Pat; she was distinctly attractive and very good company, but I wasn't in the mood for an evening out. The conversation had vaguely disquietened me. Besides it would have cost a lot of money and my bank account was running very low. I dropped Pat at her door and then went on home.

On the way I wondered what Pat was up to. The only foundation for her vague suspicions seemed to be the business about the wire contract; and surely she ought to realise that business morality and personal morality are two very different things. The former is a code imposed from without; one can either obey it or run the risk of going to jail. The latter (of course I am using the word morality in its widest sense) is an integral part of the man himself. And in this case the man himself was a man worth backing to one's last shirt if there ever was one. It was absurd to say we knew nothing about his past. We knew as much as we did about most of the people in Tsernigrad. Take the case of Pat herself; we simply knew that she had been married to a man in the Air Force who had been killed in a crash in Iraq, and we only had her word for that. I could only suppose that Pat was jealous of Vickery's paying more attention to Beryl than he did to her, or else that she was one of those women who enjoy rows and stir up trouble out of sheer devilment.

What troubled me were the signs of the first and only rift in the colony I had known since I had been in Tsernigrad. There seemed real danger of a feud, with Pemberton and the Continental Bar contingent and Pat on one side, and Vickery and the Glovers on the other. I was far too fond of both parties not to be upset at the prospect. Besides it all seemed so childish and unnecessary.

When I got back to the flat I found Beryl and Vickery sitting in the two armchairs drinking gin and angostura.

They were delighted to see me, and told me when I poured out my own drink to get ready another for Clive who was expected every minute to come in and pick up Beryl on his way home. There was such a cheerfully obvious brother-and-sisterly atmosphere about that I was doubly convinced of the absurdity of Pat's nebulous accusations. The only course was to treat the whole thing as a joke.

'I'm told,' I said, 'that people are getting quite worried at the way you two are always being seen about together.'

'I've got a better one than that,' said Vickery.

'What's yours?'

'That I'm an impostor.'

'How did that start?'

'Mr Pemberton has serious doubts as to my bona fides.'

'Isn't it frightful?' said Beryl.

'Mr Pemberton,' Vickery went on, 'is even writing to his correspondent in Warsaw to ask if he knows anything about me. As I've never heard of his correspondent it's more than likely he's never heard of me. So there it will be proved.'

'What are you going to do about it?' I asked.

'Nothing.'

'But surely you ought to do something,' said Beryl.

'My dear girl, it's all so obvious. Poor old Pemberton's rather sore at losing that wire contract, and he's getting frightened he'll lose the Mohrstadt bridge too when that comes on, so he loses his head and starts these silly rumours.'

'And I used to think he was a good sort,' said Beryl.

I wondered if Beryl was being entirely honest. Of course she had never said anything nasty about him (she never said anything nasty about anybody), but in the past when she had said nice things about him I had once or twice thought I detected a mental reservation. But then it is difficult for a woman always to be entirely just to her husband's employer.

'He is a good sort,' said Vickery. 'But he's a bit sore and jealous, and when a man's in that state he's not entirely responsible for his actions. But he'll see reason before long.'

Beryl gazed with large liquid eyes at such magnanimity. I was feeling perfectly happy again. After all, if old Pemberton chose to make a fool of himself, well, he just had to. He would see reason again before very long. There was nothing to worry about. The only person to be pitied at all was Clive, who between his wife and his boss would be in an awkward position until it all blew over. Soon afterwards Clive came in, and mindful of what Pat had said about him, I watched his eyes as they followed Beryl. There was certainly more in them than mere habit and politeness. I reflected how disappointing it is that on those very few occasions when one hears a really arresting remark one is almost sure to discover immediately afterwards that it is not fully borne out by the facts.

Beryl called to me across the room.

'Bring me an ash-tray, darling.'

It always pleased me when she started calling everybody 'darling'. It was a sign that she was feeling in good fettle. I suppose the 'darling' habit was originally invented by the section of the Bright Young People that borders on the stage, or by the section of the stage that borders on the Bright Young People, and afterwards permeated downwards and outwards through the lower theatrical strata to their friends and the friends of their friends till it reached people like Beryl who are too self-conscious to use it at all unless fortified by three glasses of gin, and even then it sounds a little awkward. But anyhow we had a very cheerful half-hour.

'What about going out somewhere to-night?' suggested
Vickery when the others had left.

'A very good idea,' I said.

I was now thoroughly in the mood.

18

In due course the Mervyn Company's Mr Scarfe arrived.
He was a big young man with a rather florid face and
beautifully if ever so slightly floridly dressed. He was
wearing the tie of a certain of our older and most expensive
public schools, which I am afraid rather put me against
him. I have met few Old Etonians and Old Wykhamists
whom I have not liked, but with this particular school I
have been less fortunate. Mr Scarfe said he had found the
Minister was out and the Commercial Secretary away on
leave, so he supposed he had to see me. He considered
Tsernigrad a bloody hole, and wondered what the hell
anybody found to do here. However, when he heard that
I had previously been for three years in Aleppo he imagined that it would be all right for me. He went on to say
that he had once thought of taking a Foreign Office job,
not the Consular Service, of course, but the Diplomatic
Service, but had chucked the idea; too bloody slow. Besides that sort of thing was out of date, nowadays anybody
who was anybody went into business.

I felt myself becoming rather distant and official and
asked what I could do for him. He said he'd come out to
collect his bloody money and find out something about
this fellow Vickery; he'd been writing to the Mervyn as if
he was the Almighty, but it wasn't in the least certain that
he'd get the agency at all. Who was the man anyway?
Was he a gentleman? I said he had not been to the same

school as Mr Scarfe. But I am afraid the point of my little joke was missed.

'He calls himself Colonel. I suppose one of these damned temporary commissions.'

'He's in an old Army List we've got here.'

'Army Service Corps?'

'The Radnorshires.'

I was given the impression that that was almost as bad.

'I've already sent a short report to your people,' I said, 'and if you want any more information you'd better go round to the bank.'

'I don't trust these bloody banks.'

'Well, you can get your information from any better source you can think of.'

'I may go round to the bank to-morrow if I have time. I'm not going to stay too long in this bloody place. I want a week-end in Le Touquet on the way back. You'd better ring up Vickery and tell him to come round here.'

'No,' I said, 'you'll have to go round and see him.'

'Well, I suppose I ought to see what his bloody office looks like. You might ring him up and say I'm coming round.'

It rather went against the grain to do anything for Mr Scarfe, but I felt that Vickery ought to know that he was here. So I rang him up and told him.

'What's he like?' came Vickery's voice down the phone.

'He's in here now.'

'A man of four letters?'

'Exactly.'

I heard Vickery's laugh.

'Send him along,' he said, 'we'll cope with him.'

Later on in the day Vickery rang up to say he was busy in the evening (I wondered whether it was the Mohrstadt bridge or Madame Silviera), so would I take Mr Scarfe out to dinner—of course at the firm's expense. He would join us at the Apollo later on. I was glad to have the chance of helping the firm without infringing the consular regulations, but felt that my task was not an easy one. I had no idea what had passed during Scarfe's visit to the office, but I did know that Vickery had taken over a fairly large debt to the Mervyn from old Sonnenschein, and also that the Mervyn business in cars and accessories was necessary to keep him going until such time as he pulled off a big government contract. I could not tell what sort of position Scarfe occupied in the firm, but as the only man to have been out on the spot his opinion would certainly carry weight. It was therefore important that he should be well disposed. However, if I spent three hours *tête à tête* with Scarfe we should be almost certain to quarrel, which would set him against Vickery as being a friend of mine. On the other hand if I took him to the Continental Bar he might pick up some anti-Vickery gossip from Pemberton. In the end I did take him to the Continental; the prospect of three hours of unadulterated Scarfe was more than I could bear.

I was lucky. Pemberton, I found, had just gone off on a business trip to Vladikop, and Grimshaw was dining out somewhere. So there was only Slaughter present who has never said a word against anybody except himself. Mr Scarfe ordered a 'Black Man's Cutie' which, of course, we had never heard of, and was very surprised at the way Weiss's education had been neglected. However in the end he consented to have a gin and mixed.

'Well,' said Slaughter, 'what's the news in dear old London?'

Mr Scarfe related an anecdote about a well-known actress whose name I omit.

'Well I'm blessed,' said Slaughter.

'Yes, but do you know what happened the other night at — ?'

(I also omit the name of the restaurant.)

'Where's that?' asked Slaughter.

'Why, I thought you lived in London.'

'So I do,' said Slaughter. 'In Leyton.'

'Oh my God!' Mr Scarfe gave up Slaughter in despair and turned to me. 'Surely you've been to — ?'

'No,' I said. 'Never.'

'Damn it, I thought everybody had been to — '

I felt myself being relegated to the social limbo of Slaughter and other untouchables.

After the second cocktail Mr Scarfe developed that curious inability, common to his type, to make any remark at all without some reference to unnatural eroticism, female anatomy, personal sanitation, venereal disease, or the sexual act. After the third cocktail he started on bawdy stories, for which I am always a poor audience. I don't regard myself as particularly strait-laced, and I am ready to admit that of the five supremely funny stories of the world three are extremely bawdy. Apparently these were the only three that Mr Scarfe did not know. In any case all of his had little more point than his normal conversation, which they otherwise so strongly resembled. I am inclined to think that my view of the dullness of the usual bawdy story is not merely a personal opinion but a general truth. I base this on the fact that it is not the hearing of such a story that constitutes the pleasure, but the feeling of importance and daring induced by the telling. At any rate, the exchange of bawdy stories is generally a kind of race game: the listeners see how quickly they can get through the minimum of laughter demanded by politeness, and the winner tells the next. In this case Mr Scarfe was lucky for Slaughter is one of the few men who are always ready to listen. Towards the end of dinner my boredom must have become apparent.

'This man's getting shocked,' said Mr Scarfe.

'It would take a lot to shock him,' said Slaughter.

During the short journey from the Continental to the Apollo Mr Scarfe, then rather drunk, confided to me the name of the lady with whom he proposed to spend his week-end at Le Touquet. He seemed disappointed that I had never heard of her. Apparently her photograph had been in the *Sketch* some three weeks before.

The Apollo was fairly full, though Vickery had not turned up yet. Zacharias made room for us at the bar, but Slaughter and I felt it would be safer to take one of the pew-like boxes.

'God, what a crew!' said Mr Scarfe looking round him.

Then he caught sight of the red-haired Russian girl sitting alone in a box opposite and went over to dance with her. In justice to Scarfe I ought to say that when sober he was probably a very good dancer indeed. But now he was merely dangerous. The girl left him in mid-air before they had been round once and came back to us.

'Your friend is drunk,' she said angrily, 'you oughtn't to have brought him down here.'

When Mr Scarfe rejoined us he was also angry.

'What the hell does this — girl think she's doing by — off like that?' He lurched forward to grab at the passing coat-tails of Zacharias. 'Here, you old — , why don't you tell your — girls to dance?'

'One moment, please,' said Zacharias, and rushed away to the opposite corner of the room. Zacharias was enough of a statesman to know that if a situation arises that you can't deal with, the best thing is to disappear in the hopes that it will deal with itself.

'We must get him away,' said Slaughter.

'Look here,' I said to Scarfe, 'if you're going to stay here you must sit down and behave yourself.'

He stared at me in resentful surprise.

'Here, you can speak this — language, why don't you tell these — '

I never heard what I was to tell them, because in his uncertain return to his chair he collided with the next table where a weedy little man was sitting by himself and upset his glass.

'Why can't you keep your bloody table to yourself?'

'Please . . . ' began the little man.

'You hold your — tongue!'

Just then Vickery came in with Cookson and Watterson, and Pujotas hanging on to their coat tails and trying to pretend he was very much of the party.

'Hullo,' said Scarfe when he saw them, 'have you brought my — money?'

'No,' said Vickery.

'Then you can — off and get it!'

I wondered how Vickery was going to take this remark, but he ignored it.

'Please,' said our weedy little neighbour, 'are you an American?'

'Look here, I told you once to go and — yourself!'

The little man turned to me as if I were the person in charge.

'Please be so good as to translate to this gentleman. I am very sorry that he should be angry with me, because I have great respect for Americans.'

'He is wanting to apologise,' explained Pujotas.

Scarfe turned a glassy stare upon the latter.

'God,' he said, 'here's another of them!'

'I am sure,' the little man went on, 'that it was quite by accident that the gentleman upset my wine, and I shall be very sad indeed if I have done anything that may have offended him.'

'These — make me tired,' said Scarfe. 'Let's take this girl to a private room and have a drink.'

He caught hold of the Russian girl by the shoulder, and her eyes glowed with fury. A large blonde in the next box began to laugh.

'Don't paw her about,' I said, 'she doesn't like it.'

'Well, what the — are these — girls here for if not to — ?'

Put in the logical way that Scarfe put it the question was unanswerable. But I was not in the mood for dialectical niceties. I got up, really angry. Scarfe got up at the same time, but tripped over the edge of the box and fell with a crash on the next table where Zacharias had just placed a fresh glass. Wine, table and Scarfe collapsed on the floor. The large blonde screamed and people came crowding round us in hopes of a row. But there was no row. Vickery picked Scarfe out of the débris, and frog-marched him, cursing and kicking, out of the room and up the stairs. Slaughter and I followed in case help was required. But it wasn't. It was a beautifully neat piece of work. Scarfe was bundled into a taxi and sent back to the Continental under the guard of the Apollo's porter to see that he stayed there. We went down and joined the others in the task of pacifying the Russian girl, and as she found herself the centre of the six most opulent looking men in the place it wasn't very difficult. Twenty minutes later the porter came back and reported. He had had some trouble at the Continental, as Scarfe had declared his intention of coming back and fighting me. However he had gone down the steps of the Tabarin (no doubt under the impression that it was the Apollo), and was last seen fighting the head waiter there. Slaughter rather wanted to go and look after him, under the unwritten law on the Continent that one Englishman must always see another Englishman back to bed, however badly he may have behaved. But it was decided that Scarfe had put himself beyond the pale.

'Will this do you any harm with the Mervyn?' I asked Vickery when the others were dancing.

'What?'

'This row.'

'No. If the Mervyn want to negotiate with me they can send out a man who can behave himself.'

'Did you fix up anything with him to-day?'

'No. And if he comes round to-morrow he's not going to put his nose inside my office until he's apologised to you and all these fellows and the girl and Zacharias.'

'Please,' said a meek voice behind us.

We looked round and saw the little man from the next table.

'Please excuse my interrupting you. But your friend went away so abruptly that I had no chance to make myself quite clear to him. I was wondering whether perhaps someone would care to pay for the two glasses of wine that happened to get upset. Thirty douros is a lot of money to me, though of course I would pay the tip for the waiter myself.'

Mr Scarfe did not attempt to call on Vickery again next morning. In fact we none of us ever saw him again, and the only one to hear him was myself. I was sitting in my office, reading a letter to *The Times* in which the writer pointed out what a pity it was that our great export firms when sending representatives abroad, did not make more use of the magnificent young men turned out by our great public schools; when the telephone rang.

'Here,' said a husky voice, 'when does that — Orient Express leave for Paris?'

'Ask the — porter,' I answered, and hung up the receiver.

19

I have not been entirely honest in the last chapter; it contains the truth and nothing but the truth, but not the whole truth. I did not explain that my own personal interest in the Russian girl, never entirely dormant, became extremely lively again. So much so indeed that after we had left the cabaret, worn out by the ceaseless din of Pujotas' voice, I could not go to sleep but had to get out of bed at 4 a.m. and smoke cigarettes and repeat to myself that I had only forty pounds in the bank, and that I wanted a new overcoat and evening shoes and a radio set; that she would probably cause me much more trouble than she was worth, and that in any case it was all damned rubbish. However, the next evening, Vickery having gone to see some municipal bigwig, I went down to the Apollo by myself.

Her name was Tala Nordova, that is, her stage name. Likewise, Russian was merely her stage nationality. Of her grandparents three had been German and the fourth Lithuanian, she was born in Riga, had lived all her life in Berlin, and spoke nothing but German. Like all cabaret girls she confessed to a fondness for country life and horses. Friends of hers had an estate near Warsaw where she had stayed from time to time and gone riding every day. She was also very interested in horse racing. She did not like cabaret work, and expected to get a proper engagement in Berlin in the winter. She had once had a film test which had come out very well, and her agent had promised to do his best for her. Still, one knew what agents are and so far nothing had happened.

All this I learnt sitting up at the bar over a couple of whiskies and sodas. I was rather surprised that she had been in Tsernigrad for over a fortnight without acquiring a protector. But of course she was obviously a girl who could afford to pick and choose or bide her time just as she wished, and no doubt a lot of gentlemen who would otherwise have been in the running were afraid she would be too expensive. And then she was of too exotic a type to be everybody's taste. Vickery, for instance, had told me that he found her 'rather too Aubrey Beardsley.'

Apparently so far she had only two declared admirers in Tsernigrad. One of them was the wife of the President of the National Bank, who daily sent her flowers and impassioned letters; but, Tala told me, that sort of thing didn't appeal to her unless of course it was something very special. The other was the little Jew I had seen with her on her first night. I told her how jealous I had been then and she giggled. (Girls who look like improper goddesses from Asia ought really not to giggle, but then Tala was only twenty.) He bored her stiff, she said. And then he was too fat. It was not that she disliked Jews, after all some of them were very nice, but when they got sentimental they were merely tiresome.

'Are you sentimental?' I asked, though perfectly certain she was as hard as nails.

'Sometimes,' she said.

She wanted to know if I was always in Tsernigrad or just on a business visit. When she heard I was stationed here she became more interested. Permanent residents are more useful to cabaret girls than mere birds of passage. She asked me if I knew the man who had been British Vice-Consul in Königsberg two years before. He had come to see her number, and had taken her out to dinner once or twice. But she had not heard from him for a long time: people didn't bother to go on writing to artists. Besides, she had been too lazy to answer.

Tala and I got on very well. I became more and more convinced that she was the most lovely creature I had ever seen, but I took care not to tell her so. Girls in her position look upon compliments with suspicion, as they meet with very few that have no interested motive behind them. When I left at about three o'clock she was insistent that I should come again the following evening – most of the guests who came were so boring. I felt that my horizon was free of dangerous rivals.

I did come down, and for the evening after invited her to dinner at the Continental, thereby conforming to the rules of courtship that Ilonka had once laid down. I did so with some misgivings. The Bowles family sometimes dined at the Continental, and if Jill were to see me there with Tala she might take it as a personal slight on herself; my conscience was still hazily (though doubtless quite unnecessarily) exercised about Jill. I was also conscious of the propriety required of His Britannic Majesty's Vice-Consul, and hoped that none of my senior colleagues would be there. But the restaurant was almost empty, and I was spared even the ribald asides that would have come if Pemberton & Co had been dining at a neighbouring table. As a matter of fact I was rather disappointed. Tala was so well turned out that I would have enjoyed being envied for having secured her. She did not look quite so beautiful, to me, in one of those little brimless hats that were then the fashion as she did in evening dress. I always think a woman looks best without a hat, and in Tala's case the full magnificence of her mouth and chin wanted the sullen glory of her hair as a balance. But her dress was excellent; very simple, rather severe, and very smart. Shoes and stockings first class; altogether very finished. In spite of the absence of an audience I enjoyed the dinner. Tala and I were tuned in. Having by now spent about eight hours *tête à tête* we were beginning to know each other fairly well. The next evening we dined together again, and feeling we had spent enough time discussing Central European race meetings I asked her if she thought we were mutually congenial enough for our relations to become more intimate. She said she didn't know; couldn't we go on just for a little as we were? She would give me an answer very soon.

The next day as Hughes-Winsor's motor-boat was by then repaired I borrowed it and took her up the Danube. When we came back she suggested a cup of tea at her hotel. She lived at the Bristol, which was not so good a hotel as the Continental but still classy enough to have two rooms with private baths. Tala had one of them. It looked over towards Miss Fraser's villa and the old Turkish cemetery, and the contrast between it and Mausi's former quarters made me vaguely uncomfortable. Tala had a large wardrobe trunk, four hat boxes and a portable gramophone in fawn leatherette. A *crêpe de Chine* dressing-gown hung over the foot of the bed. She took it and disappeared into the bathroom. On the dressing-table were a number of scent bottles of exotic shapes. Otherwise there were four elaborate and obviously expensive photographs of Tala herself, and another only less elaborate photograph of Marlene Dietrich. Tala was evidently a devotee of the Dietrich cult, for there were three biographies of the lady lying about the room. Propped against one of them was the photo of a young man who might have been a trapeze artist in private life.

'Who's this?' I asked when she reappeared.

'That? I don't know why I carry it about.'

'A colleague?'

'A colleague!' She laughed. 'No, that's a Count. He's got an estate near Warsaw.'

'Where you went riding?'

'Yes.'

'Tell me about him.'

'There's nothing to tell. I never hear from him now.'

'What happened?'

'Nothing ever happens to a cabaret dancer. Men don't bother about them.'

She changed her mood, was surprised that I liked my

tea without rum and asked me what I thought of her
room. I thought it was very nice and wondered what it
cost.

'Only a hundred and fifty douros a day.'

(Fifteen shillings, I thought.)

'That's too much.'

'I get twenty per cent off,' she said. I'll show you the
bill.'

Of course, I had been forgetting that a gentleman must
give a girl to understand what material assistance he is in
a position to offer. I became slightly alarmed. Rapid mental arithmetic told me that even with the twenty per cent
off it would come to the best part of twenty pounds a
month. And that of course was only the beginning. Tala
produced the bill. On the first of the month she had paid
one thousand and fifty douros, as the discount was only
deducted when she had paid for a fortnight. Accordingly
on the eighth she had paid six hundred and thirty. Eight
hundred and forty douros was due on the fifteenth and
twenty-second, and three hundred and sixty on the
twenty-ninth for the last three days.

'Have you got it?' I asked, wondering what I had on
me.

'I'm not quite broke yet.'

I still thought it was much too much and that at least
the hotel ought to have allowed her thirty per cent off.
She said she couldn't be bothered to haggle; also she liked
the view. We went across to the window to look at it. The
sun behind us was getting low, and threw a rosy glow on
the shoulder of the hill and Miss Fraser's villa, and the
gravestones and the little cupola of Ali Moustafa. Also, as
Tala was between myself and the light, it showed up the
lines of her figure through the *crêpe de Chine* dressing-gown.
I put my arm round her and felt the firm magnificence of
her body; nuzzled her hair and worked slowly downwards

past her ear to the throat. As I did so I wondered whether and to what extent the people in the house opposite could see us. Suddenly she broke loose and said she had to dress, but she didn't mind my staying if I promised not to look. However she seemed to doubt my ability to keep my word, for she took her things and disappeared again into the bathroom. I tried to calm myself by reading one of the lives of Miss Dietrich. When Tala re-emerged she was fully dressed and it was almost time to go out to dinner. As we went I picked up the bill which was lying on the table.

'No,' she said, and took it back again.

(Advanced technique.)

By the next day I had come to the conclusion that something drastic had to happen. I borrowed a car from Vickery and took her out in it. She wanted to drive herself through the town, chiefly, I think, in order to be seen by those of her colleagues who might be sitting outside the Café Esplanade. But I still had enough consular dignity left not to run the risk of being involved in a car accident with a cabaret girl, and wouldn't let her. We went out along the Danube road. I had heard somewhere that to be driven fast over bumpy roads is supposed to arouse the amorous instincts of the female. What with that and my own nervous exasperation I kept my foot down on the accelerator in a manner that almost took my breath away.

Anyhow it worked.

And old Pemberton was wrong again, for red-haired women do not smell foxy, not even in the most crucial moments.

Three days afterwards, a period long enough to prove to all parties that there could be no question of a mercenary motive, I had the hotel bill.

*   *   *

Our idyll was encouraged from a most unexpected quarter, namely the Foreign Office. Outside Turkey there is probably no other government department in Europe where the officials receive a large proportion of their emoluments at least two years in arrears; but that is what happens in the Levant Consular Service. An officer's pay depends largely on the difference in local prices of incongruous commodities such as rhubarb and washing soda between 1914 and now. Every year the harassed consul receives a long and formidable questionnaire, whereupon he must go out and ask the oldest inhabitant what was the price of beetroot in 1914. When this has been done, and guesses have been made at the prices of such items as the oldest inhabitant has forgotten, the consul works out the coefficient of the 1914 prices in piastres per oke as compared with present prices in douros (or dinars or drachmae or whatever it is) per kilogram. The completed questionnaires are submitted to a body of very distinguished statisticians somewhere in the bowels of Downing Street, who sit on them for eighteen months or so, and then the wheels of the Paymaster General's Department are slowly set in motion. All this is to explain why I suddenly received a cheque for ninety-three pounds in respect of my second year at Aleppo.

In American films the recognised happy ending is for the young man to drive away in a large motor-car with a supremely beautiful girl into a world of unlimited possibilities. Professional moralists, like the headmasters of our great public schools and whimsy columnists, are fond of writing to the papers to deplore the type of mind that can put forward such a state of affairs as the highest good. They write disparagingly of a material criterion; they compare quantitative with qualitative values; and usually conclude with weighty, if somewhat vague, pronouncements on true happiness. I sometimes wonder if the headmasters (imagination boggles at the whimsies) have had any personal experience of the situation which they decry.

I have. There were, of course, a few minor flaws. I used to wish every now and then that Tala had some topic of conversation other than race meetings. My vanity was sometimes piqued by the feeling that, though no doubt largely, she did not entirely love me for myself. What worried me worse was that like many professional dancers she had a few faint hairs on her upper lip that were visible in certain lights, and I was always wondering if I couldn't get her to do something about them. Then I was a little anxious about the possibility of quarrels in the colony, and my conscience pricked me occasionally as to whether my course of life was entirely in accordance with the spirit of the General Instructions to Consuls. Besides all which I was sitting up too late and smoking too much, so that I woke up every morning with the impression that something had crawled into my mouth and died there. But after all these things were not important. I had a Mervyn Dominion whenever I wanted one; I had a girl who, for me at any rate, was supremely beautiful; and, with Vickery to back me, I was setting out into a world of unlimited possibilities. I was supremely happy.

20

Discreetly I introduced Tala into local society.

'Can't you come round and dine to-night?' I asked Hughes-Winsor.

'I'd love to. But I hope there won't be a crowd. I hate crowds.'

'It's just ourselves, and a cabaret girl, and . . . '

'Oh dear. I can never think of anything to say to cabaret girls.'

'This is rather a special one. And then there'll be the Glovers.'

'I can never think of anything to say to Mrs Glover.'

'You won't have to say anything. The whole point is to introduce Beryl to the girl.'

'It sounds very unsuitable.'

'Not a bit,' I said. 'There's no more certain way of giving pleasure than introducing a respectable woman and a *demi-mondaine*. Each has just the quality that the other wants to have; it makes a little mutual admiration society. And the *demi-mondaine* goes away thinking that she's not a social outcast, and the respectable woman thinking that she might be of some use on a week-end to Brighton after all.'

'And I,' said Hughes-Winsor, 'am to be a sort of midwife to this embryonic friendship. Very well.'

The meeting between Beryl and Tala was a complete success. At first it was a little formal. There was a good deal of *Gnädige Frau* and *Gnädiges Fräulein*. Also Tala was ever so slightly embarrassed at finding herself in a company with the barbarous habit of eating asparagus with the fingers. But Beryl's admiration was so obvious and Tala was so conscientious in her advice how Beryl ought to do her hair that they were soon firm friends. We left it to them to make the running. Vickery had that curious knack of saying very little and yet always seeming to appear the centre of any group he was in. Clive had never anything to say, but he opened doors and passed things and did everything else that his hosts ought to have done. Hughes-Winsor sat in silent gloom.

I think Beryl wanted to turn the conversation round to lurid nights in Berlin, but that of course did not suit Tala at all. So we talked about country life and horses.

'I do so love riding!' said Beryl.

Hughes-Winsor asked her if she hunted, and she grew

pink with pleasure at the question. No, she had never had the chance, but she loved riding. She supposed Vickery hunted.

'No, I went out to British Columbia when I was twelve. Mills is the man for hunting. He comes from Leicestershire.'

'What is Leicestershire?' asked Tala.

It was explained to her that it was the district where the high English aristocracy went to hunt. Tala was proud of me so that I had not the heart to explain that I had never been on a horse except in my extreme youth, on the sands, during the annual month at Cromer. Also it would have been unkind to Beryl, most of whose riding had probably taken place during the annual fortnight at Herne Bay.

At a quarter to ten Tala had to go and get ready for her turn at the Apollo. I took her back in the car.

'Your friends are nice people. That woman is very much in love with Vickery.'

'Rubbish.'

'But she won't have any luck in that sort of thing. She's too fat.'

When I got back to the flat Vickery had disappeared. He had had a telephone call and gone off, promising to be back in about an hour. I supposed more intrigues with Gorkin and the Municipality. The others were having coffee out on the balcony. It was pleasantly cool out there and too high up for any mosquitoes. The night was thick and moonless. What light there was came from the glimmer of the street lamps below, reflected on the angles and surfaces of the opposite walls. The hoot of shipping on the rivers sounded distant and mellow. Every now and then came the whine and sizzle of contending cats.

'I think your friend is perfectly charming,' said Beryl.

'Very nice,' said Clive.

I felt like a popular actor taking a call after a well-deserved success. I waited for Hughes-Winsor's tribute; but apparently besides having nothing to say to cabaret girls he had nothing to say about them. It was slightly disappointing. I felt as if I was being received with rapture from the Upper Circle, but chilling silence from the stalls. I reflected, as perhaps popular actors may have done, that the stalls did not understand.

Hughes-Winsor asked if he might play the piano, and went back to the sitting-room. Ravel was a little above our heads, but sitting out there with the glow of the three cigarettes pricking out the darkness it was rather pleasant. Music, I reflected, the noisiest of the arts, should always be, as now, an unobtrusive accompaniment to summer nights. I began to feel pleasantly inconsequent.

Beryl wondered if I would mind if she asked me something very personal.

'Not in the least,' I said.

'Are you in love with her?'

I considered the matter.

'Yes,' I said. 'At the moment I don't want any other woman.'

'But I didn't mean love in that way.'

'In what way then?'

'Well, to be so much in love that you not only didn't want any other woman but you didn't want anything else at all.'

Whatever was coming over Beryl? I feared the conversation was going to get rather difficult. While there is no one (or at any rate no male) who enjoys these intense and warming talks about love more than I do, I always think that married people should not indulge in them when the conjugal partner is present. One always supposes, as a third party, that one ought to take it for granted that the proper combination of passionate desire and deep spiritual affinity does in fact exist with this particular ménage; and such a state of affairs always seems so grotesquely improbable in nearly all the married couples that one happens to meet in the flesh. It is impossible to speak one's mind without the fear of hurting somebody's feelings. The presence of Clive, clearing his throat and continually failing to keep his pipe alight, cramped my style.

'I often wonder,' I said, 'how far your style of love exists at all.'

'Oh, it does.'

'Perhaps I felt it once. At the age of ten. It was the principal girl in the Leicester pantomime of 1914. Of course I never spoke to her and she never even heard of my existence.'

'You started pretty young,' said Clive.

Beryl properly ignored him.

'I suppose,' I said, 'the most exciting adventure of my life was when I bought a picture post-card of her. It was in a little tobacconist's down by the theatre. Of course in those days I wasn't allowed in the town by myself, and I only had sevenpence in the world. I dodged my small brother's nurse who was supposed to be looking after me and went off. Once I got there I hadn't the courage to go into the shop. At that age anything to do with girls is shameful and effeminate, and I remember sitting in the tram coming back and trying to make up my mind to put away childish things. But during the night I lay awake and realised that come what might I had to go and get it. So next day I dodged the nurse again. This time I got into the shop and to my intense relief the old man didn't seem to notice I was blushing and wasn't in the least surprised at what I wanted. I had to walk all the way back because I had no money left for the tram. After that I lived in terror lest anyone should discover my precious post-card. I didn't dare leave it in my pocket at night because the maid used to brush my clothes, and I couldn't put it under the pillow because my mother sometimes turned it over when she came to tuck me up. So I had to hide it in a night sock.'

'How sweet,' said Beryl.

'I took it back to school with me and kept it hidden all through the Easter term. Just before the holidays I showed it to my dearest friend, and was very disappointed at his lack of enthusiasm. It may have been the shock of that, or else love was cooling, or perhaps the strain of keeping it hidden was getting too much for me. Anyhow during the holidays I buried it formally in a flower bed.'

'Did you cry?'

'No. I was sad for a bit. But I had that certain feeling of relief that every man has when any love affair comes to an end.'

'You're very cynical.'

'I don't think I am. Only I don't hold with love to the exclusion of everything else. That's why I get tired of novels where the people keep it up at full steam for a hundred and fifty thousand words. They don't seem normal. I'm not being cynical, I'm simply broadening the basis of romance. After all there are such a lot of other things to be done.'

'But they're none of them very important.'

'We've got our lives to make.'

In the sitting-room Hughes-Winsor had stopped playing.

'That was lovely,' said Beryl. 'Do you know Dvořák's *Humoresque*? It's my favourite piece of classical music.'

Hughes-Winsor played the *Humoresque*.

'Life is wonderfully exciting really,' said Beryl.

'Well,' said Clive, 'these Vuchinians are after me for Income Tax, so I should damn well think it was.'

'Clive, you're awful!'

They stayed on till fairly late, waiting for Vickery to come back, but he didn't. After they had left I remained on the balcony, and decided that Beryl was not in love with Vickery (or she would not have talked in the way she had done in front of Clive), but was merely exhilarated by his influence in the way that I was. So there was no need to worry for Clive's sake. Poor old Clive, he was never going to get much out of life. He would never be more than an underling with Pemberton, and at his age was unlikely ever to get a good job anywhere else. He was where he was for life. I didn't know what he was getting; certainly not more than five hundred a year. It was an awful squeeze for him and Beryl to get a fortnight at home every other summer. And yet he never seemed disappointed, which was strange, as nearly everyone one meets over forty— over thirty even—is disappointed; the Drexlers, for instance, and Bowles and Mrs Bowles and Pat McLean, and Slaughter (I remembered the way he sometimes came into the Continental Bar and sat behind his drink without saying a word); and nearly all the Levant Consular Service. And yet they all must have their secret yearnings and ambitions; most of them quite ridiculous probably. There seemed no solution for them. People with children can transfer their ambitions to their children, and eventually to their grandchildren, but the others haven't even that. And yet here was I, at the age of twenty-seven, about to conquer the world. I wondered if it was entirely due to luck or partly to my own ability.

It was past two when Vickery came back.

'They were sorry to miss you,' I said.

'I'm sorry too. Heard the news?'

'What?'

'The Mayor's dying.'

'What of?'

'Nobody knows. At least the local doctors don't. They operated on his tummy and seem to have made a mess of it. He'll be dead in three days.'

'Will that,' I asked my future partner, 'make any difference to the bus contract?'

'It'll make the difference of what he's had out of us already.'

'How much was that?'

'More than it ought to have been. I'll have to go to England for a couple of days. Moorsides will have to put up something, they can't expect us to stand all the racket. Besides the Mervyn people are still squealing for their money. I could soothe them a little.'

'Never mind,' I said. 'As soon as we pull off one big contract we're made.'

'That's the spirit. Any whisky left?'

21

It was at my private school that I first began to indulge in ardent speculations about time. I remember lying in my bed in the large bare dormitory, praying that some Slave of the Lamp would appear and at my command wipe out in the twinkling of an eye the seven weeks or whatever it was that stretched out so endlessly between now and the holidays. And when I was at home I wished the same about the interval before going to a circus or going fishing. The habit has stayed with me. I suppose at one time or another I have wished away the whole of my life except a few weeks; and when I look back and think how very little of it I would really care to live all over again I can hardly consider I have been wrong. For the few days that Vickery was away in England I had several attacks of this time-annihilating mood. My consular existence appeared more than ever insipid. I wanted to start doing things, though I was still rather vague as to what I should eventually do. I was impatient.

Before leaving Vickery had asked me to keep an eye on Mr Krompek and I went round one morning; that at least gave me the opportunity to pretend to myself that I was doing something. I found Krompek, as usual, lecturing a hot and untidy Mr Boranovitch. He received me with great ceremony, called back Mr Boranovicth to wipe the seat of my chair, and was very apologetic because he had not a more expensive brand of cigarette to offer me. I felt uncomfortable, as I always do when I meet worthy people like Mr Krompek with an exaggerated idea of my social importance; perhaps it is because I know that I shall never be able to do anything for them in return. In this case I was especially embarrassed, as Vickery had told me Krompek was no damned good and would be fired before very long.

We had nothing much to say to each other. He told me he was bringing out his mother from Mährisch-Ostrau to come and stay with him. I asked what she would find to do in Tsernigrad, and he said she would sit in the Kezbin Park and admire the view. Apparently the problem of how to keep one's parents amused is less acute in Mährisch-Ostrau than it is elsewhere. Then he took me into the next room to show me a new fire extinguisher that had just come out. It was tastefully set out on a centre table, flanked by tins of metal polish. In the corner by the window Miss Tsernigrad sat behind her typewriter, deep in a magazine about film stars. Mr Krompek told her to demonstrate the fire extinguisher.

'I don't know how to.'

'But I gave you instructions that you should learn.'

'I haven't had time.'

Miss Tsernigrad returned to her magazine, and Mr Krompek, defeated, demonstrated the fire extinguisher himself. As we went back to the inner office he shook his head very gravely over the Modern Girl.

I asked how business was, and he shook his head again, this time over the inexplicable indifference of car owners to the terrible and ever present danger of fire. I asked him if he ever tried to sell it to people who didn't own cars. A sudden light came into Mr Krompek's eyes.

'You mean, *Herr Konsul*, that to buy a fire extinguisher is the first step towards owning a motor-car?'

I hadn't meant it; but I didn't want to disillusion Mr Krompek as to what he went on to describe as my phenomenal grasp of the commercial spirit. I left him calling excitedly to Mr Boranovitch to come and take down a new circular letter. I felt his mind was filled with a vision of the office crowded with invoice clerks who all addressed him as *Herr Direktor*; while, half a mile away, his mother sat in the Kezbin Park and admired the view.

And then the Mayor died. In politics he had been a Nationalist, the same party as our friend Marinsky, and as the Opposition had been giving a lot of trouble lately the Government decided to make a big demonstration out of the funeral.

I keenly resented this decision, because when one is used to not having to get to one's office till after ten it is very annoying to have to attend a funeral at eight. In some ways perhaps we were lucky, for the Vuchinians retain the detestable Balkan habit of rising at cock-crow, and think nothing of beginning official functions at half-past six. Still, it is bad enough to have to issue forth in a morning coat at 7.40. The Cathedral was packed with notables and diplomats all treading on each other's toes in efforts to shake hands with someone just out of reach. When the service began venerable vergers, wiping their noses on the sleeves of their cassocks, distributed lighted tapers; so that we were all faced with the problem of holding a taper in one hand without damage to the top-hat in the other, and of avoiding grease being dropped down our necks from the tapers of the persons behind. As the gorgeous and interminable ritual of an Orthodox funeral service wore on there came the further problem of disposing of the spluttering ends without burning the fingers. The service lasted until half-past ten.

Once outside the diplomats and consuls gathered under the lee of the porch for a moment of respite. Everybody once more shook hands with everybody else, and enquired after healths. Cigarette cases were produced from tail pockets. Scraps of diplomatic conversation came floating through the air. Then a very hot and fussed police officer came up and asked us to take our places in the procession. At last we moved off. First of all the Boy Scouts; then the Municipal Band; then the Guard of Honour. Then the coffin on the first motor hearse ever to have been seen in Tsernigrad, with the eight strong men from the undertaker's and the undertaker himself in a new bowler hat, bursting with a very natural importance on this the proudest day of his career, and the widow supported by her four brothers-in-law. Then the Metropolitan Bishop and his eighteen attendant priests, a riot of colour in the shabby streets. Then the personal representative of the President, and the Prime Minister, and the cabinet, followed by the Roman Catholic Bishop to represent the Catholics, and the Rev. Momcilo Popoff of the American Methodist Mission to represent the Protestants, and the Chief Rabbi representing the Jews and the Grand Mufti representing the Moslems. And then the Diplomatic and Consular Corps, followed by the military and detachments of the police and the Danube Customs Guard, and the Municipal Council, and delegations from the various government departments and from the Chambers of Commerce and Industry and from the legal, medical and dental associations, and representatives of the University, and detachments of pupils and teachers from all the primary and secondary schools, and miscellaneous notables; and finally that surprisingly large body of the general public who could not be fitted into any of the above categories. The cobbled streets were very dusty and uneven, and the snail's pace at which we had to walk was especially trying.

'It is intolerable,' said Monsieur De Woutte, who was walking by my side. 'In England is the Diplomatic Corps invited to the obsequies of a mayor?'

I am afraid I had not the slightest idea as to who was officially invited to the funerals of mayors in England, but I answered the question in the way Monsieur De Woutte expected.

'One might,' continued Monsieur De Woutte, 'invite the Consular Corps, that is quite another matter. But not the Diplomatic Corps. After all, a mayor is only the functionary of a town.'

Monsieur De Woutte was looking so upset that I felt that there must be something that was worrying him even more than the indignity of having to attend in his official capacity the obsequies of a *fonctionnaire de ville*. And then I saw that quite inadvertently I was walking on his right-hand side. In many countries the right is reserved strictly for the social superiors; this has been the starting point of bitter vendettas. And here was Monsieur De Woutte, a Counsellor of Legation (par interim), walking on the inferior side of a Vice-Consul! Hastily I dodged round.

'But no, do not trouble . . . '

After a certain amount of polite jibbing I managed to install myself upon the left. Monsieur De Woutte beamed with satisfaction and gratitude.

'But, *mon cher*, you are too scrupulous. As you know, I am like you. I never attach importance to these little things. But you are always most correct. I regret extremely that I see you so seldom. In this town – ah, *mais alors*!'

This last exclamation was caused by the fact that those in front stopped suddenly, so that the procession concertina'd and we were both nearly blinded by the spikes of the Chief Rabbi's umbrella which he was using as a sunshade. By this time we had reached the main square where perhaps as many as four thousand people were gathered. The Vice-Mayor appeared at one of the windows of the Municipality and began a farewell eulogy on the deceased in his capacity as citizen.

My heart sank. Not so much at the Vice-Mayor, whose oration after all only lasted fifteen minutes, as because I knew by experience that in Tsernigrad if one speech is made there will be many more to follow. Sure enough, four hundred yards on at the corner of the Kolodvorskaya the widow's eldest brother-in-law made a speech on the late Mayor in his capacity of family man. The sun blazed down pitilessly. I eyed the Chief Rabbi with envy, and wondered if by any manoeuvre I might get some of the shade of his umbrella. Vain hope: the sun stood vertically above our heads and the Chief Rabbi was only five feet two.

On we went. By the end of the fourth speech I was so bored, tired and listless, that not even a vague disturbance at the back of the crowd could arouse my interest, though Monsieur De Woutte became very excited and declared the revolution was beginning. At the University buildings the Vice-Chancellor made a speech on the deceased in his capacity of Example to Youth. But then relief came by word being passed down that the official part of the proceedings was over. Everybody started shaking hands again, and the motor hearse rattled off towards the cemetery at twenty-five miles an hour. The crowd drifted back to the Wilsonovi to find out what the row had been about. The elder diplomats hunted for their motor-cars and the younger ones invaded a neighbouring café for a glass of beer. I went off to the Consulate to see if there were any letters to be signed before going home to change, and discovered there a round-faced little man with rimless pince-nez and a bald patch. He told me his name was Pant and that he had been sent out by Moorside, Kempton & Goodenough Ltd to make a thorough investigation into the whole position.

22

Mr Pant was a very different proposition from Mr Scarfe, and in the four days he stayed with us I got rather to like him. But he had been unfortunate in the time of his arrival, and first of all he needed calming down. Apparently there had after all been quite a serious demonstration organised by communists and students. The police had succeeded in keeping all but a very small fraction away from the route of the procession. These had created the vague disturbance we had heard near the Ministry of Communications. The main body of demonstrators, finding themselves headed off, had marched down to the railway station and started throwing stones, with the result that the station authorities and railway police had become rather rattled. Accordingly, when Mr Pant alighted from his train, he was hustled into the third-class waiting-room and locked in with a crowd of peasants, several bundles of turkeys and fourteen goats, all in a state of great excitement. From the square without came the sound of shouting. The peasants, of course, spoke no language but their own, so that Mr Pant's English and what he described as his public school French were insufficient for him to find out what was happening. Outside the shouting grew worse, and bricks and broken bottles were hurled through the windows. Then some shots were fired. Horrible stories of

Balkan war atrocities floated through Mr Pant's mind, and he wondered if the crowd outside were trying to set fire to the building and burn him alive. He hammered on the door without effect. Then at last an unshaven man in a bowler hat came in and demanded his passport, and when Mr Pant in his best public school French requested an explanation he found himself threatened with a revolver. After another wait the doors were opened and he was bundled on to the street. Eventually he had found a taxi and here he was.

'A most uncomfortable experience,' he said. 'I'm only so thankful it didn't happen to Colonel Goodman.'

'Why?' I asked.

'Well, because it was so uncomfortable.'

'But why should it have been more uncomfortable for Colonel Goodman than it was for you?'

'Oh, I wouldn't like anything of that sort to happen to Colonel Goodman.'

Hughes-Winsor came in and I introduced him. To Mr Pant, who as yet knew nothing about the funeral, it came as a further shock to find that apparently all Englishmen in Tsernigrad went about in top-hats and frock-coats. He apologised for having nothing more formal with him than his lounge suit, though considering what he had gone through at the station perhaps it was just as well.

'Why,' said Hughes-Winsor,' were you in that trouble this morning?'

'Yes, I was.'

'You were lucky.'

'I beg your pardon?'

'When they start shooting here it's generally some foreigner who gets killed.'

Mr Pant looked very perturbed.

'There'll be a revolution or a civil war here before very

long,' said Hughes-Winsor. 'The country's in a dreadful state.'

'You don't say so!'

Hughes-Winsor looked extremely gloomy, and when he had failed in the purpose which had brought him into my room (which was to induce me to take his place at a forthcoming tea-party at the Turkish Legation) he went out looking gloomier than ever. Mr Pant looked anxiously after him.

'Is the situation really as bad as that?' he enquired.

'No. Hughes-Winsor's just come back from a funeral and is rather depressed.'

Mr Pant composed his features suitably at the mention of the word funeral, and hoped it had been no near relation. I reassured him.

'So there's no real cause for alarm?' he asked.

'Not in the least.'

'Perhaps not for you, who are used to that sort of thing,' said Mr Pant. 'I read in the paper about your encounter with the brigands, which, if I may say so, was very gallant indeed. But, of course, I have to look at things from the business point of view.'

'A little dust-up like that happens every three weeks or so in the Balkans. But it doesn't mean anything. The country's perfectly stable.'

'I'm very glad to hear you say so. Of course I didn't for a moment suppose that it could be serious, or Colonel Goodman would have dealt with it. As a matter of fact it is not part of my mission to report on the political situation, but if there had been a revolution in progress I would have had to mention it, which would have been very unfortunate.'

'Unfortunate for you,' I asked, 'or for Colonel Goodman, or for Vuchinia?'

'Well, it would be very unfortunate if a subordinate like

myself made a report that did not entirely bear out Colonel Goodman's views.'

'I see.'

'I have come out really for two things. First of all I want to discuss one or two things with Colonel Vickery.'

'Well,' I said, 'he's gone back to England to see your firm.'

'But we hadn't heard anything about that.'

'He only left three days ago. He would only just have arrived.'

'Well, if he goes to see the firm it will do just as well. There has been some delay about remitting the first instalment for the wire contract. Foreign Outstandings put in quite a firm minute about it.'

'Foreign Outstandings?'

'Yes,' said Mr Pant. 'We work on the committee system, you see. Foreign Outstandings look after moneys due to us from abroad. It sits on Monday afternoons, and its recommendations go up to the Accounts A Committee who meet on Thursday afternoons.'

'Do you sit on Accounts A?'

'Oh no. I'm quite a humble person, I'm only on Overseas. We sit on Tuesday afternoons and report to Constructional Projects who sit on Friday mornings.'

'Is Colonel Goodman on Constructional Projects?'

'Oh no, he's far too important for that. He's on Managerial B, which is the Executive. They sit on alternate Wednesday mornings. It's rather unfortunate in a way, because Works Promotion sits on Wednesday afternoons and therefore sometimes has to wait a fortnight before it gets a decision.'

'But supposing there's something urgent?'

'Then the respective minute is marked urgent. Of course there is a certain delay sometimes, but it isn't altogether a bad thing because it shows our customers how carefully we work. After all, there's only one Moorsides'.'

There was such a beatific light in Mr Pant's eye as he made his declaration of faith that I thought he was going to add 'and Colonel Goodman is its prophet'. It all sounded rather odd to me and I wondered why business men made such fun of government departments. But then, of course, I knew nothing about business. I accompanied Mr Pant to his taxi. He looked anxiously up the street.

'It seems quite quiet now,' he said.

'Oh yes, it's all over now.'

'I suppose it doesn't often happen that the brigands penetrate into the town?'

'Never,' I reassured him.

The taxi bore him off, firmly clutching the handle of his umbrella, towards the Continental Hotel.

For the next three days I was intermittently pestered by Pant and by Krompek in turn. Each was highly suspicious of the other, and as they had no common language they were all the time at cross purposes. I tried to soothe Pant by explaining that Vickery must now be settling it all in London; and then Krompek got a wire from Vickery dated Paris. I suddenly realised that Madame Silviera had recently left for a fortnight in Paris, but this explanation was hardly likely to appeal to Mr Pant. The next thing was that Pant learned that the first instalment of the payment for the wire had been paid over to Vickery instead of going into a special banking account, and someone at the Ministry of Finance had said that this had been done by arrangement with the British Consul.

'Nothing of the sort,' I said.

'But they showed me the document. It was all in Vuchinian, but it had your signature and stamp at the bottom.'

'I remember now. Vuchinian government departments refuse to recognise any document in any language other than Vuchinian. So that all the papers your people sent out were useless, and Vickery had to come round here with an official from the Ministry of Communications and another from the Ministry of Finance and swear an affidavit in Vuchinian before me that he was acting as your representative. That is the document you saw and if he hadn't got it the deal wouldn't have gone through at all.'

'But don't you think you should have written to Colonel Goodman first?'

'No,' I said. 'When anyone comes round here to make an affidavit it's my business to administer the oath and collect the fee. It is not my business to hold an enquiry about what is being sworn to, unless I have any particular reason to believe that it is either illegal or false.'

Mr Pant kept on repeating that it was very grave.

'Very likely,' I told him, 'there's been a special arrangement between Goodman and Vickery about this first instalment. After all, Vickery's commission comes to about half of it, and then there are all these palms to be greased, both for this job and for future ones.'

'Palms to be greased?'

'Yes.'

'You don't mean bribery?'

'I do.'

'Oh dear,' said Mr Pant. 'I'm quite sure they heard nothing about that in Foreign Outstandings. Besides, we take a very strong line about that sort of thing in Moorsides'. I'm quite sure Colonel Goodman would never agree to anything like that, unless of course it was absolutely necessary.'

'Well, it's absolutely necessary here.'

Mr Pant looked graver than ever and went off to compose a long telegram to his firm.

Meanwhile the excitement in the town was growing. All the parties took every opportunity to make political capital out of the riot on the day of the funeral, and soon there were all the ingredients of a first-class political crisis. In Vuchinia there are no keener politicians than the civil servants, so that when Mr Pant next went to the Ministries in search of more information about the wire business he found everyone far too engrossed to attend to him. He spent two days wandering about passages and waiting outside doors and then gave up the struggle in despair. All he could think of doing, he said, was to go over to Mohrstadt and see the site of the proposed bridge. I encouraged the idea as I was beginning to get a little tired of him.

23

That afternoon Hughes-Winsor asked me if I would come and help him out with a bathing party. I was afraid it might include Jill, whose existence I was trying my best to forget. But it turned out to be only Miss Phipps, Mrs McLean and Slaughter, to none of whom, Hughes-Winsor explained, could he ever think of anything to say. The prospect appealed to me.

In the summer in Tsernigrad even political agitators take a siesta from one to three, and we went down to the river through strangely quiet streets, deserted except for dogs that lay panting in the shade of café tables. I felt I was going to enjoy myself. Lately I had been having rather too much of other people's responsibilities: Tala's finances, Mr Krompek's ledgers, Mr Pant's Foreign Outstandings. To-day I would take a holiday. I listened with a luxurious detachment to the argument between Hughes-Winsor and his chauffeur about the misbehaviour of the magneto. I flopped into the bows and refused to make any suggestion as to where we should go. Hughes-Winsor, somewhat flushed, tugged at the starter. The motor coughed, jibbed, then relented and started with a steady thug. As we turned up the Bina the yellow walls of Tsernigrad jigged before my eyes in a haze of heat. The iron railway bridge stood up hot and immemorial, like some causeway of hell; beyond was an eddy where the green waters of the Bina cut into the muddy brown of the Danube. A string of low black coal barges disappeared one by one round the bend. The current lapped against our bows.

'What a beautiful dress you've got on, Miss Phipps,' I said.

'Do you really think so? It's such an old one!'

Miss Phipps became quite pink and excited with pleasure. Pat McLean's eye met mine; a glance to say how wrong of me to pull poor Miss Phipps's leg, and how well she (Pat) understood. Now that the scientists have robbed us of our belief in causality in the so-called material world, how refreshing to find Miss Phipps and Pat reacting so perfectly in their different ways to a given stimulus! The yellow shimmering walls of Tsernigrad receded further into the distance. The ramshackle little factory frontages were all behind us; on either side were the low wooded banks. Soon we would pass the Mon Plaisir bathing establishment, the last outpost of the town. Slaughter seized his camera and demanded to be taken nearer the side. He was not unrewarded. To prevent theft the management of Mon Plaisir has very sensibly stamped the name of the establishment in large letters across the seats of bathing costumes hired out to patrons. And as we passed to our great delight three stout Vuchinian matrons were lying on the sand on their tummies. Slaughter's camera clicked. I lay back, realising I had attained perfect happiness. The chug of the motor was as music; a timeless rhythm, saving us from the loneliness of silence. Even the little physical discomforts, the hot sweatiness where my back pressed most heavily on the cushions, the squeeze of my dark horn-rimmed glasses above my ears, were but necessary reminders of the reality of my existence in this effortless world of green waters and low banks with yellow hills behind them, and blue skies and simple badinage. How clearly Nietzsche had proved his lunacy when he held that happiness was in the overcoming of difficulties! The very essence of a struggle against difficulties is the anticipation of a morrow that never comes. How infinitely better than that hot and dusty self-deception was my present withdrawal from undigested and indigestible desires. 'Incomplete Elimination', grim warning that stares at us from the pages of our morning papers, how true a diagnosis of spiritual as well as bodily ailments! Happiness is the elimination of discordant elements, the perfect harmony with the universe that I attained as I lay there above the lapping ripples.

'A penny for your thoughts!' said Miss Phipps.

'I was thinking of becoming a Buddhist.'

'Holy Christmas!' said Slaughter.

We landed eventually on the south bank, about two hours upstream from Tsernigrad, after having inspected and rejected the possibilities of an island which had an ideal strip of beach but no convenient bushes behind which Miss Phipps could disrobe. It was at a bend in the river. Behind us and about four hundred yards away rose up the little hills; between was rough pasture land with patches of bracken and thorn bushes. Away on the left was a little bluff with a ruined Turkish fort, at one time the northernmost bulwark of Islam. Otherwise there was no sign of human handiwork – just that wide spaciousness which the Danube and its greater tributaries possess. We tied up the boat, unloaded our baskets and thermos flasks; retired in our different directions to undress and reassembled and dabbled our toes in the water.

'Oh dear,' said Hughes-Winsor.

We followed his alarmed gaze. Fifty yards away a large black water-buffalo marched diffidently and clumsily out of the bracken and stood shoulder high in the water.

'He's all right,' said Miss Phipps. 'He's not doing anything.'

Slaughter tried not to laugh, but did not succeed, whereat we all laughed and Miss Phipps, pink but undaunted said what minds we all had and eventually had to laugh too.

'If only he was downstream!' said Hughes-Winsor, and everybody began to laugh again. However we marched on the invader, who stared at us with the frightened bewilderment of his kind and shambled back to the bank again. I flopped luxuriously into the stream.

I have never been enthusiastic about the sea. The sea is boring in its monotonous immensity, is unreliable, sinister, and conceals heaven knows what obscene shapes in its depths. It is prodigal of unwholesome smells at low tide. It has a deplorable influence upon the morals of sailors who ply upon it and those of ship-chandlers who ply beside it. Its shores are hideous with bathing-huts and boarding-houses, and treacherous to the feet with hard-edged rocks and jelly-fish. To those like myself who are apt to swallow water when they dive it is furthermore unpleasant to the taste. But a river is a clean and friendly thing. Thus I pondered contentedly floating on my back with the sun burning down upon my forehead and no waves to play their abominable practical jokes.

Miss Phipps was demanding that Hughes-Winsor should teach her to float and that Slaughter should behave himself while the lesson was in progress.

'Let's swim across,' said Pat to me.

'There's a hell of a current in the middle,' I answered looking at the willows on the other bank, eight hundred yards away.

'Well, if anything goes wrong you can rescue me.'

I was flattered, because Pat is a better swimmer than I am.

'We can go out a bit anyway,' I said.

So I followed her out into the middle till the others' heads were just little black blobs near the bank. A steamer came round the bend, loaded with peasants going home from the market at Tsernigrad. It loomed up so quickly that I was nearly run down, and I had to scramble away after the graceful scurry of Pat's white legs in the limpid water. The peasants stared in astonishment at our two lone figures in mid-stream; whereupon, feeling light-hearted, I sang the Vuchinian national anthem and their eyes got even rounder. Then Pat said she was getting tired and we made for the shore. I had had quite enough myself before we got there, nearly a mile away from the others for the current had carried us down. We sprawled on a little strip of sand, with the willows behind us and the great empty river in front. I watched Pat digging little holes with her toes, and reflected she was one of the first women I had ever met who could come out of the water without looking like a drowned rat.

'When am I going to be allowed to meet your harlot?' she asked. 'I hear she's perfectly lovely.'

'She is rather. You must come along for a cocktail some time.'

'What a pity she isn't here to-day!'

'Why?'

'It would have been so much more fun for you.'

'My dear Pat, as if you didn't mean more to me than fifty harlots!'

'You bloody liar.'

There was something slightly provocative about Pat's mood.

'If you call me a bloody liar,' I said, 'I shall take down your knickers and give you what you deserve.'

'If you dare to try . . . '

Pat's bathing-dress was of strong material and rather complicated design. In the middle of the scuffle a large dog appeared out of the willows and barked at us; a few seconds later came a small boy leading his cows down to water. Pat and I assumed as much of an air of dignity as was possible.

'Well,' she said. 'I suppose we'd better go back and have some tea.'

So we walked back along the bank to join the others.

'And what have you two been doing?' Miss Phipps asked archly.

'We were looking for a better place for tea,' Pat told her, 'but I caught my bathing dress against a tree and tore it.'

'Oh,' said Slaughter.

The tea was excellent. As I lay on my stomach munching cake I read (as I can never help doing) the sheet of old newspaper that was serving as cloth. It was one of the more rabid of the opposition dailies, and the article was all about the flagrant corruption that had taken place in connection with the recent contract for telegraph wire. In another mood such reading might have made me anxious. But now I didn't care in the least. The sun and the river had raised me worlds above such things. Besides was I not quite a devil with the ladies?

After tea we bathed again, but Pat and I had no further chance of getting away from the others. Later on when the sun went down and mosquitoes began to ping around the willows we packed up and went home.

'It really has been wonderful,' said Miss Phipps.

And I heartily agreed with her.

We travelled back in twilight above a dark and gleaming river. Hughes-Winsor produced a portable gramophone and some dance records and their tinny sentimentalities blended with the chug of the motor. I plied Pat with cigarettes; accused Miss Phipps of playing tangle-toes with Slaughter; laughed lazily at simple and primeval jokes. Life was so easy and uncomplicated. But later as the music and the warm night air began to take effect I began to remember Pat's slim legs and her toes digging holes in the sand. And then I thought of Tala again, and was conscious of definite anticipations. Buddhism is a different creed.

24

When we got back to town Slaughter and I suggested taking Pat out to dinner. She wanted to come, but was dining with her chief and couldn't. So we dropped her and Miss Phipps at their respective doors, left Hughes-Winsor bemoaning an unavoidable dinner at the Polish Legation, and went on ourselves to the Continental. In the lounge we came across Mr Pant looking so depressed that we took him up to the bar with us. Pemberton and Grimshaw were already there, so I introduced them and ordered drinks and enquired about the afternoon in Mohrstadt.

'It was really most unfortunate,' said Mr Pant.

Apparently Mr Pant had got over to Mohrstadt without other incident than having to show his passport to a policeman, and had gone on and inspected what he took to be the probable site of the bridge. Then he had returned to the ferry. Meanwhile, however, some ingenious oppositionist had conceived the idea of organising a demonstration against the Government on the part of the professional ladies who inhabited the licensed houses. Accordingly Mr Pant was sitting quietly in the steamer waiting for it to start when there came an invasion of some hundred and twenty stalwart harridans, aged between fifteen and fifty, in every state of undress and all intensely excited. They stormed the steamer, forced the captain to start off for Tsernigrad, and spent the twenty minutes of the voyage in dancing round and shouting for Liberty and Clean Administration. Mr Pant was terrorised into going through the motions of shouting with them. The Mohrstadt authorities of course telephoned across to Tsernigrad, and when they arrived a large detachment of police were waiting for them. The ladies put up a very gallant fight; two policemen were thrown into the Danube and Mr Pant had his glasses broken and lost his hat before the Amazons were overpowered and led off to the police station. Mr Pant of course was suspected of being a ringleader and taken with them, but he managed to explain himself and here he was.

'Though, of course,' he concluded dolefully, 'the police could not help me about my glasses or my hat.'

'They'll go down in your expense sheet,' suggested Slaughter.

'You know, I really think they should. After all the whole expedition was on the business of the firm.'

'I wish I knew a firm like that,' said Pemberton.

'Why, whatever do you mean?'

'I wish I knew a firm whose business it was to have an afternoon on the river with a boat-load of wenches.'

'But surely you don't suppose . . . '

It wouldn't be human to miss a chance like that.'

'Good gracious me!' cried poor Mr Pant in horror.

On the way up to dinner he asked me if he was right in thinking that Pemberton was pulling his leg; I assured him he was. Then of course it was all right, he said; he had a sense of humour and could enjoy a joke himself. Though naturally he hoped this particular one wouldn't go too far. If the Mohrstadt bridge contract came off he might have to spend some time in Tsernigrad, and he had thought of bringing the wife out with him. And though the wife had a sense of humour too, there was, of course, a certain type of joke that ladies did not like.

I gave him half a litre of rather generous red wine at dinner which cheered him up a little. But he was far more cheered by a telegram which arrived towards the end of the meal. It was from Moorsides' to say that Vickery had called at the London office and that Pant was to return at once. He had just time to pack his things and catch the evening train.

While they were bringing his bill he wrote out a telegram to Mrs Pant and gave it me to read: *Shipping one husband express per tonight's train fully insured love Norman.*

'I think I told you,' said Mr Pant, 'the wife has a sense of humour.'

25

Four days later when I returned to the flat in the evening Agnes told me that Vickery was back. I at once had a feeling of elation and relief; I was no longer responsible for people like Mr Pant and Mr Krompek. I found Vickery in the bathroom with head and shoulders rising out of a sea of lather.

'I'm awfully glad to see you back,' I said.

And I'm damned glad to see you, old man. What's the news?'

I told him about Mr Pant and his adventures which amused him very much. He was also amused that I had guessed all about Madame Silviera. Apparently the weekend in Paris had been a very successful one. Then he had gone on to England to discuss things with Moorsides'. The chief thing he had wanted to get settled was this advance payment by the Vuchinian Government. He had explained things to Goodman and it was all fixed up. He (Vickery) was to keep the whole of it as an advance on future commission, so that he should have something in hand to grease the various palms and secure more business. Apparently Goodman – who seemed to be the Great Panjandrum of Moorsides' – had known nothing about Pant's being sent out, and had made a frightful fuss when he had heard; the various departmental managers and committees were still quaking. Vickery had meant to go on and arrange matters with the Mervyn as well, but had read such alarming reports in the London papers about the political crisis in Vuchinia that he thought it best to hurry back.

'What do you make of it, old man? Is there going to be a dictatorship?'

'It doesn't make much difference if there is,' I said. 'A dictatorship in the Balkans simply means that the gang in power issues a decree to abolish the opposition and carries on just as before. As long as we're good friends with the crowd on top we're all right.'

'So you're optimistic?'

'Absolutely.'

It was true. Now that Vickery was back I was serenely confident about everything. He pulled out the plug and turned on the shower. I watched his muscles ripple under his skin as the little shining water-drops splashed off him. Irrelevantly I wondered if Madame Silviera had a cold shower after her bath.

'Any other news?' he asked.

I told him that Mr Krompek, at my instigation, was in hopes of selling a fire extinguisher at trade terms to Mr Yoshogi.

'How's my friend Pemberton?'

'Much the same.'

Then the telephone went and I went out to answer it. By a strange coincidence it was Pemberton himself. He wanted to know if Vickery was back and said he was coming round at once to see him.

'Damn the fellow,' said Vickery.

Ten minutes later Pemberton appeared. He was feeling the heat very perceptibly, which was not surprising for the flat was on the third floor and as the staircase was on the south side of the building it became like an oven towards the end of a summer's day.

'Have a drink,' I suggested.

'No thanks.'

'That sounds very serious.'

'It is.'

Vickery who had meanwhile come in in a blue silk dressing-gown told him to sit down at any rate. We waited.

'I want to talk to you privately,' said Pemberton to Vickery.

'There's nothing you can't talk about in front of Mills.'

'It's for his sake as much as yours. He's in an official position.'

'Anyhow I'm in my private capacity now,' I said. 'Too damned hot for anything else.'

'Well, I don't mind,' said Pemberton.

We sat round in a semi-circle and waited again.

It's this, to put it shortly,' said Pemberton at last, looking at Vickery. 'I think you'd better pack up and clear out of this place.'

'Really?'

'Otherwise you may be leaving in a hurry.'

'Indeed.'

Vickery and Pemberton sitting there looked exactly so like the hero and villain of a highly coloured American film drama that I was struck with a sense of unreality.

'Do you know Riga?' asked Pemberton.

'I've been through it.'

'Do you know the Baltic and Eastern Industrial Bank?

'I've heard of it.'

'That ought to be enough.'

'Honestly,' I said, 'it seems a bit far-fetched that a man should have to pack up and clear out just because he's heard of the Baltic and Eastern Industrial Bank.'

Pemberton ignored me.

'I haven't got full information yet,' he went on. 'But what I have is quite enough. I don't want to make a fuss and I don't want to cause any unpleasantness. But you're not going to stay on here. It's not going to do any good to the British commercial community to have you about, and it's not fair on this lad here. As I said, when the truth gets out you'll have to leave in a hurry. So it would be best for all concerned if you cleared off within the next few days.'

'Well, there is the door, and I suggest you clear off in the next two minutes. If it wasn't Mills's flat I would help you to go.'

'All right,' said Pemberton, 'if you care to take it that way.'

He got up and I went to the door with him to let him out.

'I'm perfectly sure this is a mare's nest,' I told him.

'You can believe whomever you like,' he answered. 'Time will show.'

When I got back to the sitting-room Vickery was pouring himself out a whisky and soda.

'Is there any truth in it?' I asked.

He looked round at me.

'In what?'

'In these vague and mysterious stories about Riga.'

'Of course there isn't.'

'It's not so much the moral side of it,' I said. 'I have my own ideas about right and wrong, and don't have to take them second-hand from the Latvian Commercial Code. I wouldn't be in the least horrified to hear you'd done down a lot of sharks in Riga. It's all in the game. But if there was anything in it I could probably help you more if I knew the truth.'

'That's all right, old man. It's pure invention.'

'All of it?'

'Every damned word of it.'

'That's good enough for me. But how did Pemberton get hold of it?'

'I wonder.'

'After all, Pemberton must have heard some rumour. It's up to us to prove him wrong. Suppose I write and ask the consul in Riga?'

'I think you'd better. After all you're an official and you can't afford to share a flat with a crook. You ought to write at once.'

'Damn it all, I wasn't thinking about my official position. I'm old enough to look after myself. I was thinking of you.'

'Oh, I'm quite happy,' he said. 'If Pemberton wants a fight he can have one.'

'It's a pity there's no libel in this country.'

'There's a pretty stiff law against unfair competition, as he'll find out before long.'

He got up and took a cigarette from the box on the piano.

'I'm going to break Master Pemberton,' he said.

Then he went into the bedroom and came back and dropped his passport into my lap.

'There's a proof. You can see the dates I entered and left Latvia.'

The passport was a mass of visas and frontier control stamps – Chinese, Russian, Korean, Polish. He leaned over my shoulder and found the place.

'Do you see? Entered Latvia on November 18th and left November 19th. If you look up the time-table you'll find the train stops fifty minutes in Riga. That was all the time I could have had to carry out any nefarious campaign about the Baltic and Eastern Industrial Bank.'

'I suppose it was. There aren't any other Latvian entries here.'

'Do you believe me now?'

'Yes,' I said.

I supposed I did. I didn't know. It seemed so immaterial whether he had or had not been mixed up in some doubtful business on the Baltic, and so important that he should trust me to back him, right or wrong, through everything. But now he evidently wanted me to believe him so that I should not be compromised. And very probably his version was the true one. In any case he would learn to trust me before long.

'I doubt,' I went on, 'if even you could organise and carry a bank swindle in fifty minutes.'

'You were rather inclined to believe Pemberton at first.'

'Perhaps I was rather hoping there was something in his story. You see it would have given me a chance of pulling my weight. I look like being such a damned passenger in this concern.'

He laughed.

'You'll have plenty of chance to pull your weight, old man.'

Then he went back to fill up his glass and pour out one for me. We drank as if celebrating a rite of blood-brotherhood. I felt with a certain thrill that things were going to start happening. But I wished the fight hadn't got to be against Pemberton. I had always liked old Pemberton.

26

Two days later when Vickery was out on some mysterious visit to Marinsky and Tala was busy with her hairdresser I dropped in to have a cup of tea with Beryl Glover. I had seen little of Beryl lately, but in the days before life had become so complicated with love affairs I used to go round on an average two afternoons a week. Clive was always away at the office, and Beryl and I used to have long heart-to-heart talks which we both thoroughly enjoyed. On this particular afternoon Beryl seemed to have something on her mind. I waited till the small maid had cleared away the tea things and then it all came out.

'I think Pemberton's going mad,' she said suddenly.

'Why, what's happened?'

'He told Clive in the office this morning that he'd prefer him to see as little as possible of Vickery in the future, and suggested that I ought to see nothing of him either.'

'What did Clive say to that?'

'Well, he naturally said that I was certain to ask why. And then Pemberton said he wasn't that sort of person a man would like his wife to associate with.'

'That's pretty vague,' I said.

'It's damned impertinence. And coming from Pemberton of all people! Of course Vickery drinks a good deal, but he never shows it, which is more than one can say of Pemberton. As for going with girls from the Tabarin, I'm sure none of the girls would go with Pemberton unless he paid them. And as if anybody cared about that!'

'It can't be that.'

'I know it can't. That's why I wanted to ask you.'

I felt I ought to be cautious. After all Pemberton was Clive's boss, and at all costs Clive and Beryl must be kept out of the coming scrap.

'Did he give any other reason to Clive?' I asked.

'Oh, there was something about his being mixed up in something or other before he came here. But it was all very vague. As I told Clive, if anyone starts stories like that one's got to prove them.'

'It's all very awkward for poor old Clive."

'I don't see why it should be. He's not a slave. Outside the office he's got a perfect right to see whom he likes. He should have told Pemberton to go to hell.'

Beryl's eyes glowed with the eternal indignation of the female at the cowardice and apathy of the male.

'Yes, my dear,' I said, 'but would it have done any good if he had?'

'It would have done Pemberton good. And I shouldn't mind in the least if Clive lost his job. After all it isn't anything of a job. When we first came out five years ago the idea was that Clive should eventually be taken into parnership, but Pemberton seems to have forgotten all about that.'

'The last year or two have been very poor ones for business.'

'I never thought you would side with Pemberton.'

'My dear Beryl,' I said, 'you're being unreasonable. You know perfectly well how fond I am of you and Clive, and you also know that in any row between Vickery and Pemberton my sympathies are entirely with Vickery. I'm simply saying that it wouldn't help anybody if Clive were to get mixed up in it.'

'Clive could perfectly easily get another job.'

'Very likely he could, though of course there aren't many jobs going.'

'I shouldn't be at all surprised if Vickery didn't ask him to go in with him.'

'Vickery's only just beginning himself,' I said. Much as I liked Clive I had an unworthy feeling that I didn't want too many of us to share the proceeds of the Mohrstadt bridge.

'Vickery's going to make good,' said Beryl. 'And I hope he takes every single bit of business away from Pemberton. And you and Clive can do what you like, but I'm not going to let anyone interfere with me.'

I went away rather unhappily. This was a very different Beryl from the absurd and delightful creature I used to go and have tea with and discuss why Frenchwomen like niggers or whether Hughes-Winsor wasn't really a homo-sexual manqué. This intense and crusading spirit didn't suit her.

I went on to the Continental Bar. There was nobody there yet, so I sent Weiss down for an evening paper. He brought me the *Narodnyaya Krva*, the organ of the Independent Anti-Semites, and I was struck by an enormous headline 'Marinsky is a Thief.' This, of course, meant that the Anti-Semites had broken away from the Government coalition. That in itself was not very important. The Anti-Semites made a lot of noise, but they only had half a dozen deputies, and nobody took them at all seriously. But on the other hand it wasn't going to do us any good to have political capital made out of the wire contract, and if the Anti-Semites could launch attacks like that with inpunity it might be a sign that Marinsky's position was weakening. I put the paper down with some annoyance.

'Weiss,' I said, 'there is a particularly nasty smell in here to-day.'

There was. Mr Weiss after one or two deprecatory sniffs agreed with me. We shut the window and opened the door, and also the door of the bedroom opposite which was then unoccupied. The faint current of air brought in slight but perceptible reminiscences of the atmosphere in which generations of Central European commercial travellers prefer to sleep.

'Weiss,' I said, 'shut that bedroom door again.'

'Very good, *Herr Konsul.*'

Then Slaughter came in with news of a rare old shi-mozzle that was going on in the town. The entire issue of the *Narodnyaya Krva* was being confiscated by the police, and half-way up the Wilsonovi a band of determined Anti-Semites were defending a newspaper kiosk with stones and broken bottles. Slaughter wondered what the offending article had been about.

'Here it is,' I said.

'I can't read this damned language. What's it all about?'

'It's an attack on Marinsky.'

'The old scoundrel.'

Slaughter lit a cigarette.

'Is there anything there about the wire contract?'' he asked. 'Poor old Pemberton was very cut up about that.'

'I really don't see why he should have been. He ought to know this country well enough to realise that's quite a normal way of doing government business.'

'Yes, one knows what the officials are like, but it's a bit thick when an Englishman comes along and eggs them on to be even worse.'

I realised that Slaughter was definitely of the anti-Vickery party. I was just going to explain to him how un-reasonable he was being about the wire contract, when in came Pemberton with Pat McLean and Grimshaw.

'Hullo,' they said to me, 'you haven't been here for ages. Here, Weiss, there's a damned awful stink here!'

Mr Weiss apologised and said he knew there was. He had already been down to complain to the porter, but so far nothing had been done.

'You don't notice it so much after a time,' said Slaughter.

As the dice were going round Pemberton asked me if I had been thinking over the little matter discussed when last we met. I said I had, and was quite sure it was a mare's nest. He shook his head omnisciently.

'But I've got proofs,' I said.

'Proofs of what?'

'That the man never spent more than fifty minutes in the town you mentioned.'

'Don't you believe it.'

Then it was Pemberton's turn to shoot, and the argument dropped. The drinks arrived. Grimshaw had a new story about Mrs Bowles. I played up to Pat, and Pat showed herself very ready to be played up to. But somehow there was not the old atmosphere that we used to have in the Continental Bar. There were clouds in the air. I felt that if I were to go the others would at once start discussing Vickery.

And then, unexpectedly, Vickery himself came in. He ordered his drink and sat down between Slaughter and me. He was perfectly unconcerned and seemed secretly amused about something.

'Well, how's everybody?'

Slaughter and Grimshaw, obviously embarrassed, returned his greeting. Pat asked him how London was and where he had stayed. He had stayed at the Dorchester. Pat hadn't been to the Dorchester yet, and wanted to know all about it. Vickery told her.

'Marvellous!' said Pat.

Of course it might have been true that Pat didn't like these frightfully good-looking fair men, but one couldn't have guessed it from the way she looked at Vickery. Pemberton became very restive.

'When you've finished your drink,' he said to Pat, 'we'll go on and have some dinner. This place smells.'

They all got up and asked me if I was coming with them, but I was staying on a bit with Vickery.

'Just as you like.'

They went out, and Pat, the baggage, gave us a beaming smile over her shoulder as she left. Vickery called to Weiss for two more gins.

'You've driven old Pemberton out of here all right,' I said.

'He'll be driven out of a lot of other places before I've done with him.'

'Have you seen the *Narodnyaya Krva*?'

'Yes.'

'I know it's been suppressed but it's rather a nuisance.'

'That doesn't matter. I've just been with Marinsky.'

'What has he got to say?'

'A lot. They're dissolving Parliament at once.'

'Are they?'

'New elections at the end of next week.'

'That's pretty rapid.'

'That's on purpose, of course, to give the opposition no time to get going. Marinsky tells me there's not the slightest doubt as to the result. All the officials are either Liberals or Nationalists. They may lose a set or two in the big towns, but they'll get every one of the country seats. There'll be some dirty work at one or two of those police stations!'

'I bet there will,' I said.

'There's going to be no more nonsense after the elections. Marinsky will probably be Minister of the Interior himself. These damned fellows like the Anti-Semites will either behave or find themselves in quod.'

'What about your business schemes?'

'There'll be no time wasted at all. Old Marinsky takes a lot of persuading, but now he's made up his mind to come in solid with us there's no stopping him. As soon as the elections are over he's going to make a clean sweep of this Municipality here and put his own lot in. We'll form a company, Tsernigrad Transport Ltd, to start a new bus service and take over the trams and the ferries. We shall probably take over the light and power as well, but that will come later. I shall be Managing Director. Gorkin will be on the board, Marinsky, of course, can't be on it himself. Then Miss Fraser . . . '

'Good Lord!'

'As long as she's there it will stop any agitation about rich foreign capitalists grinding down the poor Vuchinian.'

'But will she agree?' I asked.

'Oh yes, I can persuade her all right. Then there'll be two more Vuchinians, dummies, of course. Then there'll be one director to represent the English group that puts up the money – I talked it all over with Goodman when I was at home. And one other.'

'Who'll he be?'

'He will be a Mr Mills, late of His Britannic Majesty's Consular Service.'

As he said it the nightmare that had haunted me for so long, the nightmare of being transferred to some forlorn little wilderness at the back of the world and left there to rot, all vanished into the air. It was only when it was gone that I dared to realise how much it had frightened me.

'Mr Weiss,' I said, 'two more pink gins.'

'As soon as the elections are over,' Vickery went on, 'you'd better send in your resignation to the Foreign Office. There'll be a lot for you to do.'

'What am I to live on till it all gets going?'

(I wasn't really bothering about that; I was merely mentally touching wood for fear it was all too good to be true.)

'That'll be all right. Goodman tells me that if we can get a government guarantee, which, of course, Marinsky can arrange, there won't be any difficulty in raising three hundred thousand pounds. And we shall get three per cent commission for raising it. Of course old Marinsky will want

his share, but there'll be plenty left to buy a glass of gin.
with. We might even pay off those bloody Mervyn people.

'Anything doing about the Mohrstadt bridge?'

'I shall be wiring Goodman next week to send his experts out to have a look at the place. That's where you come in. I'll be taken up with getting the transport company going, and you can start the negotiations about the bridge.'

'So things are moving.'

'By God they are.'

To me the stuffy little bar seemed to be dancing.

'I can't get over your asking me to come in on all this,' I said.

'Damn it all, old man, when I arrived here three months ago without a bean and not knowing a soul you believed in me and you backed me up. That ought to count for something.'

27

The next day there were huge black headlines in all the papers and the election campaign was in full swing. Excited little knots gathered in cafés and at corners of streets, and large unshaven men in morning coats and bowler hats were bumped triumphantly over the cobbles in ramshackle motor-cars amid the cheers of their supporters. Police patrols were doubled, and often at night one could notice pale-faced handcuffed men being jostled along side lanes by plain clothes detectives towards the main police station. Marinsky and his friends were taking no chances.

But for the first few days at any rate there was no real disturbance. In fact the only pitched battle took place in the Apollo, where, unfortunately, the members of two rival committees adjourned after a late night sitting, and came to blows. The police were called in and the Apollo was closed for a week. This was hard luck on Zacharias who, of course, was in no way responsible and who now saw all his clients diverted to the Tabarin. It was also hard on those girls who had no gentleman friends to support them, because for that week Zacharias naturally refused to pay any salaries. Tala celebrated her unexpected holiday by getting up at noon instead of three in the afternoon as she generally did, and coming to the flat for lunch. Afterwards she took a siesta in my room.

I remember how her perfume used to cling about the sheets though I have forgotten the name of it; and how the dull rich tangle of her hair showed up against the white of the pillow. It is the fashion for novelists nowadays to grow lyrical about breasts and even bellies, but I decided as I watched Tala one afternoon that after all the naked female form is seen to best advantage from behind. Tala's back was immortal in its perfect simplicity of line; with the firm but provocative curve of the haunch. Seen from in front nearly every female figure is in some attitude untidy; besides, their knees are always hideous. Tala turned her head lazily and saw me.

'You mustn't look at me,' she said. 'It's bad for you.'

'It isn't in the least.'

No more it was at that moment. In the terrific heat of a Balkan summer afternoon vitality requires a long recuperation. My appreciation of Tala's back was purely aesthetic, as if I were looking at a statue. It resembled it also inasmuch that after looking at a statue for a certain time one wants to go on and look at another statue or at any rate do something else. I remembered rather wistfully that there was a new number of *Blackwood's* which Vickery had brought back with him and left on the sideboard in the dining-room. But Agnes might be clearing lunch away, so if I went into the dining-room I should have to put on pyjamas or a dressing-gown, and that meant going and fishing them out of the wardrobe. Besides Tala who never read anything herself generally made it impossible for anyone else to read in the same room. And there were no comfortable chairs in the dining-room and the sitting-room faced south and was unbearable until the evening. It was all very complicated. I wondered what Tala was thinking about.

'What do you really want to get out of life?' I asked her.

'What do you mean?'

She rolled over, stretching herself with a supreme self-assurance.

'What do you really want?' I repeated.

'An eight-cylinder Mercedes-Benz.'

'What would you do with it?'

'I'd go to Nice.'

'You can't go to Nice in July.'

'Then I'd go to Deauville and go on to Nice in the winter.'

'Don't you ever want anything more than to drive about France in a big motor-car?'

'You're very serious.'

There was that slightly amused gleam in Tala's eyes that nearly always came when I tried to talk to her seriously. It was rather like a worldly wise and indulgent aunt listening to an earnest recital of nursery problems.

'Everybody wants something,' I said. 'Even the most brazenly self-satisfied people like judges and self-made millionaires, inside they're just suffering mortals, all wanting something and terribly afraid they won't get it.'

Tala was graciously pleased to fall into my mood.

'I should like a place in the country with horses and dogs.'

'Would that be enough?' I asked

'Well, I should want a husband.'

'Would he be enough?'

'Yes, if he was the right one.'

I wondered if she was thinking of the Polish Count who looked like a trapeze artist.

'He'd be lucky to have me as a wife. In the drawing-room a lady, in the kitchen a housekeeper, and in bed – do you know it?'

I did. Tala giggled with a false prudery.

'You're getting a stomach!' she said suddenly.

'I'm not.'

'Now you're holding it in, but you are getting one. Love's supposed to make a man thin so all you feel for me must be just platonic . . . '

We were interrupted by Agnes knocking at the door and saying that a lady was there who wanted to speak to me at once. I dived into my clothes, devoutly hoping that, in the event of its being Mrs Bowles, Tala had not left any of her things lying about in the sitting-room. But it was Mrs Brinkworth. She was full of apologies for disturbing my sleep, but she had to get off a governess by the evening train to Vienna, and she wasn't quite sure whether her passport was in order. I reassured her and she was just going away again when the front door bell rang, and Agnes, with a ghost of a twinkle in her eye, ushered in Tala who was fully dressed, hatted, and incredibly demure. I introduced her as the duaghter of an impoverished but noble Russian family, who had to earn her own living and had been thrown out of work by the election disturbances. Tala unblushingly said how glad she was to find Mrs Brinkworth there; I had asked her and some friends to tea, she must have come rather early, and it would have been very uncomfortable for her to have had to wait unchaperoned in a bachelor's flat until the others came. Mrs Brinkworth (who had her governess waiting downstairs) made light of these scruples, and said she was sure that two young people would get on much better without an old fogy like her. She left in a flutter of archness and gratitude.

'What on earth did you mean by it?' I asked Tala.

'I wanted to see what your lady friends were like. So I dressed and went round by the kitchen. But I needn't be jealous of that.'

I would not let Tala laugh at Mrs Brinkworth. But I was gratified at the only indication of anything approaching jealously that she had ever shown me.

Later on I asked her what she wanted to do that evening. We might take Hughes-Winsor's motor-boat and go up the Bina.

'But there are so many mosquitoes,' she objected.

'Not in mid-stream.'

'I don't know. Let's go to the Tabarin.'

"But my good girl, for three hundred and sixty-three nights every year you sit about in various cabarets saying how much you wished you lived in the country, and now when at last you get a night off you want to go and sit in another cabaret.'

Besides all which my ninety-three pounds were melting away very rapidly, and a night at the Tabarin with Tala wanting to show off to the girls engaged there was likely to be expensive.

'I'd rather go to the Tabarin,' she said.

28

That week passed intolerably slowly. Outside there was the increasing rumble of the elections, and in the office my consular duties seemed more than usually futile. Mr Dutt wrote to me again about his bicycle. My old friend the Russian refugee informed me that owing to his great admiration for the British Government he was willing to hand over his invention for a hundred pounds, but that, of course, would have to be paid at once. Another Russian offered to raise a division of his compatriots and go to India to capture Mr Gandhi dead or alive. Miss Jones wrote that she had lost her passport. And a firm of sanitary engineers, happily ignorant of Balkan proclivities, asked for a list of 'gentlemen of good standing likely to be interested in closet seats and flush tanks.'

One morning Bowles called. He said he seemed to be seeing very little of me nowadays, and I ought to come round to tea some Sunday; Pujotas and a lot of Jill's other friends usually turned up. Then he said what a nuisance the elections were and how they held up business. Finally, having broken the ice, he wondered if he might ask me one or two questions and if our little chat could be regarded as strictly confidential. I told him of course it could be.

'You're sharing a flat with Colonel Vickery; do you know at all what he was doing before he came here?'

I told him all I knew about Vickery's past, and referred him to the Army List, to Colonel Goodman, and, if he wished, to General Lih Fing. Bowles, I think, felt this last suggestion was rather flippant and looked very solemn indeed.

'Of course this isn't very much,' he said.

'Could you tell why you're asking this?'

'I hear he is negotiating for certain important public contracts, and as the manager of the British bank I feel I should find out if certain rumours that I have heard are true.'

'You mean,' I said, 'about the Baltic and Eastern Industrial Bank?'

'So you have heard that. Have you made any enquiries?'

'I haven't heard what the rumour is, I've simply heard there is a rumour. But one can see from the endorsements on Vickery's passport that he can't have spent more than fifty minutes in Riga in the last five years.'

'Oh.'

'As you're a banker,' I said, 'why don't you write direct to the Baltic and Eastern Industrial Bank yourself?'

'I am writing. They're in liquidation, of course, but it's possible I may hear something. Have you spoken to the Minister about all this?'

'No.'

'Don't you think it might be as well?'

'I certainly don't. There's nothing to talk to him about.'

'Of course it's all very vague.'

'Don't you think all these stories are largely due to personal jealousy?'

'No, most emphatically I do not.'

'Well, I do,' I said.

'I am sure there is no one in the colony who would act from motives of that sort. Mind you I myself have nothing against Vickery, and I shall be only too pleased to find that these stories are mere gossip. I've only met him superficially, but he seems a very charming fellow. Though he does seem to spend a good deal of time in places like the Tabarin.'

'No more than I do.'

'Well, of course, it's no business of mine,' said Bowles, 'and I think it's only right that a young unmarried man in a place like this should have a little jollity now and then. But one or two people – as I'm a good deal older than you, you won't mind my telling you – one or two people in the colony have been thinking you spend rather too much time in cabarets.'

'Is this anything to do with Vickery?' I asked.

'Now you musn't think . . .'

But I never learnt what I musn't think for just then Mr

Aquilina announced Miss Fraser. She marched in, sat down in Bowle's chair and lit a cigarette.

'You're both looking very serious,' she said tartly. 'I hope I'm not intruding.'

'Miss Fraser knows Vickery very well,' I remarked.

Bowles looked very uncomfortable. It was rather unfair of me to bring Miss Fraser into it, but I resented the moral lecture.

'What about Vickery?' asked Miss Fraser.

'Mr Bowles was asking what he had been doing before he came here.'

'Then Mr Bowles had better go and ask him himself.'

'Well,' said Bowles, 'it happens there have been one or two stories going about . . . '

'That is all the more reason to go and ask the man himself.'

'But, Miss Fraser, there is very possibly no truth in them. No one would be more pleased than myself if that was the case. But as a bank manager and the senior British resident I feel it my duty to make enquiries, to ensure that no injustice is done and at the same time that the community is not exposed to the danger of having their confidence misplaced.'

'And you achieve that by going round and spreading gossip.'

Poor Bowles got very hot and indignant.

'Miss Fraser, I cannot allow a remark of that sort. There is no question of spreading gossip. As I have told you I am simply making confidential enquiries.'

'You can call it whatever you like.'

'Miss Fraser, I can see no point in our continuing this conversation.'

'Nor can I,' said Miss Fraser.

Bowles got up, rather red and very dignified, and went out.

'I always knew that man was a fool,' said Miss Fraser. 'That ridiculous wife of his has been egging him on.'

'Are you as brutal to Mrs Bowles as you are to Bowles?' I asked.

Miss Fraser smiled. She was, I think, rather flattered.

'I am never brutal.'

She pressed the end of her cigarette into the ash-tray.

'I hear we are going to be colleagues,' she said.

'Oh good. I'm so glad you've decided to come in.'

'I haven't definitely decided yet. I strongly disapprove of women sitting on boards. They ought to stay at home. But in this case I think I shall till I find someone to take my place.'

'It's going to be a wonderful show.'

'I hope it will be. I am only sorry that Marinsky is so mixed up with it. I don't trust the man; he will be simply out to make money for himself and perfectly willing to exploit the wretched public in every possible way.'

'He won't have much chance if you're there.'

'That of course, is why I'm joining. Vickery will be far too busy to see to everything himself. So I shall do what I can and Vickery tells me you will help me. He seems to have a very high opinion of your abilities.'

'He's got a soft spot for me,' I said. 'He thinks I helped him a little when he first came.'

Miss Fraser got up to go.

'However,' she said, 'I still think it is extremely foolish of you to leave your present job.'

'But I've got nothing to do in it. Or is that what you meant?'

Miss Fraser laughed.

29

There was serious trouble in Vladikop on the day of the elections and the police had to use their firearms, but in Tsernigrad things were fairly quiet. After dinner Vickery and I sat out on the balcony. We had neither of us much to say. It was not that we were nervous as to the result of the voting, but after all one wouldn't really definitely know until to-morrow. Faintly the noises of the town came up to us; among them the distant squeak of bagpipes and banging of a drum. Somewhere the gipsies must be having a high old time. Gipsies like general elections. They can generally reckon on at least the equivalent of eighteen pence per vote, and sometimes it is possible to sell the same vote in advance to two or three different parties. In any case one can get a lot of *slivovica* for eighteen pence. I thought of that last time I had heard the gipsies, it seemed years ago, the evening Jill and I had gone up to the President's villa.

'Let's go out and hear the results,' said Vickery.

The main square was beginning to fill when we arrived and the surrounding cafés were crowded. However, Gorkin appeared from somewhere and managed to find us seats at a corner table. He was very excited and dishevelled. Things were going quite well, he thought. The opposition had shown unexpected strength in the South, but the Government had taken firm measures. He gave details of faked registers, falsified returns, broken heads and crowded prisons. These last seemed to give him particular pleasure.

I leant back in my seat, listening to the account of these manoeuvres which were to result in an amusing and lucrative existence for myself. Behind us was the din and clatter of the café and in front the uneasy silence of the great square. The irregular roofs of the houses opposite were silhouetted against a starlit sky. About fifteen yards away stood a group of students from the University, callow youths in cheap ill-fitting clothes, talking excitedly about Liberty and Justice. They were evidently supporters of the opposition. I felt sorry for them although they were my enemies. They would never get anything out of life. After they had scraped and starved themselves through the very second-rate courses provided by the Tsernigrad University the best they could hope for was to become village school-masters. They would spend their lives begetting more children than they could afford to bring up, talking the same half-baked rubbish about Education and Science that they now talked about Liberty and Justice, becoming more and more of a butt for the neighbouring peasants; and finally die.

There was a stir in the crowd. An announcer came out on the balcony of the Municipality. I caught the word 'Vladikop', but the rest of what he said was drowned in a burst of cheering with a few cat-calls. The students became jubilant.

'Bloody young fools!' snarled Gorkin.

'What was it?'

He did not answer me for a moment, as he was leaning forward to whisper to a man who was passing. It might have been a member of the secret police.

'Vladikop,' said Gorkin when he had done. 'One Liberal one Democrat, three Progressives.'

'Not very good.'

'It doesn't matter. We knew something like that would happen there. They are all bloody swine in Vladikop.'

The crowd in the square was warming up. I could see the glint of excited eyes. Newcomers arrived and tried to press through towards the front. There must have been nearly four thousand altogether: all of them shabbily dressed, most of them unshaven, many under-nourished.

Here and there was a little group of peasants, staring round them in rustic bewilderment. A police patrol moved up towards us.

The announcement came out again and a stir went through the crowd.

'Tsernigrad.'

The silence became so complete that even I could hear.

'Liberals two mandates, Progressives two, Independent Anti-Semites one, Jewish Party one.'

There was a deafening roar of applause and the students threw their hats into the air.

'Long live Liberty and Justice!' they shouted. 'Down with Marinsky! Down with Tyranny and Corruption!'

A gendarme stepped across and slashed his truncheon down on the nearest student's head. The boy fell in a limp heap.

'That will teach him,' said Gorkin.

There was a movement among the other students to go and help their comrade; but then suddenly they saw the police and faltered. In the light from the café I could see their pale frightened faces. Then they broke and fled, the police after them. I heard the thud of the truncheons on their bodies ; one of them began to scream with pain. Gorkin laughed. The student on the ground feebly tried to get up, but a policeman kicked him in the face and he dropped again. Then a second policeman arrived, put his foot on his head and started beating him unmercifully. I got up in a fury, but Vickery caught hold of my wrist.

'Sit down, old man.'

'Do you see those swine?'

'Sit down, old man, you can't do any good.'

The student was up on his feet again now, a gendarme holding each arm. His face was a dead white and he was bleeding at the mouth.

'You must not be so tender-hearted,' said Gorkin.

I felt the man was laughing at me and hated him.

'Where are these gendarmes taking him?'

'They'll just go to the police station and have a little fun. He won't do much shouting at the next elections.'

'Well, stop it,' I said. 'Tell your detective friend to make them let him go.'

'You'd better,' said Vickery. 'You don't want foreigners to see too much of that sort of thing.'

Gorkin reluctantly got up and went off after the two gendarmes.

'I've got no brief for the students,' I said to Vickery. 'But after all he was only shouting for his own side, and I know what goes on in these police stations.'

'You're quite right, but we can't alter the customs of the country. What's worrying me are these bloody results. None of Marinsky's Nationalists has got a seat so far.'

Gorkin came back and said he had arranged that the student should be let go. I wondered if he had; but I hadn't the moral courage to go and make sure for myself.

'That sort of thing is nothing,' said Gorkin. 'You should have been here during the war.'

He went on to describe in detail what had happened to certain Austrian prisoners of war. I felt rather sick.

The announcer came out again with news of a neighbouring agricultural constituency; three Nationalists, two Progressives and one Liberal. That was better. Then came five or six more in which the Liberals and the Nationalists together had a big majority.

'It's quite all right,' said Gorkin. 'I told you we would have all the country districts.'

Vickery thought it wasn't worth while waiting any longer, and suggested going to the Apollo for a night-cap. But I left them and went back to bed. I had had rather too much of Gorkin. Besides, I was dead tired.

PART THREE

THE ROMANTIC ADVENTURER

30

I had just finished my early tea next morning when
Vickery came into my room with the paper.

'Is it all right?' I asked.

'It was a damned near squeak.'

He gave me the paper and sat down on the foot of my
bed while I read. The results were:

Government Bloc:

Liberals	197
Nationalists	43
Jewish Party	6
Total	246

Opposition:

Progressives	98
Democrats	57
Agrarians	30
National Minorities	21
Anti-Semites	11
Miscellaneous	6
Total	223

There were about fifteen results still to come in, but they
were expected to be evenly divided and anyhow could
make no real difference.

'Well,' I said, 'at least it's a clear majority, even if the
Jews drop out. You're looking awfully tired.'

He had dark circles under his eyes and his face looked

thinner than ever. For the first time since I had known him he looked over forty rather than under.

'I didn't sleep much last night,' he said. 'Just after you'd gone the news from the south came through; every bloody seat for the Progressives.'

'Still, it's all right now.'

'Yes, I suppose it is. It's the hell of a relief. Look here, I want to get Marinsky to dine here to-night.'

'Won't he be busy?'

'He's never too busy for a bottle of fizz. Have we got any, by the way?'

'I'll see we have by this evening. We'll celebrate the victory. I take it we don't want Tala?'

'Not this time, old man. We've got to talk business.'

'All right. I'll spend my morning drafting my letter of resignation to the Foreign Office.'

'Good.'

He went off into the bathroom, and I lay back luxuriously for the last half-hour in bed, and thought about that letter of resignation. Very courteous it was to be, almost courtly; but making it perfectly clear that a man of my exceptional talents and temperament must be given sufficient scope.

The greater part of my day was entirely uneventful. I arranged for the dinner. I went down to the office and had a great spring cleaning of old files, being determined to leave everything in apple-pie order. I even wrote two very firm letters on the subject of Mr Dutt and his bicycle. Pat rang up to ask me to a little party she was giving that evening, but I had to refuse because of our dinner. Tala came to lunch. She had had a good offer for Prague for next month and wanted to know if she should take it.

'What would you like to do yourself?' I asked.

'I should like to stay on here with you.'

I was flattered and rather elated; until half an hour later

when she told me that her birthday was next month, and that last year when she was at Budapest her friend had given her a gold and platinum wrist-watch. At half-past five she had a fitting at her dressmakers. I took her there in a taxi and then walked back. On the way I met Watterson who told me, with that very trying air of omniscience assumed by journalists in times of crisis, that the Government bloc were negotiating with the Democrats. As soon as I got home I rang up Vickery, in case he didn't know already, but was told he hadn't been at the office all the afternoon. It occurred to me that Madame Silviera was due back, and I took up a book. However, I don't know why, I felt mildly uneasy, and an hour later I rang up again. This time he answered the phone himself.

'Have you heard about the Government negotiations?' I asked.

'Yes.'

'I hope it will turn out all right for us.'

'So do I.'

'Is the dinner still on?'

'Yes.'

'When will you be here?'

'About half-past eight, I expect. We may be a bit late.'

'Very good. So long.'

'So long.'

I hung up the receiver and began to wonder what birthday present I could get for Tala that would be expensive to look at but not too expensive to buy.

At seven o'clock I put the champagne into the ice chest. At eight I made a final inspection of the dining-room. It really looked extremely nice; a fitting scene for politics and high finance. I went into the kitchen and complimented Agnes. Then I changed. At a quarter to nine, to make waiting pleasanter I mixed myself a cocktail. Just after nine was a tremendous bellow of newsboys in the street below and I went down and got an evening paper. In the light of the entrance hall I read that there was a definite split between the Liberals and the Nationalists, and that the Liberals were now negotiating with the Progressives. I ran up the stairs again and rang up Vickery's office. After a long time the exchange told me that nobody answered.

If what the papers said was true, Marinsky's support was useless and our whole scheme, for the time at any rate, had fallen through. I poured myself out another gin and French, not sparing the gin. Local papers were notoriously unreliable, and even if this time they were right, it was always possible that to-morrow the Progressives would quarrel with the Liberals and the Nationalists would be in the saddle again. But, of course, the opposite was just as possible; and that meant no more champagne, no birthday present for Tala, no letter of resignation to the Office, and all this waiting and scheming and nervous exhaustion all over again.

The telephone went, but it was only Beryl who wanted to talk to Vickery.

I made an ineffective attempt to read. At half-past nine I tried to comfort myself with the thought that I was worrying in advance, and troubles one worries about in advance seldom seem to materialise. The real tragedies of life always fall out of a clear sky. At ten o'clock I told Agnes to go to bed; if the others turned up after all we could always fish out something cold. Agnes waited for another half-hour and then went off. I got out the bridge table and two packs of cards and played patience.

It must have been a little after eleven that I heard a key turn in the lock and Vickery's steps in the hall. But instead of coming in to where I was they went up the passage to the dining-room. I heard the chink and splash of a siphon. I went to the dining-room myself and found him standing by the sideboard.

'You're damned late,' I said.

'Sorry, old man. I know I am.'

'Where's Marinsky?'

'In jail.'

'What?'

He turned round and took a long pull at his glass.

'I wanted that,' he said. 'Yes, Marinsky was arrested an hour ago on a charge of corruption. The Liberals weren't content with that small majority. They made overtures to the Democrats, but they weren't having any, so they tried the Progressives who would only come in on condition the Nationalists were dropped and Marinsky prosecuted. So there you are. They've got Gorkin locked up too."

'Are they bringing up the wire contract?'

'Yes, among other things.'

'But there's no danger of your being dragged into it?'

'Two detectives followed me back here. Does this flat enjoy extra-territoriality?'

'No,' I said. 'A consul's office does, but a consul's private residence doesn't. But they aren't likely to come in.'

'That'll give us an hour or so.'

'You mustn't take it all so seriously; this is Tsernigrad. It's quite on the cards Marinsky will be out of jail tomorrow, and even Prime Minister the day after.'

'Let's go into the other room. I've got something to tell you.'

I followed him into the sitting-room. He had looked tired this morning, but now he seemed like a man at the end of his tether. His voice had no life in it. He wanted help and encouragement; at last there was a chance for me to be something more than a passenger. I became very confident and rather exhilarated.

He sat down and felt for a cigarette in the box at his elbow.

'Have you sent in your resignation yet?' he asked.

'No.'

'That's something to be thankful for.'

He jigged at his lighter that would not take fire. I waited for what was coming.

'Do you remember Pemberton's story about my being mixed up in a ramp with the Baltic and Eastern Industrial Bank?'

'Yes,' I said.

'Well, it's true.'

'But you weren't in Riga.'

'No, but it wasn't the Riga office. It was the branch in Reval. Otherwise the story's true enough. Old man, I'm a crook.'

'Do you suppose I care tuppence?'

He smiled.

'That particular show was merely that I was trying to do the dirty on a party of scallywags who were trying to do the dirty on me. And in the end we both of us lost our money. But that's not my only escapade. I had a little contretemps at Shanghai, and when I left China finally I left it rather hurriedly with two thousand pounds in my pocket belonging to General Lih Fing. He'd stolen it himself, and as we were parting company in any case I thought I could look after it just as well as he could.'

'I quite agree with you.'

'Yes, old boy, but the law doesn't.

'Well, I don't suppose Vuchinia has an extradition treaty either with China or Esthonia.'

' It's not as simple as all that."

From away on the river came the hoot of the last ferry steamer to Mohrstadt.

'Why didn't you tell me before?' I asked. 'I'd have been perfectly safe.'

'Good Lord, old man, I know you would. But it would

have put you in an impossible position, a consul sharing a flat with a crook. But even so I would have told you if there had been anything you could have done. But there wasn't. There's nothing to be done now, but I'd like to tell you all the same. When I was at home I went to see the Mervyn people.'

'So you did go there after all?'

'I got as far as the front door and there I bumped into a man who had known me in Shanghai. So I naturally turned round and walked out. I just hoped he hadn't recognised me. But he must have. Thereupon the Mervyn people seem to have got into touch with Goodman. The next thing that happened was that my own lawyer here received instructions from a firm of solicitors in London to start proceedings against me for embezzlement, on behalf of Moorsides' and the Mervyn.'

'Criminal proceedings?'

'Yes. Apparently out here you can't sue for recovery in these cases unless criminal proceedings were started first.'

'But what grounds had they?'

'First of all the Mervyn credits are still in a mess, and then there's this payment for the wire contract.'

'But you fixed that up with Goodman.'

'Only on condition that the balance due to Moorsides' was paid into a separate banking account in their name. When I came back here I found Marinsky willing to close for a consideration. After he'd had the consideration there was nothing to open the banking account with. It was the chance of a lifetime. If I'd lost time in referring it all back to England he might have fixed up with somebody else.'

'Good Lord.'

'My lawyer got all this four days ago. Then of course he thought I was the coming man, and wired back to say he was representing me and they must find somebody else. I wasn't very worried. I knew the people were only panicking for their money, and once they'd got it they'd drop the case. If the elections had turned out all right with Marinsky on top, I, as a friend of his, could have borrowed three thousand pounds from any bank in the place. Then I could have paid them off, and Goodman would have had to come back to me, for no one else could have put through the Mohrstadt bridge or the Tsernigrad transport.'

'Isn't there any chance of raising the money as it is?'

'None whatever.'

'Have you tried Bowles?'

'Yes. Damned old woman.'

'I've got a hundred pounds in War Loan,' I said.

He smiled.

'Of course that's a fat lot of use,' I added.

I felt I was being just about as inadequate an adviser as I was a financier.

'So I may be arrested any moment,' he said. 'Rather comic, isn't it? Just when I was really trying to turn over a new leaf and go straight; and with your help succeeding.'

'But they can't have you for embezzlement. You've simply spent the money for the firms. Not a penny went into your own pocket.'

'One doesn't get a receipt for a bribe. And then they'll start digging my past up. Sorry, old man, but it can't be done. Besides, bribing a politician who's fallen is a damned sight worse crime in the eyes of the courts here than stinging Goodman for a few hundred.'

Everything seemed unreal to me; the hot room and the clammy feel of my shirt, the dust on Vickery's shoes, the moist warmth of my pipe and this impossible story.

'I can't believe it,' I said, 'I can't believe you're beaten.'

'Well, I am. It's all in the game.

'You must get away.'

He turned out the light so that our silhouettes could not be seen from outside and took me to the window. Two figures were loafing in a doorway twenty yards down the street.

'Besides,' he said, 'they'll be watching the station and all the roads as well as warning the frontier posts.'

We went back into the middle of the room and turned on the light again.

'I've thought it all out,' he said. 'I've got a revolver, but that's a cowardly way. Besides, it's too messy. There's only one thing to be done. I give myself up to you as Consul, and you send me back to England to stand my trial. I'd sooner do time in Wandsworth than in one of these prisons.

'No,' I said.

'It's the only way, old man. Besides, it's the only way I can make any return to you. Your association with me isn't going to do you any good with the Foreign Office; you might just as well have the credit of catching the thief.'

'No,' I said. 'All this is far too noble and just a little out of date. It's like one of Gerald du Maurier's productions in about 1905. You've got to get away. We'll think of something. At the moment I'm bloody hungry.'

As we went back to the dining-room the telephone rang and I went to it. Vickery told me that if it was for him he hadn't come back yet unless it was Madame Silviera. But it wasn't Madam Silviera.

'It's Beryl,' I said with my hand over the mouthpiece.

'What the devil does she want?'

'She wants to know if you're back yet. She rang up before.'

'Well, I'm not.'

Beryl's voice at the other end was very agitated; but I told her I hadn't the slightest idea when he would be in.

I remembered there was caviare in the ice chest, and fished it out. Vickery would eat nothing.

'What you want,' I told him, 'is a glass of wine.'

'Very likely.'

I got out the champagne with which we had been going to celebrate our victory. I poured out two glasses, and added to each a third as much again of brandy. It made us feel better.

'We'll have our next when I come out of jail.'

'Don't talk rubbish. We could get out of this house by the fire-escape at the back. Then get hold of a car and make a dash for it.'

'They're watching the roads, old man. And then all the frontiers are too far for that. Except Roumania, and there's that bloody river in between.'

A brain wave struck me.

'It's easy,' I said. 'We'll take Hughes-Winsor's boat. We could get to Roumania in about an hour.'

'Where does he keep his boat?'

'I know.'

'Damn it all, I'm not going to drag you into this.'

'You've got to. There's got to be someone to bring the boat back. Otherwise it would help them to trace you, and if it were lost or stolen it would be rather rough luck on poor old Hughes-Winsor.'

I wasn't tired or depressed any more. I was confident again, radiant.

'I've been a passenger in this show of ours ever since it started,' I said. 'Now I've got a chance of doing something I'm not going to miss it.'

'I can't let you. You've risked quite enough already.'

'You've talked quite enough. Go and pack.'

'Old man … ' He tried to go on but couldn't. I followed him into the bedroom and watched him pack his suit case. He didn't take much: a spare suit and a pair of shoes, half a dozen shirts, a flask, his decorations, a few letters.

'This isn't just heroics on my part,' I said. 'It's a purely commercial speculation I know perfectly well you'll come out on top sooner or later. And when you do you'll send me a post-card and the old firm of Vickery & Mills will get busy.'

'You bet it will.'

It wasn't long before he had finished his packing.

'What do I owe you for the housekeeping?' he asked.

'Nothing.'

'Don't be an idiot I've got plenty of money.'

'You'll want it all. I'll give you a bill when we next meet.'

'Mind you do. Anyway this is for Agnes.'

He took out a thousand douro note and laid it on the dressing-table. We went back into the sitting-room and had a final drink, our last together in Tsernigrad.

'I shall miss this flat,' he said. 'I once thought I'd taught myself not to regret anything, but this flat, and you, old man, God, it's a wrench.'

'We'll have a better flat somewhere else.'

He ground the stub of his cigarette into the ash-tray.

'It's rotten not being able to say good-bye to Consuelo,' he said.

(I had never known that that was her name.)

'Can't you write her a line?' I suggested.

'Too risky. Her husband might find it. Could I send her one of your books?'

'If you can find one that will do.'

As I looked at the book-case I rather doubted it. *The Anatomy of Melancholy*, Pepys, Johnson's *Lives of the Poets*, *Pride and Prejudice*, *Revolt in the Desert*; they all seemed very unsuitable. He searched for a moment and then took down a volume of Donne and turned over the pages.

'Yes, this,' he said. 'Will you send her this with the page turned down here?'

'All right.'

I looked.

When I am gone, dreame me some happinesse,
Nor let thy lookes our long hid love confesse,
Nor praise nor dispraise me, nor blame nor curse . . .
Augure me better chance, except dread Jove
Think it enough for me to have had thy love.

I felt it was all rather above Madame Silviera, but then I may have been jealous; this parting should have been a parting with me, with no shadow of feminine interference.

'What about your other girl friends?' I asked.

'They can go to hell.'

'We'd better be starting.'

'All right.'

31

For safety's sake I went first; climbing out of the skylight in the scullery and down the iron fire-escape. I have a bad head for heights and was afraid to look down. The rust on the rungs peeled off in my hot moist hands, and I was seized by an absurd terror that the ladder was not properly fastened to the wall and would fall away. At last I reached the roof of a store house. I walked across it and it was an easy drop to the pavement. A stray dog asleep in a gateway woke up frightened and barked at me; but otherwise there was no sign of life in the mean little street.

I struck a match as a sign that all was clear. Three minutes later Vickery was down by my side with his suitcase. We had about fifteen minutes' walk to get to the Rowing Club where the boat was. As we turned the first corner we ran into a policeman and my heart gave a jump. I felt certain I would arouse his suspicions by the unnatural way I was walking. I felt I was a fool ever to have started on this adventure at all.

' If we're caught, old man, remember I've told you nothing about my troubles.'

'We shan't be caught,' I said.

My voice encouraged me; it really sounded quite confident.

We went down the hill over uneven cobbles. The houses were all dark and shuttered except here and there a café with its gipsy musicians and stench of *slivovica* and much breathed air. We passed the disorderly tangle of the quays, crossed over an open space strewn with the gutted bowels of ships' engines and reached the wooden fence of the Rowing Club.

'The caretaker sleeps in the Club House,' I said, 'but if we're quiet I don't think he'll wake.'

The fence creaked rather as we climbed over, but no one stirred. The boat was in her usual place. We got in, untied her and paddled silently into mid-stream, so that the current might carry us out of hearing of the town.

'What about petrol?'

'That's all right,' I explained. 'Last year I borrowed it to take a girl out, and the petrol ran out so that we were stuck in mid-stream, and I very nearly had to marry her. Old Hughes-Winsor got such a shock when he heard that he's kept two spare tins on board ever since.'

The Berlin-Athens express loomed out of the darkness to our left, rolled over the bridge with a growl and a rattle, swung round towards the station in the town. Then all was quiet again except the whisper of the ripples my under paddle. We drifted under the railway bridge, past the little spit of sand with its red light where the Bina joined the Danube. To our left were the few scattered lights of Mohrstadt station. To our right was Tsernigrad: the flares in front of night watchman's shelters along the quay; then humps of buildings guessed at in the darkness, thin points of street lamps; the dim circle of the illuminated clock on

235

the Municipal Hall; and above the deep blue velvet of an August night. A locomotive whistled in the station; far away a dog barked. Slowly the town was left behind us.

'We might start her up now.'

I tugged at the cord. The engine coughed, and the echo rattled over the waters so that I feared the whole of Vuchinia would be roused. She warmed up quickly; the current was with us and soon we must have been doing twenty miles an hour. We were off! My spirits began to dance with the thrum of the engine. This was my show, I felt, my first adventure. The episode of the brigands a few weeks before had been an accident, and, for me, an in-glorious one. But this was an adventure of my own de-vising. I felt that I was backing my luck against all the Goodmans of the world with all their money and lawyers and public opinion; and getting away with it.

The hills on our right receded into the gloom, and the south bank became low and wooded like its fellow. Vic-kery's cigarette glowed in the darkness in front of me.

'Going well.'

'Yes. Roumania in fifty minutes.'

We switched on the lights; we were making a good deal of noise, and if we continued lightless there was the danger that some officious customs launch might put out after us to investigate. An infant moon came up over the hills behind us, and the reflection sparkled in the broken whiteness of our wake. We threaded between two islands, low and wooded like the banks.

'I love this river,' I said.

'You know it damned well.'

It was just as well I did. The Danube is nowhere easy to navigate, and this particular stretch was full of little shoals and sandbanks that might have given trouble even to a boat with so shallow a draught as ours. The moon rose rapidly. On the left bank we passed a sleeping village; a cluster of little dark houses huddled round the church spire.

'That's the last village in Vuchinia,' I said. 'The frontier's about four miles on.'

We discussed his plans. We were to get well inside the Roumanian frontier before I put him ashore. Then he would go inland till he struck a village. He would give himself out as a geologist: all Englishmen found wandering about off the beaten track in the Balkans are readily believed to be officials of some oil or mining company. It might be that a policeman would notice that his passport bore no Roumanian visa, but in these hard times a pound or two mean a lot to a Roumanian village policeman. He would then go on to the railway line from Sibiu to Temesvar. And then?

'Heaven knows, old man. Perhaps I'll go and have a look at Bucharest.'

Far away on the left bank was a little hut with a light showing at the window. It was the frontier post. Then at last I realised that Vickery was really going away; that I wouldn't see him for months, perhaps years. I tried to think of life without him, and was frightened; life would have no zest, no punch in it.

We discussed ways of communication. There was the danger that the Vuchinian post office would keep a watch on letters to me, as a means of tracing his movements. He promised to send me a post-card in an assumed hand and with a false name from the first town he struck just to show he was all right; then he would write to me properly care of the Foreign Office so that the letter would come out in the Foreign Office bag.

'Putting the King's Messenger to use for criminal purposes, what?'

'It's just as well he should have some use,' I said. 'And don't forget, wherever you are and whatever you're doing, you've only got to send the word, and I shall come along in my best suit with my hundred pounds of War Loan and join up. Don't forget that.'

'You bet I shan't.'

We rounded a bend, and ten minutes later decided that we had come far enough. We switched off the lights, went down to half speed and crept in towards the left bank. A little strip of sand showed up white under the dark shadows of the trees.

'This will do.'

I switched off the engine and ran her in, felt her nose run upon the soft sand. Vickery picked up his suitcase and threw it ashore.

'I'm not going to thank you, old man,' he said. 'I'm not even going to try. But you know.'

'This isn't good-bye,' I answered. 'It's only *au revoir*.'

'Of course.'

'Till then, good luck.'

I felt his grip on my hand.

'When you think of me,' he said, 'try and think sometimes that I'm not quite such a blackguard as they'll all try and make out.'

He jumped across to the bank, making the little boat shake.

'Do you want a shove off?'

'No thanks, I can manage with the paddle.'

I pushed her clear. He was standing by his suitcase, very tall and straight and slender in the shadow of the trees. I turned the boat's head round.

'Good luck,' I shouted again.

'Good luck to you.'

'To us both.'

I started the engine and looked round and waved to him. He waved back. Then he was gone.

32

Going back against a five miles an hour current was slower work. I thought out how I could cover up my tracks. The best plan would be to deny having seen Vickery at all that evening. I would say I had gone out immediately after Agnes left. There had been a good half-hour between Agnes's departure and the time the detectives followed Vickery home; so that nobody could prove I hadn't gone out. If anyone wanted to know where I had been I could hint at amorous adventure and refuse to say anything that might compromise a woman's honour, etc. It all seemed fairly fool-proof.

As I passed the frontier post again I thought I heard a hail: but the river was wide there and I was almost half a mile away, so that I felt I was safe in holding on. But I was relieved when it was not repeated. Rounding the island I was nearly fouled by a tug of the *Donau Dampf-schiffahrtgesellschaft*, labouring with a string of deep-bellied barges: after which I switched on the lights again.

I tried to make plans for the future – chiefly to quell the sense of loss. But there was nothing much for me to do: just wait for Vickery to give a sign, and meanwhile amuse myself as well as I could. All the time complacency kept breaking through my scheming. All my life I had tried to pose as the dashing unconventional young man, who when the moment came would show himself capable of doing great things. The moment had come and I had not missed the bus. I had done something. And damn it all, if I had done something once, I could do it again. This civil service career was just an episode. Vickery would start some show somewhere and I would go and join him. We'd beat the world yet. Thug-thug-thug went the engine. Tunes danced in my head.

Adieu, mein kleiner Gardeoffizier, adieu, adieu,
  Und vergiss mich nicht, und vergiss mich nicht.

I looked in the locker to see if Hughes-Winsor kept his gramophone there. I was in a festive mood. But apparently he kept it in the Club House.

After a time I got sleepier. Dawn came, first of all a pale grey gleam in the north-east that slowly spread across the sky. Then the hills to the south stood out again. By the time I got back it was daylight. The great stack of the power station towered over the other factory chimneys and its smoke cloud hung heavy in the still air. I rounded the final bend and saw Tsernigrad itself with its white houses and irregular roofs, very cool and clear. The hands of the municipal clock pointed to half-past three.

All was quiet at the Rowing Club. I tied up the boat, slipped over the palings and walked up towards the town. It wasn't late; the Apollo would still be open and I thought for a minute of going in and having a drink with Tala. It would give me an alibi. But I decided that after these hours in the open air the atmosphere of the Apollo would be unbearable. Besides, I wanted to put the flat straight before Agnes came in the morning.

The peasant carts were rumbling in to market. I stopped one of them and bought some pears.

There were no detectives watching our door, or if there were they were too well hidden for me to notice. The sixty-two steps to my flat seemed an intolerably weary climb. I went up trying to determine whether I should eat my pears first and put the flat straight afterwards or vice versa. I had reached my floor before I had made my mind up. I went into the sitting-room.

'Hullo.'

'Beryl, what on earth are you doing here?'

She was sitting, looking very tired, bunched up in a corner of the sofa.

'Where is he?' she asked.

'He's not here.'

'They're going to arrest him.'

'They won't do that. He's gone.'

'Gone?'

'Yes. How on earth did you get in?'

'The key was in the lock.'

I supposed Vickery must have left it there when he came up. Beryl told me that half-way through Pat's party Watterson had turned up and told them that Marinsky had been arrested and Vickery would be the next. Pat's telephone was in the bedroom, so Beryl had gone in there and rung up our flat; an hour and a half later she had tried again. Clive had been tired and gone back to bed early. Beryl herself had been seen home by Slaughter about one; but she had waited at the door till the taxi had gone on and then come along to us on foot. No one had answered the bell, so she had come in and sat down and waited for Vickery.

'He came in just after you'd rung up the second time,' I said.

'How did he get away?'

'Oh, we managed to smuggle him out.'

'Did you tell him I'd rung up.'

'Yes, of course.'

'Well, why couldn't you have let me know when he came in? You knew I was at Pat's.'

'My dear, the police were probably listening in to this number. We simply couldn't risk it.'

'I wanted to say good-bye to him.'

'He gave me all sorts of messages for you,' I lied.

'I wanted to see him. Surely you could have rung me

up. I'd have understood. And then I could have slipped round here.'

Then she broke down altogether and began to sob. I felt stupid and embarrassed.

'Don't cry,' I said. 'He'll be all right.'

'I'd have ... " She was sobbing and I could not catch what she said. It might have been: 'I'd have gone with him.' Poor old Beryl. My brain kept buzzing with the thought. 'For heaven's sake stop it. He doesn't want you, and never will want you. Don't make such a fool of yourself.' There was something pathetic and ridiculous about this fat woman sobbing her heart out into the corner of my sofa. I couldn't stand it any longer and went into the dining-room. There was still a little champagne in the bottle we had opened four hours before. I added an equal quantity of brandy and brought it back to her.

'This will do you good,' I said.

She made an effort to control herself.

'I'm sorry to be such a bloody fool.'

'You'll feel better now. Besides, your nose wants powdering.'

'I bet it does.' She pulled out her glass and looked at herself. 'Lord, what a mess!' she said.

'Drink some more.'

She emptied the glass.

'That's wonderful stuff.'

'His special. Guaranteed never to fail.'

I told her how he got away. She was really pulling herself together very well.

'Who marked this in the book?' she asked.

The works of John Donne were lying on the sofa beside her.

When I am gone, dreame me some happinesse.

I was tempted to pretend that it was Vickery's farewell message to her, but realised that that would be futile.

'I did,' I said. 'The first line would do so well for a theme song of a sentimental talkie.'

'It's a funny book.'

I guessed she had been hoping that Vickery had marked it for her, and fearing he had marked it for some other woman.

'Have you been reading it?' I asked.

'I looked at it. Some of it's rather amusing: *To His Mistress going to Bed*. I thought all your books were stuffy.'

I wondered whether I could cheer Beryl up by introducing her to *Love's Progress*, which she would think salacious. But I was too tired.

'Clive will imagine you're dead or eloped,' I said.

'So he will – why, it's after four! I simply must get back.'

We walked as far as the Continental and took one of the taxis that were waiting there for stragglers from the Tabarin. As we pulled up in front of the Glovers' house Clive opened the door. He was wearing very crumpled pyjamas and looked pale and anxious.

'Wherever have you been?' he asked.

'We've been out for a drive,' said Beryl. 'But no luck, my dear, you can't get a divorce. The taxi man was with us all the time.'

I felt it was just as well that Beryl had Clive to invent stories for. It was at least something else for her to think about. I left them and went back home. My sixty-two steps seemed more unending than ever. I tidied up the sitting-room and Vickery's bedroom and ate my pears. Then I undressed. As I got into bed I was too tired to think of either my own problems or anybody else's.

33

I was still very tired when I woke up next morning, and had to listen to Agnes's surprise and anxiety at having found Vickery's bed not slept in. It was late when I got to the office. The local papers were, of course, very full of the news of Marinsky's arrest, but there was nothing about the wire contract and no mention of Vickery's name. However, the Progressives, who had five portfolios in the new cabinet, seemed out to do all they could to discredit the Nationalists completely and finally. So it would certainly be brought up sooner or later. My official mail was very small and dull and I had no callers. I duly sent the works of John Donne round to the Argentine Legation, and wondered what Madame Silviera would make of them. Then I began to wonder what I could do about Tala. At about twelve o'clock Sir William sent for me.

As I opened the door it gave me rather a shock to see Colonel Goodman there. With him was a thick-set man whose name I did not catch – someone from the Mervyn Company. The atmosphere was hostile and I felt the interview was not going to be an easy one: I wished I wasn't feeling so morning-afterish. Sir William explained that the gentleman wished to ask me a few questions, and Goodman who had scarcely troubled to say good morning started off.

'Where's this man Vickery?'

'I don't know,' I said.

'Was he in your flat last night?'

'I don't know.'

'How can you say you don't know?'

'I was out myself.'

'When did you get back?'

'About four o'clock.'

'Where had you been?'

'Surely that concerns only myself. May I ask what all this is about?'

'You'll know in good time.'

'I hope so.'

So far I had been holding my own rather well. Also I knew how much the Minister hated being pestered by visitors of this sort and felt that his sympathies were on my side.

'The situation is this,' said the Mervyn man. 'As you probably know, both Colonel Goodman's firm and my own have been in business relations with Vickery. We recently obtained certain information as to Vickery's past, and this, coupled with developments out here, made it seem desirable for me to come out, and for Colonel Goodman to interrupt his engagements in Berlin and come out also. We arrived last night, and have spent this morning making enquiries. Vickery is believed to have returned to your flat at about eleven last night; but after that his movements cannot be traced. The housekeeper tells us that she left at ten, and now you tell us that you did not return till four. However, his whereabouts are a matter for the police. What is very interesting is that almost everywhere we have been, in the Government Departments for instance, and in Vickery's own office, where we interviewed a certain Krompek, we have been referred to you. Now it was you who first introduced Vickery to Colonel Goodman, and the first time that we in the Mervyn Company ever heard of him was through a letter of recommendation from you. Do you remember that letter?'

'Yes,' I said.

'You told us you had inspected the accounts, and considered Vickery's report on the position to be correct.'

'I think I said I had no reason to believe . . . '

'Yes, you worded your letter cautiously, but the natural inference was that the man was all right. Do you agree?'

'Yes.'

'I looked at those books myself this morning. Would you be surprised to hear that Vickery's report was completely misleading?'

'I would,' I said. 'Very surprised.'

'Well, it was. How much time did you spend inspecting those books?"

'About an hour. But I think I told you in my letter that my inspection was superficial.'

'Then what was the point of it?'

' It was a sign of good faith on Vickery's part giving me the books to inspect.'

'Did he know that you knew nothing about accountancy?'

'I haven't the slightest idea,' I said.

I felt that the Mervyn man, in spite of his quiet manner, was a more formidable customer than Goodman.

'When you wrote to us,' he went on, 'you were a friend of Vickery's?'

'Yes.'

'But you knew nothing about his past?'

'Very little beyond what he told me himself?'

'Did you make any effort to check or amplify it? For instance, he told you he was in Warsaw; did you think of writing to the Consul there?'

'He didn't know him.'

'I see, Vickery said he didn't know him and therefore you did not write.'

'May I ask what you're driving at?'

'It will be quite clear very soon if you will excuse me a little longer. Did you subsequently hear anything about his past from other sources?'

'No.'

'Mr Bowles tells us that he had a conversation with you on the subject of the Baltic and Eastern Industrial Bank.'

'I heard there were certain vague rumours about him, but I had evidence from his passport that he hadn't done more than pass through Riga in the train.'

'So you didn't think it worth while to make further enquiries?'

'No.'

'Nor to communicate either with Colonel Goodman or with us?'

'By the time I'd heard these rumours you'd both of you sent out men of your own here, so you ought to have known more about his standing than I did. What did your Mr Scarfe report?'

The Mervyn man did not seem to welcome reference to Mr Scarfe, and I felt I had scored.

'Besides,' I added, 'one could tell by the man himself. He was one of the straightest men I ever met.'

'So you would also be surprised to hear that we were obliged to instruct a local lawyer to start criminal proceedings for misappropriation.'

I did my best to look surprised.

'Then you made a great mistake,' I said. 'If he used any money it was simply and solely to give presents to officials in order to secure more business for you.'

'We have been told at the banks that yesterday he withdrew some nine hundred pounds in cash.'

'Well it was for bribes.'

'That seems rather improbable. Balkan elections are uncertain things, and it seems unlikely that an intelligent man such as Vickery undoubtedly was would pay out large sums before the political situation was clear enough for him to judge whether the individuals concerned would be in a position to help him.'

'He was convinced, like everybody else, that Marinsky would come out on top,' I said.

'On the other hand he could see perfectly well that if Marinsky did not come out on top his own position would be desperate and he would have to do a bolt in any case.'

There was no doubt about it that the Mervyn man was a nuisance. I remembered the two thousand pounds of General Lih Fing. Well, if Vickery had gone off with it I was damned glad. I was only sorry I could not say so.

'Apart from that,' the Mervyn man went on, 'he seems to have lived in a very extravagant manner.'

'He was living with me.'

'Yes,' said Goodman, 'that's the point. You keep recommending the fellow, and that flat of yours – it's notorious all over the town – was full of champagne and women the whole time. Who was paying for it all?'

'If you want to be offensive you can go home and be offensive to your own staff. Apparently that's all they're paid for."

Then there was a row, a real Billingsgate row, such as, I hope, has never before or since disgraced the private sanctum of one of His Majesty's Ministers Plenipotentiary. Goodman completely lost his temper and told me I was a whelp, a liar, a wastrel, a drunkard, a womaniser, a scandal to the colony, a disgrace to the British name and the cause of losses of thousands to British trade. I lost my temper and told him he had made a complete fool of himself and was simply trying to shift the blame on to somebody else. That set him off again of course. Suddenly it struck me how futile it all was, and I just lay back in my chair and watched the quiver of Goodman's moustache and the sparkle of his saliva, and Sir William's ineffectual efforts to intervene. I was too tired even to laugh. In the end Goodman came to the end of his breath and Sir William told me I ought to apologise. I flatly refused. The Mervyn man saw there was no use in staying and got up to go. Goodman got up with him.

'No doubt I shall see you later,' said Sir William.

'While you have subordinates like this,' Goodman answered him, 'I'm not coming into this building again. I shall send a full report to the Foreign Office.'

Whereupon he stalked out, his friend with him.

'Goodman and his pals lost £150,000 of Moorsides' money last year,' I said. 'A few more hundreds won't make much difference.

Sir William was not listening.

'What do you mean by it?' he said.

'By what?'

'By behaving as you did. Did you hear me tell you to apologise?'

I realised the Minister was extremely angry with me for being the cause of a row in his room and of a probable consequent enquiry from the Foreign Office.

'The man ought to apologise to me,' I said.

'You had no business to let your conduct expose you to insinuations of that sort. What's all this about your being a scandal to the colony?'

'You'd better ask Colonel Goodman.'

'I'm asking you.'

'Honestly, Sir William, I feel I've been cross-examined quite enough for one morning. I am not ashamed of anything I have done either in the office or out of it. If I am supposed to have been a scandal to the colony the only thing to do is to ask the colony.'

And I walked out. I suppose in the Army if a subaltern walks out in the middle of a lecture of his commanding officer, he is shot at dawn. Fortunately discipline in the Foreign Office is more elastic. Nevertheless when I got back to my own room I was vaguely apprehensive. But I was too tired to try and think out the situation. Now that

the battle was over I felt limp and lifeless. I sat chewing
the stem of my pipe and scribbling little designs on the
blotting-paper. At last I went out for lunch. In the street
Hughes-Winsor was getting into his car, and he offered
me a lift.

'I'm awfully sorry about this business,' he said.

'About Vickery?'

'Well, more for your sake. I've just been in with the
Minister.'

'He was rather worked up.'

'He doesn't know what to make of it. We've got to hold
an enquiry.'

'On what?'

'Oh, on your behaviour generally.'

'That'll be interesting.'

'Oh, I hate these enquiries. We had one of them at my
last post. A very nice fellow it was – a very clever fellow
too – but, of course, he had to leave the Service. He
couldn't get another job and afterwards he was found in
some lodging house bedroom with a bullet through his
head.'

'You're very cheerful.'

'I don't suppose for a minute you're likely to do that,
but all the same I hate these enquiries.'

Hughes-Winsor dropped me at my door, and drove on
looking extremely doleful.

34

I wanted to sleep all the afternoon, wake up for a little
soup at dinner-time and then go to sleep again. But I had
to see Tala; it was now absolutely necessary for her to get
that engagement at Prague. I took her over to Mohrstadt
and gave her dinner in a restaurant there in a courtyard

with lime-trees. The proprietor was a stout and kindly little German with a son in Detroit and therefore very eager to believe I was an American. His menu was made out in English, German, French and Vuchinian. I remember the English was rather curious; *salami* was 'summer sausage', and *plats du jour* 'ready messes'. A friendly dog came and wagged his tail at us.

'But it can't be so bad as you make out,' said Tala, 'you still have your salary as Consul.'

'That's not enough to keep an expensive bit of goods like you on. Every other penny I had went in the crash.'

As I said it I wondered at the curious instinct that prompts men to make quite unfounded boasts of their financial losses to their women friends.

'It is bad luck,' said Tala, 'I'm just getting really fond of you and you lose all your money.'

'You'll have to love me for myself for the next week and then go off to Prague.'

'I must telegraph.'

The waiter brought us a telegraph form and she wrote out her wire while we were waiting. (We had ordered roast chicken, which came under the heading *A la minute* – 'Messes to order'.) The dog nuzzled our knees enquiringly. We offered him bread which he sniffed at politely, but gave us to understand he would prefer to wait for the chicken. The twilight deepened and our host turned on the lights, little coloured bulbs hanging from wires between the lime-trees.

'Take off your hat,' I said to Tala.

'Do you want me to?'

'Yes.'

She took it off, and I realised that in spite of a five weeks' intimacy she was still, for me, supremely beautiful.

By the time we came back in the ferry it was quite dark, and Tsernigrad stood up across the waters in its pyramids of twinkling lights. I felt sentimental and squeezed Tala's hand. She squeezed mine back.

'Tell me,' I said, 'suppose your Polish Count had lost all his money, every single bean, and had asked you to go away with him and live in a furnished bedroom on tuppence a week, would you have gone?'

'I was very young and foolish then. I might have done all sorts of silly things.'

I felt she was thinking I was very young and foolish myself, but that I had my troubles and she ought to be kind to me.

'Of course I'm very fond of you,' she said. 'But I'm not really in love with you. How could I be? After all, I've only known you five weeks.'

I left it at that.

*   *   *

The next day Tala got a favourable reply from Prague, which was a relief. There was no post-card from Sibiu or Temesvar; but I couldn't expect one just yet. Goodman and the Mervyn man went off, and though there was a good deal of stir about the Vickery business no one approached me again; so that when first Beryl and then Miss Fraser rang me up for news I had none to give them. I lay very low and saw nobody. Two days later Mr Krompek came to see me. His fat round face was a picture of woe.

'This is a very unfortunate business, *Herr Konsul*.'

'It is, Mr Krompek.'

The firm was being wound up, and the various lawyers, who seemed to be the only people likely to get anything out of it, had told Mr Krompek that he could go. They had even been rather rude to him, implying that he was partly to blame.

'Did you see *Herr Generaldirektor* Vickery before he left, *Herr Konsul*?'

'No. You see it all happened so suddenly.'

'Of course. Of course, *Herr Konsul*. I was only wondering if *Herr Generaldirektor* had said anything to you about my salary.'

'What about it?'

'My salary for this current month.'

'He didn't. But I suppose you get that from the liquidator.'

'The lawyers all told me that I shall get nothing.'

'But surely salaries for the staff are always a first charge on the assets.'

'There are no assets, *Herr Konsul*. There is an overdraft at the bank. The stock is all on consignment and belongs to the Mervyn Company but the bank say that part of it is a security for the overdraft. Also Sonnenschein is making a claim under his agreement.'

'There are the office furniture and fittings.'

'They were all supplied on part payments and belong to the supplier. Only two instalments have been paid.'

'Isn't the lease worth anything?'

'We owe money to the landlord.'

What a mess it all was!

'I am very sorry, *Her Konsul*, to have troubled you with all this. But I thought *Herr Generaldirektor* might have spoken to you about my salary. It is a very difficult situation for me. I have just brought my mother out from Mährisch-Ostrau, which was very expensive, and now I cannot get another situation in Tsernigrad, and have no money at all for the journey back home.'

Suddenly an impulse came to me, one of the few that I can look back on with a certain degree of satisfaction.

'Look here,' I said, 'I owed Colonel Vickery a little money privately, and I am quite sure he would wish me to pay it out to you.'

'That is very good of you, *Herr Konsul*.'

'You quite understand this was an entirely private transaction. You won't say anything about it to the liquidator?'

'Of course not, I quite understand, *Herr Konsul*.'

'You were getting five pounds a week?'

'Twenty pounds a month.'

I pulled out my cheque-book. As I looked at the counterfoils one side of me cried out that I was making a fool of myself. After the £20 were gone there would be £28 left: and there was Tala's last week at the Bristol, and her sleeper to Prague, and Agnes's wages, and two or three bills, and nothing due in for another five weeks. The image of a dumb and perspiring Mr Boranovitch rose up before me and I tried to steel my heart. But I couldn't.

'And Mr Boranovitch?'

'Oh, there is no need to do anything about Mr Boranovitch, *Herr Konsul*. I had given him notice, He had no proper grasp of the commercial spirit. Besides, the liquidator will be keeping him on for another week or so to help in the winding up.'

I felt very relieved.

'And the girl has already gone, *Herr Konsul*.'

'What, Miss Tsernigrad? What's she doing?'

'She has become a film actress.'

'Gone to Hollywood?'

'No, she is here in Tsernigrad. They are making the first Vuchinian talking film. It is called *The Fox Trot King and the Seven Merry Female Bathers*.'

'And she's going to be one of the seven?'

'Yes, *Herr Konsul*.'

I wrote out the cheque and Mr Krompek took it and went away full of gratitude. He and his mother intended to go back home at once. Then he would have to look out for another job. In spite of his diploma it wasn't going to be any too easy, because there were a number of qualified men in Mährisch-Ostrau and there was the commercial depression there like everywhere else. So Mr Krompek passed out of my life, and I never heard of him again. I hope he did eventually manage to find some job or other. He may have been very stupid, but I liked the creature.

A week later Tala left. She was a good sort, was Tala. After all, if it was anybody's fault it was mine, certainly not hers, that I had not made more of an impression on her. She was fond of me in her way, and was always perfectly straight with me. She never bored me, as poor Mausi had: when she started her endless stories about Berlin race meetings I simply didn't listen. At any hour of the day or night she could be relied upon to to look quite beautiful and be perfectly turned out. And then one knew she could look after herself; she involved no moral responsibilities. In fact she was the perfect mistress; for six weeks at any rate. She seemed quite content to spend her last few days very quietly, and even suggested, if I was quite broke, that she could pay for her sleeper to Prague herself. But for me it was a point of pride.

When I installed her in her train in her sleeper, with her wardrobe trunk and her hat-boxes and her gramophone, I was reminded of Mausi's wicker basket. Tala thought she would probably go on to Budapest after Prague, and we made plans for my taking a week's leave and coming over to see her if in the meantime I managed to save enough to pay my railway fare. She made humorous suggestions as to how I could economise when I got there. I could live on paprika, and as nobody ever goes to bed in Budapest I could save the hotel. I thought she was very lovely, even in a hat. Two over-dressed young Greeks who were on the same train evidently thought so too. I reflected somewhat bitterly that they would certainly be paying for her dinner on the train that night; my only comfort was that they would have to pay a great deal more before they got any further.

The whistle blew and the train slowly pulled out. *Athênes*

– Tsernigrad – Beograd – Budapest (Keleti) – Praha – Berlin.
Tala leant out and waved to me. Half a minute later she
was gone. I turned and walked along the endless platform.
I realised with a certain relief that I would now be able to
go home and read *The Times* undisturbed.

An hour later I read *The Times* from cover to cover and
there was nothing to do. I set up the bridge table and
began to play patience.

35

Looking back on it now it is easy to understand my state
of mind during those few days. For the last six weeks I had
been drinking too much and smoking too much. There had
been far too much excitement and far too little sleep.
Besides which it was no sinecure being Tala's boy friend.
Now that it was all over I had neither stimulus to spur me
on nor nervous reserves on which to draw. I just flopped.

I was frightened. Every day I opened the local paper
with the dread of reading the news of Vickery's arrest: I
imagined him being brought back to Tsernigrad to stand
his trial, myself being called as a witness. I expected every
minute to be summoned to Sir William's room and be confronted with some official who had found out the manner
of Vickery's departure. I pictured Vickery going to prison
and myself dismissed from the service. This last might perfectly easily happen as it was a result of Goodman's com-
plaints and the subsequent enquiry. And supposing it did
happen, what was I to do then? Go home and become an
articled clerk in my father's office? It wasn't going to do a
provincial solicitor any good to have anyone with my
record. Besides, there wasn't the work for me there. If they
did take me in they would be doing it for charity. I thought
of going and living at home with perhaps a pound a week

pocket money: patronised by my younger brother; resented probably by my sister-in-law as claiming a share of what was due to her husband and her child. I, the 'clever' one of the family, who was going to do such great things abroad! It was unthinkable. For better or for worse I had cut myself loose from the family. Pride if nothing else would never let me go back. But what else was I to do? Who was going to employ me when the City was full of good men, qualified men, looking for a job at any salary? I knew nothing of business. It was no use sending me round even with refrigerators or encyclopaedias from door to door. I would never sell one.

Sitting on those breathless afternoons in the sitting-room shuffling the patience cards I used to cling desperately at any straws of hope. That I didn't hear from Vickery was perhaps a good sign: he was waiting perhaps for a day or two so as to be able to send good news when he did write. And anyhow the idea of sending a post-card was absurd and rather risky. He would write care of the Foreign Office and I would get the letter with the bag next Friday. But Friday came and there was no letter.

I would have to wait till the following Friday. Meanwhile I could comfort myself with the thought that at any rate he had not been arrested, and that as time went on there was less and less likelihood of our midnight dash down the Danube coming to light. Moreover Sir William's report on my behaviour had been sent off some days ago, and no telegram had come ordering me to return home immediately. The whole thing might just fizzle out, like so many other things.

So I hoped in my more cheerful moments: and then I would get depressed again and go back to my patience cards and numb imaginings. I was listless and lifeless, and utterly alone. I did not even ask Hughes-Winsor to show me the copy of the report about me, though he probably would have done so. Apart from Agnes in the flat and Mr Aquilina in the office, I spoke to no one. I could not go to the Continental Bar; in siding with Vickery I had thrown down the gauntlet to them. True, they had not taken it up, but that only made it all the worse. They must think I had made a fool of myself; I had no means of convincing them that I was right, and as they had always been just as friendly to me as ever, to go there simply for the purpose of quarrelling with them would be futile. Besides, I had neither the energy nor the money to pay for cocktails.

Beryl rang me up twice and wanted me to go round; but I didn't go. I knew she only wanted a chance to let herself go, and I was far too fond of Beryl to be willing to see her make herself ridiculous. For poor Beryl as a tragic figure of romance could only be ridiculous. Perhaps it was because I felt that what romance there had been was wholly mine. That was my secret comfort in those days. At night sometimes when I went out for solitary rambles along the silent streets, or stood in the Kezbin Park looking over to the lights of Mohrstadt across the river, or sat on the balcony at home, I used to remember that whatever might happen to me and whatever the verdict of the world might be, there was at least one opportunity that I had not missed. I would always have the thought that once when a friend of mine had his back to the wall and the world against him I had had the guts to come in and help him. It might be objected that I had not done very much. Perhaps not; but I had done something. I had done what I could.

36

One day, it was a Thursday, the office telephone rang and a woman's voice said 'Hullo.'

'Who's speaking?' I asked.

'Pat.'

'Hullo, why, how are you?'

'You don't seem very pleased.'

'I'm sorry, my dear.'

'I'm very angry with you.'

'Why?'

'It's ages since you asked me round for a drink.'

'Well . . . '

'It's no use using your harlot as an excuse because I know she left ten days ago.'

'It's simply because I'm broke.'

'Then come and have a drink with me.'

'Well, I might be able to rise to a couple of *slivovicas*. What about Uncle Bozha's?'

'Rather. Seven o'clock?'

'Very good.'

After all I couldn't go on living like a hermit for ever. There was a new Third Secretary coming out, and the Commercial Secretary was due back from leave; and then the Bishop in South-eastern Europe was threatening to visit us again, which meant a tea-party at the Legation which I would have to organise. I would have to re-emerge into society more or less before long. I might just as well begin with Pat as anyone else.

At seven o'clock I was in the little yard surrounded by the cats and Pat turned up very soon after.

'All the crowd in the Continental Bar are wondering why you never come there now,' she said.

'The enemy's camp.'

'Who do you call the enemy?'

'I suppose Pemberton for one,' I said.

'My dear, don't talk such rubbish. Pemberton's very annoyed at the way Vickery let you down.'

'Vickery never let me down.'

'Well, it's no good arguing about that. Vickery's gone,

anyway. And I don't see why you should want to carry on
a sort of vendetta against Pemberton. After all he was a
friend of yours long before Vickery came, and then look at
the way he stuck up for you lately.'

'Who?'

'Pemberton.'

'How?' I asked as dryly as I could.

'In this absurd enquiry into your behaviour. Surely you
know.'

'I don't know anything about it.'

Pat told me. Apparently when the news got round that
I was in disgrace the Continental Bar had sat in committee
upon the matter and decided to take action. The next day
Pemberton, Grimshaw, Slaughter and Watterson had
marched to the Legation and explained that I was an
innocent and virtuous young man who had had the ill luck
to trust an adventurer.

'He might have been an adventurer,' I said. 'But he was
the straightest man I've ever known. And these damned
people are making me out to be a child!'

'My dear, aren't we all children when it comes to that?'

'We don't like being told so.'

'I don't see why you should quarrel with these people
because they tried to help you. It was rather good of them.'

I pondered.

'Yes,' I said, 'it was. It's no help my saying that as Pemberton had won he could afford to be generous. I'll simply
say it was damned good of them.'

I had a tremendous feeling of relief.

'Of course,' said Pat, 'the whole thing was too funny for
words. Slaughter made himself a sort of secretary and
roped in everyone he could. Miss Phipps and Torrens, and
of course the Glovers . . . '

'Not Mrs Bowles?' I asked.

'No, not Mrs Bowles. But practically everybody else.

And they all went along and swore that you were a tee-totaller and a virgo intacta and everything else you possibly could be.'

'But the Minister is no fool,' I said. 'He can't have believed all this.'

'I honestly don't think it matters if he did or not. If nine-tenths of the colony come along and swear you are he's simply got to believe it.'

'But how did they get over Tala?'

'Oh, we all said she was a Russian aristocrat whose family had been ruined by the revolution and had known your uncle, and how you felt you had to be kind to her now that she had come down in the world. Beryl Glover had met her at dinner and that made it all much easier. Oh, and the trump card was Mrs Brinkworth who seems to have met her – my dear, it was too mean of you to have introduced her to Mrs Brinkworth when you never would let me see her . . . '

'She surprised us in the flat one day.'

'Anyhow Mrs Brinkworth said she seemed a very nice refined girl, and knowing you as we all did, it was quite unthinkable that you would ever try to take advantage of her circumstances.'

'Splendid.'

'My dear, it was perfectly marvellous!'

Pat wanted me to come on to the Continental Bar at once, but I was feeling rather light-headed and wanted time to adjust my ideas. I dropped Pat and went back to a cold supper in my flat.

It was only then that I realised how much of my depression had been due to fears for my own skin. Now these fears, or ninety per cent. of them at any rate, were gone. And that feeling of loneliness was gone too. I reflected as to whether my going again to the Continental Bar implied disloyalty to Vickery; and decided it did not. I couldn't afford to go there often, but that didn't matter very much. Apart from that I wouldn't want much money now that Tala was gone. I would cut out the Apollo altogether. If I felt the need (as I probably would) of feminine society there was Pat. I had been rather an idiot, with Pat in the town, ever to have bothered about Mausi or Tala, not to mention Jill. Pat and I spoke the same language, liked the same jokes. Pat was used to being poor and making the best of it. Of course she wouldn't go on to Prague or Belgrade at the end of the month as cabaret girls so conveniently did. Man likes a week-end at Brighton; but Woman (even a baggage like Pat) is annoyingly apt to want some more permanent arrangement – no doubt as the result of generations of economic subjection. But there was no need to start worrying my head about that.

In any case I was going to enjoy the rest of my stay in Tsernigrad. I felt happy again. And as I went to bed I had a sure and certain presentiment that to-morrow, Friday, there would be a letter from Vickery in the Foreign Office bag.

37

My good spirits lasted till the morning. I remember I sang in my bath. There was quite a stir in the Legation when I got there. The Commercial Secretary had come back from his leave and looked in to see me. I was so confident again that I myself broached the subject of Goodman and Vickery, and the Commercial Secretary, who was a cheerful soul, laughed heartily and said that from all he had heard Goodman was a man of four letters and Moorsides' would never do any good again till they had got rid of him. This, of course, I much enjoyed hearing. An hour later, when I was arranging for the invitation cards for the

Episcopal tea-party, Hughes-Winsor brought in the new Third Secretary. He was a young man even more beautifully dressed than Hughes-Winsor himself, and spoke so high and so fast that I had great difficulty in understanding what he said. I relished in anticipation the comments that would be passed upon him in the Continental Bar. Soon after they had gone the consular mail from the bag was brought in. There was no letter from Vickery, and I was annoyed at the carelessness of the people in the chancery. I rang them up on the house telephone.

'Where's the rest of my post?'

'It's all gone up to you. Haven't you got it?'

'There must be some more. I'm expecting a private letter.'

'All that came for you has gone up.'

More bewildered than disappointed I rang up Hughes-Winsor to see if by any chance it had got mixed up with his letters. But it hadn't.

Everything seemed dull and colourless again. I looked, without interest, at the official mail. Two letters were addressed to me personally. I opened one of them.

Dear Mills.

It was from one of the bigwigs of the Consular Department. He told me that, as I was probably aware, serious allegations had been made concerning me by the representative of an important British firm. Sir Willian Drexler had instituted enquiries, and his report, the writer was glad to say, had shown that the graver charges were not substantiated. On the other hand it seemed clear that greater prudence and diligence on my part would have materially assisted in preventing the losses suffered by the firms involved, and in my private capacity I had not shown that steadiness of conduct and discretion which the general Regulations to Consuls require. Accordingly while it had been decided that no special disciplinary action was necessary I was to take this letter as a reprimand.

Well, I thought, a little pompous perhaps, but not unfair. After all, the Foreign Office, though often the butt of
uninformed wit, is probably the most sensible and reasonable of departments. The great thing was that the incident was now closed: there was no need for me to worry
any more about it. I opened the other letter.

Sir,

*I am directed by the Secretary of State to inform you that you
have been appointed His Majesty's Vice-Consul for the Vilayets
of Bitlis and Van, to reside at Bitlis.*

*2. You will hand over the Vice-Consulate at Tsernigrad to HM
Commercial Secretary and proceed to your new post without delay.*

I didn't bother to read all the rest, duties, emoluments,
travelling allowance, I knew it all by heart. I stared out
of the window at the lime-tree where the jackdaws were
fussing, and at the vine-covered roofs beyond.

Bitlis.

I thought of a cluster of squalid little houses weeks away
from anywhere among the dreary Anatolian hills: of the
emptiness and loneliness of life with nothing whatever to
do and nobody to do it with. I thought of my guest at
Aleppo two years before, and what Bitlis had made out of
him. Of course I wasn't going to stay there eight years; I
should have joined Vickery long before that. At least I
hoped so. But it might be years before I did.

Mechanically I looked throught the rest of the mail. The
ordinary post came in and with it a letter from Mausi.
Belgrade hadn't been bad, she said, but she didn't like it
much. I mustn't be angry with her, but she felt she simply
must come back to Tsernigrad. She had fixed up with the
Tabarin for September. This would probably be an unpleasant surprise for me, but she promised not to be in the

way. All she asked was that I should come down just once to the Tabarin to see her, to show I wasn't angry.

Well, Bitlis had settled the Mausi problem.

I picked up the two Foreign Office letters and went in and showed them to the Minister.

'Of course we shall be sorry to lose you,' he said. 'But it's just as well that you should leave here. How do you like the idea of Bitlis?'

'Loathe it.'

'Oh, I don't know. In the old days it used to be a wonderful place for picking up carpets. They brought them across from Tabriz.'

'I'm afraid I don't know anything about carpets.'

'Well, it will be a very good opportunity to learn. When are you thinking of leaving?'

'As soon as I can. I expect next Tuesday or Wednesday.'

'Oh, I should give yourself a few days more if you like. It isn't really as urgent as all that.'

'I should prefer to go at once.'

It is true that things are seldom quite as urgent as the Foreign Office is apt to maintain, but I am one of those people who, if they have to have a tooth out, want it out at once.

On my way back to my own room, I had a sudden idea to write to Mausi and ask her to come to Bitlis with me. She would come like a shot: would ask for nothing better.

But then I reflected that if I got tired of her in a month in Tsernigrad I should certainly very soon get tired of her in Bitlis. Besides what was going to happen when I came back to civilisation again and she had lost her looks and her figure and couldn't go back to cabarets? I decided it wouldn't do. It wouldn't be fair on either of us.

The next three days I was too busy even to go to the Continental Bar; there was the Consulate to hand over and my things to pack, and the future of Agnes and my flat to be settled. Fortunately the new Third Secretary was willing to take on both the flat and Agnes. I had to make farewell calls on all my colleagues and the local authorities, who then came back and called on me: that is all of them except Monsieur De Woutte who merely sent a p.p.c. card with the top left-hand corner turned down. And there were various farewell meals. Lunch at the Legation, where Lady Drexler asked if I would soon be solving crossword puzzles in Turkish. Dinner at Beryl's where I met Miss Phipps who supposed that they were sending me to Bitlis to stamp out the brigands. Lunch with Mr Yoshogi who with a temperature of 98 in the shade gave me the sort of meal he hoped would remind me of home, that is thick soup, fish pie, turkey, roast beef and plum pudding. I can see him now, beads of perspiration standing out on his forehead, as he tried, by force of example, to spur my flagging appetite, and apologised profusely for the absence of Yorkshire pudding, which his cook did not know how to make. Mr Yoshogi was perhaps the only colleague I was genuinely sorry to leave: and perhaps the only one who was at all sorry I was going.

'Now you will go,' he said, 'I do not know with whom I can talk English. I am very fond of English language. It is very fitted to express the deep philosophical truths.'

Before I left he showed me his fire extinguisher and said he would always think of me when he looked at it. It seemed years and years since the time when I had bothered about fire extinguishers. And then there was dinner with Hughes-Winsor and the new Third Secretary, who talked in very high fast Mayfair voices about the merits and demerits of the various local doctors, not, as the new Third Secretary was careful to explain, that one was ill, but because it would be so uncomfortable to feel that one might get ill and not know which was the best doctor to send for.

My last evening I had reserved for the Continental Bar. In the afternoon I remembered my racquet was still at the Tennis Club. There was no prospect of my using it in the next few years but I did not want to lose it altogether, so I walked over to the club. The streets were filling again after the midday siesta. Never again, I felt, would I see these irregular cobbles and low, uneven houses and dusty acacias; or the shabby crowded tramcars; or the ponderous unshaven citizens drinking *slivovica* outside cafés; or the incredibly ragged little newsboys; or the bright-eyed silk-stockinged girls looking at the stills outside the cinemas; or the long-tailed strident cats; or the hawkers with their great bleeding segments of water-melon. I became sentimental and unutterably sad.

The Diplomatic Tennis Club was not so full as it had been two months ago. Many of its members were away on leave. Still, there were enough ladies left for a couple of bridge tables. Madame Silviera, more beautifully turned out than ever, barely acknowledged my bow and looked back at her cards. I wondered what she had made of Donne; but I would never know. I retrieved my racquet and was just going away again when I noticed Jill sitting by herself. I felt I ought to say good-bye to her; I had made no farewell call on Mrs Bowles as a p.p.c. card had seemed enough. I went and took an empty chair next to her.

'So you've appeared again,' she said.

'Yes.'

'I'm off on Friday.'

'Are you?' I asked. 'Where to.'

'To Scotland.'

It showed how cut off I had been lately from local society. I had no idea that she was leaving so soon.

'You're going too, aren't you?'

'Yes, to Bitlis.'

'Where's that?'

'At the back of Turkey.'

'That will be jolly for you.'

I felt she was still thinking she owed it to her self-respect to put me in my place, but didn't quite know how to set about it. There was a pause.

'What are you going to do in Bitlis?' she asked.

'Nothing.'

'I mean, what's your work?'

'There is no work.'

'Then why do they have a Consul there at all?'

'Because there always was one there in the past, and the powers that be can't be bothered to close the post down. They have far more important things to think of.'

'It sounds very silly.'

'It is.'

There was another pause. The sun was sinking behind us, and threw a rich glow on the beginnings of the presidential villa on the top of the hill. If the policeman had not disturbed us on that night in May everything might have turned out very differently.

'You won't have much gay life in Bitlis,' said Jill.

'That doesn't matter very much. The trouble about these little Eastern towns is the animals. They're all full of wretched starving dogs who whine all night in the summer because they're hungry and all night in the winter because they're cold. And they're all mangy and most of them going blind. And the horses are covered with sores where the harness rubs them. And they're all frightened because they're badly treated. You can never do anything for them and never get away from them.'

'How beastly,' said Jill.

Slowly the glow on the presidential villa grew deeper.

'What I probably ought to have done,' I said, 'was to fall in love with you.'

'Good Lord!'

'You needn't have reacted at all; it wouldn't have worried you. Besides I didn't mean anything very desperate. Just an honest manly love.'

'Do you ever talk seriously?'

'I'm being perfectly serious now. It would have kept me from dry rot in Bitlis.'

Pujotas and three of his friends had just finished a set on one of the far courts and were coming noisily towards us. I got up and picked up my racquet.

'Good-bye,' I said.

'Good-bye. I hope Bitlis won't be too foul.'

I went down the little path to the gate. In Victorian times on an occasion like this I supposed the man went up to the girl and told her how he realised what a fool he had been and how he was now going to pay the penalty; but all the time he spent in the wilds her picture would be in his heart and he would try to make himself less unworthy of her. Or something of the sort. And the girl would be quite thrilled. How sensible the Victorians were I reflected. A scene like that would for years afterwards fill both parties with the comfortable glow of self-conscious nobility.

I went up to my flat and sat among the packing-cases.

38

Word had got round that I was going to make my final appearance in the Continental Bar, and when I arrived they were all there: Pat, and Beryl and Clive, and Pemberton, Grimshaw, Slaughter and Watterson.

'Here he is,' they said, making room for me. 'Where's that damned fellow Weiss got to? No, you can't pay for any drinks your last night. Weiss, one more gin and French.'

'It's quite like old times again,' said Beryl.

She was right. It was. I felt the warm glow of loved and familiar things.

'It's about time you came along to look after me,' said Slaughter. Whereat Grimshaw and Watterson haw-hawed, and Slaughter told us how that morning at 4.30 a.m. he had come out of the Tabarin and got into a taxi and as the driver didn't know where he lived, had told him to drive straight on till he stopped him. But he at once fell asleep in the taxi, and when he woke up they were ten miles out of town, bowling merrily along towards the Bulgarian frontier. And when he got back he had a row with the man about the fare. Everybody enjoyed the story, none more than Slaughter himself. And then Pemberton said that was all very well but it was a damned pity I was going; and Grimshaw gloomily predicted my successor would probably be some damned Cissie like the new Third Secretary. Pat said he wasn't a Cissie, so Watterson asked her how she was in a position to tell; which caused much laughter. Then Grimshaw, who liked to repeat jokes, said that really as the fellow had only been here three days it was pretty quick work on Pat's part. So we laughed again, and Pat said we were all idiots and she wanted another drink.

Perhaps it was nothing special in the way of conversation; but as I so keenly realised it was something better. Good company is not intellectual company, nor, as we are apt to think in our extreme youth, company in which we ourselves sparkle. For good company, that one sure comfort for our failures and disappointments, is the sinking of our own personal pettiness in an overwhelming consciousness of common humanity; quickened, if possible, by a common appreciation of gin. This was good company, here in the Continental Bar; something that I should badly need until I found Vickery again and had something to fight for.

'Of course,' I heard Pemberton's voice across the group, 'what I can't forgive him for was not playing straight with our friend here.'

'He played absolutely straight with me,' I said hotly.

Pemberton smiled; an omniscient smile implying that I was very young but he didn't want to quarrel my last night. I caught Beryl's eye and felt her support and understanding. But I didn't want to quarrel either; partly because it would only cause bad feeling between Beryl and Pemberton, but chiefly because this last night of mine was a luxury I could not afford to spoil. Then Slaughter wondered if the Legation would rise to whisky and soda on the occasion of the tea-party for the Bishop, and Grimshaw remembered the Bishop's last visit when he had to christen the American Consul's baby, and kept on mistaking Miss Phipps for the mother.

Mr Weiss was kept very busy and Beryl began to call everybody darling. When we looked at the time we found it was too late to have dinner anywhere else so we all trooped up to the restaurant. By the time we had finished, the programme at the Tabarin had begun, so we all trooped down again to that.

We were very noisy spectators and applauded all the turns vociferously. And Grimshaw whispered to Beryl that Slaughter had said he would rather take her (Beryl) for a week-end to Budapest than any of the girls on the stage. Beryl asked Slaughter if it was true and Slaughter got flustered and said of course it wasn't. Whereupon Beryl said it was very rude of him, and Slaughter, still flustered but always the gentleman, said it was what he would have liked to say if he had been ten years younger and twenty times better looking.

The last turn was a Japanese conjuror. Pemberton thought it was extraordinarily good though he had seen it six times already in the last fortnight. By that time it was half-past one and Pat and Beryl began to wonder if they oughtn't to go home to bed (not that they wanted to in the least, but they were afraid of being in the way if they stayed on). So we crowded into two taxis, and Pat sat on my lap, partly, I think, because she liked it and partly to show off to Beryl. We dropped Beryl and Clive, who told me not to say good-bye because they'd be on the station to-morrow. Then we went on to Pat's place, and though there was now more room, Pat said she was quite comfortable sitting where she was and didn't intend to move. I got very sentimental and squeezed her leg all the way. When we reached her door she also told me not to say good-bye because she'd be on the station to-morrow. I got out to open the door for her.

'*When I am gone*,' I said, '*dreame me some happinesse*.'

'My dear, I'll dream you anything you like.'

She kissed me in front of the others who said 'my word,' they felt they were rather in the way. Pat went in and we got back into the taxis and drove back to the Apollo. Zacharias welcomed us very fulsomely and shooed all the girls away from the bar to make room. Pemberton looked round disparagingly and said they really were a bloody poor lot that month; at which Zacharias began to rub his hands and explain how difficult it was to get hold of really first-class talent at that time of year, but if we would only wait till next month . . .'

'What's the good of next month? My friend here's going away to-morrow.'

Zacharias looked very upset – as well he might be when he remembered all I had spent there with Tala – and said he hoped I would soon come back.

We all sat at the bar and the band started up again for our benefit. Two Hungarian blondes were very anxious to be taken notice of and moved from table to table so as to be in our direct line of vision. When that didn't work they came and sat beside us at the bar and asked the barman for a glass of water.

'You ought to take those two with you to Bitlis,' said Grimshaw.

'There was once a consul,' I told them, 'Who was sent somewhere into Turkey, and picked up two sisters in the Moulin Rouge at Marseilles and took them with him. But then the missionaries at his town wrote to the Embassy that their good work was being undone by the ostentatious immorality of the British Consul. So the Ambassador wrote to say his behaviour must cease. But the Consul had a marriage licence and married himself to one, and of course the sister stayed on with them. Next time he was in Constantinople he took his wife and sister-in-law to call on the Ambassador's wife: and there was a row, so he was transferred at once to Yenbo on the Red Sea where he died nine years afterwards.'

'Dirty luck.'

The barman measured out another five whiskies.

But I could get no elation from alcohol that night.

'Do you hear that?' shouted Watterson, 'Zacharias is going to get a gigolo for the autumn!'

'Zacharias, what do you mean by it?'

'We must have someone here to start dancing with the girls. Sometimes the guests are too shy to start the dancing.'

'Who's too shy?'

'I was not speaking of you gentlemen, I was speaking of the other guests. Besides, sometimes elderly gentlemen come down with ladies and like to have somebody to dance with them.'

'Why, then there's Mr. Slaughter.'

Zacharias laughed a rather thin laugh that was intended to express as much appreciation of Pemberton's joke as was compatible with proper respect for Slaughter.

I realised I should never see the gigolo, never hear Pembertons' comments upon him. Just as I would never see that masterpiece of the talking film – *The Fox Trot King and The Seven Merry Female Bathers*. Just then Snowball began priming himself, looking rather embarrassed and foolish, and the band struck up his piece:

'*Elszallt a dál* . . . "

Yes. For me the song was ended.

The two Hungarian blondes had at last succeeded in attaching themselves to our party. One of them who was sitting next to me told me she was rather lonely. Tsernigrad was not bad as a town – she thought she liked it better than Belgrade – but of course that was not enough. She wondered if she would be able to find a nice friend.

'It's a most awful wrench,' I said to the others, 'to have to leave you fellows. I don't bother about the general foulness of the place I'm going to and the flies and the dust and the prickly heat and the boils. All that doesn't matter so much. But to wake up to-morrow morning and realise I shall never have the chance to hang round this bar with you, or roll up at the Continental again, well, it's perfectly bloody. Anyhow I've got to say you've all been damned good to me while I've been here, damned good, and I shall never forget it.'

'That's all right. You'll be coming through here on your next leave.'

As they said it Pemberton and Grimshaw exchanged glances, and I noticed a gleam of satisfaction. They had done their duty. They had fulfilled the last rite for the departing friend. They were getting me drunk at last.

'In a night club,' said the second Hungarian blonde, who of course had not understood a word of my outburst, 'one must not think serious thoughts. One must be cheerful. Why don't you come and dance?'

So I went and danced with her. She danced rather well.

But four o'clock came and the barman began making out his chits.

'Are you coming along?' Pemberton asked. 'Or are you going home with the cuties?'

'I'm coming with you,' I said. 'I've drunk too much whisky to be any good to these girls.'

I knew perfectly well that after three months of Bitlis the thought of even one Hungarian blonde would seem far too good to be true. But I wanted the luxury of walking back this last time with the others through the cool morning air along a still and shuttered Wilsonovi, and meeting the peasant carts coming in to market.

39

My train went at seven. By half-past five my packing-cases had all been fetched and I had taken leave of Agnes and wound up finally and completely my life at Tsernigrad. And then I realised that I had not said good-bye to Miss Fraser, not seen her even since Vickery had gone though she had once telephoned. I had just time to climb the hill and call upon her.

When I got up to the villa I saw a notice board hanging on the fence: 'TO BE SOLD'. It seemed quite incredible. However there was Miss Fraser, looking just the same as ever, sitting on the verandah and hammering away at her typewriter.

'I've come to say good-bye,' I said.

'I thought you'd come and see me before you left.'

She called to the servant girl to bring out half a litre of the home-grown wine.

'Well,' said Miss Fraser, 'so you aren't going to take that niece of the Bowles's to Bitlis.'

'No.'

'It's possibly just as well. Very likely she wouldn't have appreciated it.'

'I doubt if I shall appreciate it very much.'

'Nonsense. It's a wonderful opportunity for you to get to know the Kurds.'

'I don't know that either I or the Kurds would mind very much if I never saw one. Anyhow I hate leaving Tsernigrad. Miss Fraser, you aren't going away, are you?'

'I don't know.'

'I saw that board outside.'

'Yes.' She hesitated a little. 'I shall have to sell this house in any case. It is my contribution to Tsernigrad Transport Ltd.'

'What, to Vickery?'

'Yes. I lent him some money soon after he arrived, no doubt extremely foolishly. It was arranged that he should pay me back in shares in the new company.'

'But hasn't he written to you?'

'I have neither heard from him nor seen him since three days before his disappearance.'

'Then he must be simply waiting for a chance to send you the money,' I said. 'He may have been an adventurer. I grant that. And he hadn't the slightest scruples in doing down people like Goodman or General Lih Fing. But to anyone he liked he was the straightest man on earth.'

'He was a common swindler,' said Miss Fraser.

I had a curious empty feeling.

'How much was it?' I asked.

'About six hundred pounds.'

If he had had over nine hundred pounds in cash he could just as easily have got me to pass six hundred to Miss Fraser as a book to the Argentine Legation. I remembered little things: Krompek's salary, the young Vuchinian at the language school.

Pemberton had been right.

'It's partly my fault your losing your money,' I said. 'He had more than that on him when he went away, though I didn't know it at the time, and I helped him to escape."

'You did?'

I told her the story of how Vickery had come back that evening; and how we climbed down the fire escape and over the fence of the Rowing Club; and of our dash down the Danube to Roumania.

'You were perfectly right,' said Miss Fraser.

There was something about the way she said it that took my mind back to a conversation I had once with Pat in Uncle Bozha's little yard. Could it be that Miss Fraser still wanted romance? I felt embarrassed and a little frightened.

'It's terrible about your money,' I said.

'Not very,' said Miss Fraser.

I realised how futile it was to talk about money.

'There was something about the man,' I went on. 'For me at any rate. You know the idea was that I should join him and be his partner. Of course, the idea was attractive to me because I thought I was going to be rich. But it wasn't only that; there was the man himself. In a world of hedgers and compromisers and petty excusers here at last was somebody absolutely without fear, moral or physical, a man who was willing to take on anything and never ask for justice or fair play. There was something worth while in joining up with a man like that.'

'I understand.'

'And then that last night we arranged that as soon as he had settled down somewhere I should leave the service and join him and we should try our luck against the world together and the idea of that has more or less kept me going ever since. But now I see quite plainly that he'll never send for me. He doesn't want me any more than he wants – well, a certain woman here who thought he was going to take her with him. And now that that prospect's gone everything seems so perfectly futile.'

Miss Fraser lit a cigarette and looked out over the plain in front of us.

'I've got the disease that all my generation has got,' I said, 'we're all dressed up and have nowhere to go. It was all very well for the Victorians to wave each other Upwards and Onwards with their umbrellas. They ignored the fact that if you got to the top there was only another mountain the other side. But we can't. We aren't materialists because science has knocked the bottom out of materialism, we've got a certain capacity for devotion, but we haven't got a cause with a big C.'

'You'd better stay on another week,' said Miss Fraser, dryly, 'and talk to the Bishop about it.'

'I know perfectly well what he'd say. Devote myself to my work and all the opportunities of doing good that I shall doubtless find there. Knock off cocktails and take plenty of exercise. Oh yes, and there was a red-haired creature here last month whom I thought rather beautiful: knock her off too.'

'Very sensible advice.'

'But it's negative. That's the whole tragedy of people like Bishops and schoolmasters. They haven't the courage to give one a lead. It's no good giving up a girl just for the sake of giving her up. There must be something positive – some big spiritual adventure. If the Bishop were to suggest my going out to take charge of a leper island I might go.'

'Possibly the Bishop could arrange for a leper island.'

'I know it sounds as if I was talking rubbish, and I know if he did suggest a leper island that the chances are a thousand to one I wouldn't have the guts to go. But there is one chance that I might, and that's the chance he ought to back. Life's like Yadil.'

'Like what?'

'Like Yadil. You can analyse it down as much as you like but there's something left you can't explain.'

'I haven't the slightest idea what you're talking about.'

'Very likely it's nonsense. You know sometimes I think I've made no progress mentally or morally since I was sixteen.'

'Perhaps that's a sign that you're growing up,' said Miss Fraser.

Perhaps it was. But it didn't seem very probable. And then I realised that Miss Fraser was not paying much attention to our conversation; she was thinking of that hour before dawn on the Roumanian bank when Vickery had disappeared among the willows.

I looked at my watch. It was nearly half-past six and my friends would soon be waiting for me on the platform. Miss Fraser walked with me to the gate and wished me good-bye. I left her there and went on down the hill, and looked for the last time at the sun going down in a riot of crimson over the two great rivers and the miles of golden maize.